Gwen saw h⋯ ⋯e pulled⋯

Drew.

He was the tall one with the sure stance, waiting for her with a group of other people. Relief eased some of the tightness in her chest.

She straightened and walked to the hangar. She was at least one hundred feet from the open doors and the welcoming group, but Drew's features were as sharp as if he stood six inches away.

His sunglasses hid his eyes so she had only his facial features and posture by which to judge his demeanor. He looked taller, his face defined, more mature. Not as young as she'd remembered him for six long months.

Before she finished her train of thought, Drew was in front of her. She hesitated. Was he angry about taking her in? Having her stay at his house?

"Gwen." He closed the distance between them and embraced her. He kept his arms tightly around her, and she relished the feel of his winter jacket against her cheek. Relished the way she could almost convince herself she still had him to come home. That this was real.

She felt a sudden urge to pull back, look him in the eye and tell him that now she understood what really mattered in life.

Dear Reader,

Thank you so much for your support of the Whidbey Island series! Your positive comments on Facebook and Twitter, and your emails, mean so much to me. It's heartening to know you've enjoyed meeting the fictional heroes and heroines of Naval Air Station, Whidbey Island, as much as I've enjoyed writing them. While my characters are always made up, their virtues are not—courage under fire being the most common. Whether the heat is felt on a war-torn battlefield or in the home of a military spouse who's keeping the family together while his or her warrior is deployed, it's what makes today's military family stronger than ever. I'm honored to bring you these stories, and I hope they lift the spirits of our friends and families in service.

Navy Rescue started in my mind years ago when I had the gift of a conversation with a senior enlisted aircrew man who survived a P-3C ditch in the ocean. Unfortunately I don't remember his name but I'll never forget how he so honestly described the details of the ditch. His real-life story made me think about the repercussions of one of the crew getting lost at sea, and how difficult it would be to come back home after being assumed dead.

Gwen and Drew have been divorced for several years when the story starts. Two life-changing events for both of them force the reassessment of why they split, and make them consider whether the love they shared is worth resurrecting. Or maybe they now have a chance at a newer, deeper love.

I look forward to your thoughts on Facebook, Twitter and Goodreads. For the latest news on the next book in the Whidbey Island series, check out my website, www.gerikrotow.com, and sign up for my newsletter. As always, thank you for your unwavering support of our men and women in uniform and the families they love.

Peace,

Geri Krotow

GERI
KROTOW

—

Navy Rescue

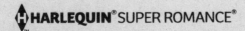
HARLEQUIN® SUPER ROMANCE®

Recycling programs
for this product may
not exist in your area.

ISBN-13: 978-0-373-60849-2

NAVY RESCUE

Printed in U.S.A.

ABOUT THE AUTHOR

Former naval intelligence officer and U.S. Naval Academy graduate Geri Krotow draws inspiration from the global situations she's experienced. Geri loves to hear from her readers. You can email her via her website and blog, www.gerikrotow.com.

Books by Geri Krotow

HARLEQUIN SUPERROMANCE

HARLEQUIN EVERLASTING LOVE

*Whidbey Island books

Other titles by this author available in ebook format.

For Bob Coughlin and Jack Stoner,
two heroes who rescued me when I didn't even
realize I needed rescuing!

Acknowledgments:

Much appreciation to John Weiss, DPT, and his
staff for their professional insight and patience
with my *very* fictional questions.

PROLOGUE

COMMANDER GWENDOLYN BRETT adjusted the power levers on her P-3C-Orion aircraft as another gust of wind racked the airframe. Lightning lit up the night sky over the Philippine Sea and she wished they'd finished the mission hours earlier.

Terrorist insurgents in the remote southern islands of the Philippines hadn't shown their hand until the last possible moment before she had to turn the plane around while there was still enough fuel to make it back to base. Besides streaming live video to government troops on the ground, her crew got their location, captured excellent photos of their camp and transmitted them via satellite to be disseminated to the intel weenies who'd figure out what it all meant.

They'd completed the mission; now she had to get her crew back to base.

Alive.

Thirteen souls, including herself.

That awareness kept her from letting the monotonous drone of the four turbo-prop engines lull her into drifting off—into thinking about anything other than the flight...

For some reason, the image of Drew as she'd driven off just before deployment had haunted her all day. She'd wondered why he'd bothered, why he showed up at the hangar. He'd said, *no one should go off on deployment alone.* He'd given her a friendly hug.

They *were* friends, in spite of all the hell they'd put each other through as young junior officers. So why had his platonic hug been worse than if he'd tortured her with a kiss, reminded her of all she'd lost when they'd divorced five years ago? More important, why was she allowing thoughts of him now, during a key mission?

The old mesh fabric pilot's seat gave little support to her spine, and she shifted her position, trying to stretch her lower back.

"You've got to do those ab moves I told you about, XO." Her copilot's gentle chiding made her smile.

"No amount of exercise is going to shave the years off me, David."

"Aw, ma'am, you're still young."

She chuckled, even as the sharp stab of a lower back spasm made her wince. Simple tasks that she'd managed through brute strength as a junior officer were becoming more difficult as her birthdays added up.

Thirty-seven was young in the civilian world, but not in the navy.

She was tired of the constant reminders of the years passing too quickly. When she got back from deployment she was going to follow her best friend, Ro's, advice and get herself back into the dating scene.

Not that she'd ever been *in* the dating scene. *Because of Drew.* Because they'd been together since flight school in Pensacola, Florida.

From the beginning they knew their marriage faced more challenges than most—long deployments, geographical separation, war. Hurdles that wouldn't go away until one or both of them resigned from the navy. Drew didn't have the passion for flying that Gwen did and they'd agreed that she'd stay in while he got out. They both assumed Gwen would eventually resign her commission and fly for a commercial airline.

They'd survived three intense years after Drew got out of the navy and went back to school to earn his doctorate in Physical Therapy. His PT practice had thrived after only a year.

As his career took off, so did hers. Unfortunately, their marriage tanked.

She still mentally kicked herself for not seeing the inevitability of their divorce. That would've saved them both so much emotional distress. Very few dual-active-duty couples made it for the long haul.

Factor in how young they'd been when they got married, and the odds had never been in their favor.

The long deployments and wartime assignments had been hell for both of them, but her performance earned her top marks and led to this tour. The ultimate goal all career officers chased after—the command tour.

Serving as the Executive Officer of Patrol Squadron Five-Two, the Grey Sharks, she'd had two more months until she'd become the commanding officer. A coveted twelve-month stint that had taken her entire career to reach and taken her marriage with it.

Her squadron's mission was to conduct reconnaissance and antisubmarine warfare all over the globe. They provided real-time intelligence to operational ground forces and operational commands, no matter which theater they flew in. Often her missions kept civilians safe from unspeakable terrorist events. Sometimes it was simply reconnaissance. Other times, Gwen's aircraft carried weapons, or helped others aim their weapons on the enemy target.

"See the flashes, XO?" David pointed starboard of the nose, to where sharp points of light lit up the not-distant-enough horizon.

"They're not happy. Good. That's our job." She referred to the insurgents who were shooting off AAA, antiaircraft artillery, in an effort to take her aircraft down.

"We're too far away for those triple-A rounds,

Commander," one of the radar operators said over the ICS or intercommunications system.

"And we're going to keep it that way, crew." Gwen spoke into her microphone as she eyed her fuel levels.

She glanced over at her copilot, his profile relaxed but alert in the starboard seat. Young and supersmart, he reminded her of Drew and of herself. Once again she lamented that they'd been so *young* when they started out in the navy and in life. Too young to know how to make a marriage work.

She contracted and relaxed her abs and her glutes. It eased the discomfort in her lower back.

At least she and Drew had remained good friends. That was more important than a marriage, in so many ways.

Drew hadn't been impressed with her selection to command. He was proud of her, unquestionably. He'd supported her through the wartime deployments—by getting her mail, doing basic admin stuff a spouse often did, handling household responsibilities. But they'd been divorced for five years when she left last month. Neither of them had remarried, but she expected he'd be the first one to make that leap.

He'd wanted to start a family. She'd wanted to wait.

Tonight, at the end of a long mission, flying through a hell of a storm, she wondered if she'd been nuts to stay in the navy, to go through so much, for this last operational tour. Had it been worth it, giving up so much to become a commanding officer?

Lately she'd begun to suspect that she'd lost more than her marriage in the process. She didn't know who she was anymore, except for her military vocation. If she hadn't screened for command, would she have stayed in to make the twenty-year mark required for retirement?

"Shit! Incoming starboard, three o'clock! Probable missile!" The aft observer's scream in her headset shattered her thoughts.

"Confirmed surface-to-air. Son of a bitch!" The radar operator validated that the sighting wasn't another aircraft or fireworks.

Cold dread gripped her.

"I see it. Hell, it's closing, XO!" Her copilot had his hands on the yoke, his head swiveled around to the right as he sighted the missile off their starboard side.

Preflight intel confirmed the existence of AAA during their mission brief, but never mentioned manpads—portable surface-to-air missiles.

They had an incoming that could blow them all to bits.

She heard screams and shouted curses over the ICS.

Drew.

Shudders buffeted the fuselage of the P-3, and Gwen's operational instincts pushed anything else out of her mind. The plane rolled alarmingly to port and she threw a quick shout at her copilot. "Help me out here, David!"

"Engine number four, gone. Wing on fire."

She never lifted her gaze from the control panel, where she confirmed that they'd lost an engine. Annunciator lights in the cockpit also indicated that number three, the other engine on the starboard wing, looked as if it was going to quit at any moment.

"We've lost both hydraulic systems," the FE shouted.

"Roger. Pull the boost out handles!"

The FE leaned down and pulled the three yellow-and-black striped handles by his feet.

This left them with only manual control of the aircraft.

"What's next, XO?" David yelled into his mic, even though he was right next to her. They'd never hear each other over the roar of the aircraft as it struggled to maintain altitude.

It was a losing battle. The altimeter showed they were dropping at an alarming rate.

One, maybe two minutes was all she had to prepare her crew.

They'd trained with the hope of three minutes.

"We'll never make it to land, David." She tore her gaze from the instrument panel and looked at him. His profile was set and determined, but she recognized the same fear she felt.

No one wanted to die. Not like this.

"You with me?"

He turned his stare on her and an understanding passed between them.

Whatever it takes.

Yells and shouts mixed with expletives over the ICS as the crew went through their trained-for responses.

The flight engineer pushed the button that issued the deadly warning—one long ring on the command bell. The sound she never wanted to hear while flying a P-3 reverberated through the entire aircraft.

They were going to ditch.

"Prepare to ditch!" She yelled what might be her last command—she had no choice. They'd lost two engines and were damned lucky they were still airborne.

The controlled panic of the crew aft of the flight station was palpable. Gwen heard swear words, prayers then silence as the country's best-trained professionals prepared to fight for their lives.

Lives in her hands.

"Everyone got their LPAs on?" She referred to the survival vests that would be their only flotation device, other than the three life rafts, once they were in the harsh seas.

"Condition One set!" Lizzie, the TACCO or tactical communications officer, confirmed that everyone was prepared to ditch.

God help us all.

Ten thousand feet above the Pacific Ocean, approximately five miles off the southwest tip of the Philippines, they were about to ditch. The condition of the sea was abysmal, with waves that were ten feet and higher, And it was quarter past midnight.

Pitch blackness.

Her worst nightmare come true—a nighttime ditch in rough seas, miles from land, oceans from the nearest naval vessel.

Robert "Mac" MacCallister, the flight engineer, worked in sync with the copilot to complete the ditching checklist. It was standard procedure they'd all practiced and prayed they'd never need to use.

I'm ditching in the ocean.

She'd practiced it in the flight simulator countless times, mentally rehearsed the most undesirable event for any naval aviator.

"I'm here if you need relief, XO." The voice of the third pilot rose above the rush of air that swept through the cabin. He clutched the back of the copilot's seat as he shouted in her ear.

Gwen couldn't spare him a look.

"Go back to your station and strap your ass in, Aidan!" If any of them were going to survive they had to be properly secured. She had to bring the bird onto the water safely and in one piece so they could get out before it sank.

"But ma'am, if you—"

"Take the freaking order!" Before she even finished her statement, Gwen had to grab the yoke back after it was wrenched out of her hands.

"Help me out here, David!" she shouted to her copilot.

"I'm pulling as hard as I can!"

Gwen didn't have to see David's face to know the young officer spoke through clenched teeth.

"Come on, gal, give us one more break!" Gwen yelled at the old bird, then groaned as she stretched her shoulder and back muscles to their limit in her effort to pull back. Losing hydraulics after two engines had been blown apart by the surface-to-air missile wasn't just bad luck.

It was fatal.

She had to beat it.

That was her crew's only chance.

"Five thousand feet." Scott reported each time the altitude dropped another thousand feet. Soon it would be every hundred feet.

"Wind direction is two-four-five at 45 knots," her navigator, Bryce Griswald, shouted from the nav station, aft of the cockpit.

"Roger, Grizzy."

Gwen checked the compass heading and was grateful for one small miracle in this hell. She was taking the plane down at the right angle of descent to keep the waves from becoming brick walls lying in wait to destroy the aircraft.

Forgotten images of her life appeared before her in quick succession. The first time she rode her bicycle without training wheels, her dad's smile, Mom's hugs, Drew's first kiss, her graduation from Annapolis.

Their wedding.

Drew.

"This plane is coming down in one piece. We're all getting out." It might be the last thing she ever did for them.

"Two hundred feet!" David hadn't missed a beat.

"One hundred feet!" David's shout reached Gwen just before she saw the last glint of white-capped waves through the night darkness.

"Hang on!" She pulled back on the yoke with all her strength.

"Fifty feet!"

David's last report.

"Hands off power levers!" Gwen shouted the order for David to join her in letting go of the power levers and gripping the yoke. They'd lose their fingers if they didn't release the levers.

For the length of an indrawn gasp, the world stood still as she waited for touchdown. Her mind struggled to convince her that this was like any other landing, the end of any other mission she'd be able to walk away from.

That delusion shattered when the plane hit water. What remained of the two operating engines' combined ninety-two-hundred shaft horsepower screeched to a halt as metal propellers met the ocean surface with such a violent impact she was sure they were finished. Panic threatened to drown them before their greatest enemy did. The sea.

Not yet.

Water sprayed against the windshield and blinded her. It took all her mental discipline to ride out the ditch, hands on yoke. Each creak, groan and shudder as the aircraft broke apart echoed in her bones.

After interminable moments, the aircraft's forward motion stopped and the race for their lives began.

"Out, out, out, let's go!" Gwen used her deepest shout, the one that had its origins in her plebe summer at the Naval Academy, to motivate her crew. Not that they needed any motivation—their quick decisive actions flashed in front of her as if they ditched regularly.

Mac crouched next to her, shoving the copilot out the upper hatch. They were up to their chests in water and jet fuel, so every movement became slow and difficult. Her flight suit provided no protection from the ocean or the thousands of gallons of aviation fuel that had spilled from the torn wing tanks.

"Anyone else?" Mac yelled as he pointed directly above his head to the cockpit hatch.

"No, everyone else will exit the over-wing hatches." They couldn't go back to help anyone now, and she had to trust that the rest of the crew had survived the ditch. Her toe met a hard, unmovable steel bulkhead as she fought to hang on to the hatch rim while Mac, the flight engineer, prepared to egress.

Gwen prayed the crew who'd been strapped in back were out over the wing hatches, along with the life rafts. She wouldn't know until she was out.

The fuselage tilted dangerously forward. They had precious minutes to get out and away from the sinking wreckage.

"Go ahead, Mac." She gave him a shove and watched as his body disappeared up the hatch. Seconds later Mac's hand reached down and grabbed the top of her helmet.

"Up here, ma'am! Let me pull you."

Gwen complied and allowed him to save her life. As the plane commander, Gwen was responsible for each crew member's life. She *had* to be the last one out.

She grabbed the edge of the hatch as soon as her arms were past the entrance and pushed herself up into the raging storm. The sting of salt water and the howl of the wind shocked her, and she had to take several gulps of air before she could ascertain where the life rafts were. In doing so, she breathed in the aircraft's fuel fumes. Her eyes and throat burned and her stomach heaved. She had no choice but to vomit on the spot.

She saw David's face, illuminated by his flashlight. The copilot was safe with the navigator and the second flight engineer. She couldn't see any farther into the menacing darkness.

"How many?" Gwen screamed across the waves and the rapidly sinking P-3 to the first of the life rafts.

"All here, XO."

Gwen couldn't allow time for relief. She sought out the second and third life rafts.

"We're missing the TACCO!" The shout from the second raft elicited immediate action from Gwen. Lizzie was still stuck in the aircraft.

Gwen had to go back in and get her.

Lizzie.

Going back the way she'd exited was risky, especially if Lizzie was unconscious. Gwen couldn't inflate her LPA or she'd never get back in the fuselage. She made a quick guess as to where the over-wing hatch was positioned on the now-sinking aircraft.

She had seconds.

Gwen took a deep breath and dived into the thrashing sea, holding on to the aircraft as a guide. She found the over-wing hatch and went in.

Total darkness meant that feeling her way through the fuel-filled cabin was a challenge, but Gwen knew she had to get Lizzie. *Get your shipmate or die with her.*

She ignored her need for air and felt forward to the TACCO station. Lizzie was still strapped in her seat, only her face above the waterline.

Gwen drew in great gasps of air as she struggled to release Lizzie's seat belts.

"C'mon, Lizzie Lady." She used Lizzie's call sign and grimaced with relief when her fingers managed to unbuckle Lizzie's straps.

"You with me, Liz?"

"I'm here. Hit my head." The whispered reply was all Gwen needed. Lizzie was still alive and had a chance if Gwen could get them out of the destroyed fuselage.

"I need you to take a deep breath. Hang on to me and I'll do this as fast as I can."

"I'll try."

"Okay. One, two, three."

Gwen went under with her arm around Lizzie's chest, pulling her through the totally submerged aft cabin. Their progress was excruciatingly slow and Gwen sent up a prayer that they'd make it to the over-wing hatch.

The fuselage groaned with each wave that hit the steel frame, sounding deadly, final.

Gwen's fingers caught on the rim of the hatch and she pulled both herself and Lizzie through it. Something scraped her arm and a piece of metal clanged on the top of Gwen's helmet.

She didn't stop. She couldn't, wouldn't. She was Lizzie's only chance.

Her own lungs burned and she was afraid that Lizzie had sucked in fuel or seawater in an effort to breathe. Gwen felt the tug of the aircraft's drag once they were free of the fuselage. They had seconds to clear the area. She reached over to Lizzie's

LPA handle and pulled. Lizzie left Gwen's arms as though a great arm had stretched down and pulled her up. Gwen grabbed her own beaded handle and yanked. Her LPA inflated and bolted her to surface.

The black spots that she'd tried to fight off dissipated as she gulped in the salty, wet air. She blinked. Lizzie floated a few meters away from her. She swam over and wanted to scream when she saw Lizzie's closed eyes and blank expression.

Please let her be unconscious, not dead.

She tried to hook their LPAs together but the rough seas only allowed her to clutch Lizzie's vest collar as they were tossed like pieces of trash.

"XO, over here!"

Gwen couldn't tell whose voice was behind the flashlight beams as she started swimming toward them, Lizzie in tow.

Get away from the aircraft. Get away. Get away.

Hours of training in simulated ditches had drilled into her the necessity of putting as much distance as possible between her and the ditched craft. It was moments from sinking and would take down everything around it.

She pushed and kicked and hung on to Lizzie. After what seemed like hours, they arrived at the side of life raft number two. Number one was attached to the right of it. She couldn't see the third raft.

"Get her up—she's injured." Gwen pushed Lizzie

as hard as she could, watching as the hands of two crew members reached over to haul her up.

She saw Lizzie's boots go over and into the life raft.

She'd done her job. All crew members safe, in their rafts.

"Grab my hand!" The second flight engineer leaned over the raft and held out his arm.

Gwen prayed it wasn't too late. Exhaustion weakened every muscle and she couldn't lift her arm out of the water.

"Go, report it." She wasn't sure he'd heard her, and the sea spray threatened to choke her each time she opened her mouth.

Drew.

She had to fight, to get back, to get home. A sob escaped her throat as she willed her booted feet, so heavy, to move, damn it! Her life, her hope, was on Whidbey Island.

Not lost at sea.

"Please. Let me get there." Her words came out as the tiniest of whispers.

She focused on the FE's outstretched hand and dug deep for the core of her will, her remaining physical strength, to grasp it.

To save her life.

A wave crashed over her and made it impossible.

If she was going to survive, it would be on her own. She didn't have control over the ocean any more than she did the memories that clawed at her.

The family room with its woodstove burning while the Christmas tree twinkled... She and Drew wrapped in each other's arms in front of the fire.

CHAPTER ONE

Six months later

"You've gained twenty-six degrees in your mobility over the last six months, Helen." Drew smiled at his prize patient and snapped his protractor closed. Helen Burkoven was sixty-two, and had presented with a frozen right shoulder, due in part to her competitive tennis practice of the past fifty years. She made a lot of his younger clients appear lazy.

"I can't tell you how great it is to be able to pull weeds again, Drew. The brambles had taken over my rose garden!"

"As long as you keep doing the exercises we've gone over, you'll be fine—but take it easy on the tennis court, okay?"

Helen grunted and walked over to the chair, where she waited while Drew got an ice gel pack out of the chiller.

He arranged the pillow under her arm to make her more comfortable before he placed the gel pack over her injured shoulder.

Helen groaned in pleasure. "Oh, that always feels so good after all the work you make me do."

"Sit tight and enjoy. You're free to go in fifteen minutes." He set the timer near Helen's chair and went to see his other client, Tom, who was doing leg exercises for his knee on a wheeled office chair.

Drew relished the modern layout of his clinic. One large room held the equipment and therapy tables for up to six clients at a time.

"How's it going, Tom?"

"Fine, doc. But I feel like a crab on the beach, walking around while I'm sitting on this stool."

"It's going to help your knees, trust me."

"Drew?" Serena Delgado, his receptionist, interrupted him.

Drew looked at her sharply, but his annoyance dissipated at the stunned expression on her beautiful face. Whatever it was, she wouldn't express it in front of his clients. Serena didn't normally interrupt his consultations. The last time she'd burst in like this—

Gwen's plane had gone down.

That was well over six months ago, but damned if he didn't tense up and expect Serena to give him more bad news.

There isn't anything worse than knowing Gwen's never coming home.

"You have some visitors. It's very important."

The dread that had simmered in his gut since the minute he'd learned Gwen was missing erupted into an all-out boil.

They've found her body.

As much as every piece of naval intelligence that he'd been told about, not to mention logic, indicated that Gwen had perished in the South Pacific six months ago, he'd held out hope. That she'd survived—that she'd come back. That, somehow, against all the odds, she'd made it.

He shook off the fantasy.

If she'd lived, if she came back, they'd only be the friends they'd become since the divorce.

"Drew?" Serena stared at him. He swung his gaze to Helen, his rotator cuff patient. She hadn't said a word, but she wasn't deaf. Her eyes sparked with knowing. Hell, the whole town knew what he'd been through. The P-3 ditch. Gwen's role in it— she'd saved her crew. The entire damned crew had returned safely to Whidbey Island. To their families.

Except Gwen.

Gwen didn't have a family to return to anymore. Only him, her ex-husband, and their shared pets. The island newspaper had detailed Gwen's naval career as well as her personal bio, including their divorce. Her MIA status had been picked up by the national news, as well.

While locals like Helen knew an awful lot more about his personal life than he'd choose, they didn't know the half of it.

"Go ahead, Drew. You're done with me." Helen's eyes didn't twinkle any longer, and her expression was gentle. Motherly. "We're all praying for you."

"Thanks."

After a quick nod at Helen, he followed Serena to the back office, behind the therapy room.

He stopped at the threshold when he saw the occupants.

"Ro."

Lieutenant Commander Roanna Mikowski, his wife's best friend since they'd been midshipmen at the Naval Academy, stood with her hands clasped in front of her. She was still on active duty, but had put in her resignation so she could remain in the same place as her husband, Chief Warrant Officer Miles Mikowski. A stab of envy broke through his shock as he saw the obviously happy couple.

Why couldn't Gwen have resigned, too?

It wouldn't change who we both are. We'd still be divorced.

Miles stood next to Ro and offered Drew a slight smile. "Drew."

"Miles."

Silence stretched between them. They'd shared an awful lot of grief these past several months. Tension seemed to crackle off Ro and Miles. They were going to confirm his worst fears, the news they'd all dreaded.

"Do I need to sit down?" His voice sounded sane, steady, but he couldn't feel his mouth move with the words.

"Yes." They spoke in unison, then glanced at each other. It was the kind of look that only a couple who knew and deeply loved each other exchanged. Drew missed that kind of intimacy.

He sank into the leather office chair, unable to relax.

"Spit it out." He wanted to run away, leave the office, leave Oak Harbor, charter a flight off Whidbey Island. Destination: Anywhere But Here.

It wouldn't change the truth.

"Drew, they've found Gwen." Ro's voice was low and steady. He gave her credit for being so strong.

He couldn't stop the tears that squeezed past his closed eyes. "Where?"

"Drew, look at me. You don't understand."

He opened his eyes and saw that Ro's eyes glistened with unshed tears, too.

"She's *alive,* Drew. She made it."

"She—" His voice crapped out on him. Miles nodded in affirmation. Relief bloomed in his chest. And then common sense shut it down.

"That's impossible."

"Ro's not kidding, Drew. She's alive! She was caught by insurgents but escaped from their prison camp after two weeks."

Gwen. Alive.

Drew jumped out of the chair and grabbed the edge of his desk. "Where was she for the past five months? Where is she now?"

"Apparently, she found a small village where she hid out until she had a chance to walk out of the jungle. She got to our embassy in Manila via the

Philippine government, once she was able to reach them. She saved a baby's life while she was out there." Ro paused. "That, of course, is classified."

He blinked, grateful that Ro was willing to risk telling him something she probably shouldn't have.

"I appreciate it, Ro." He turned to each of them. "Thanks for sharing this with me. I'll call her mother."

Ro shook her head. "She's probably already called her. It's going to hit the news any moment."

"Got it." Drew was grateful they'd come and told him in person, so he wouldn't hear it first on the radio or see it on TV. Now he needed them out of here. They were waiting for a reaction he couldn't give them. No matter what he'd told them when Gwen had gone missing, it didn't change who he and Gwen were. They were friends. Exes who'd outgrown their youthful first love.

"She'll be coming home in about a week. She's being flown from Manila to Seattle, and examined down at Madigan for several days." Madigan Army Hospital was three hours away, south of Seattle.

"I'm sure they'll take good care of her," he said. "She's tough, we all know that." He stood up as if to go into the therapy room. It had to be enough of a hint for them.

"No, Drew, stop." Ro walked around the desk and put her hand on his arm. He stared down at her hand.

"She needs some time to come to grips with

it all, to adjust to the reality that she got out of there alive."

"You talked to her?"

"No, not yet. I'm telling you this ahead of the call you're going to get from the commodore. I couldn't bear the thought of you finding out alone. We wanted to be with you."

He looked at Ro, then Miles.

"You know this doesn't change anything," Drew said. "We'll never be more than friends." He didn't mean to say that out loud, but there it was.

"This isn't the time to worry about that, bud." Miles gave him a long look. "What you told Ro and me, it's just between us."

Drew wasn't so much in shock that he didn't know bullshit when he heard it. Ro was Gwen's best friend since they'd been on the same sailing team together. Gwen was like a sister to Ro. Drew shook his head and walked to the side of the desk. He beckoned to Miles and Ro, and enveloped them both in a hug.

"She's alive. Nothing else matters."

He'd been given what he'd prayed for. The chance he'd bargained for with God. He'd promised he'd accept that they were friends, and never hold another angry thought about the fact that they weren't destined to be more.

Surprisingly, Gwen's disappearance had taught him to be grateful for the entire time he'd known her—not only the good years of their marriage but

the tough years, too. It had all brought him to where
he was today, enjoying the career he'd dreamed of
in his favorite place on earth, Whidbey Island.

He couldn't go back to regrets or what-ifs.

To the reasons for a divorce that had become
final five years ago, after nine years of marriage.

Miles pulled back from Drew's embrace but Ro
stayed by his side, her expression hopeful as she
kept glancing over at Miles as if for support.

*Please don't bring up the possibility of recon-
ciliation.*

"There's a detail we still have to take care of,
Drew."

"Yeah?"

"She has to stay with you."

Drew pulled back and dropped his arms. He
rubbed his face.

"I'm willing to help her out, Ro," he said after a
moment, "but living with me? Not going to happen.
She'd never agree to it. Besides, I'm sure Brenda
will take her home before the week's out." Let her
mother, Brenda, help her out for once.

He could be her friend, but not in such close
proximity. Not day after day, in a situation he might
mistake for more than it was.

They'd all thought she was dead.

You knew she was still alive.

"She'll want to come here. Whidbey is home to
her. And you know Brenda's not who Gwen needs
right now. She needs someone who's had PTSD,

who's been through a war. Someone who understands what she's got ahead of her."

Leave it to Ro to pull out the big guns.

"I went through my issues a decade ago, Ro."
Miles was watching him with wary alertness.

"Ro and I just finished going through our 'issues.' None of us will forget the hell it can be once
we're back. You'll be able to support Gwen like no
one else can. You've known her almost as long as
Ro has." Miles didn't add the "you've been married to her" part. He didn't have to.

No. Freaking. Way.

Gwen in his house? Living under the same roof
again?

No.

"You're still forgetting that Gwen has to agree
to this."

"Her apartment's been rented out. You have all
her stuff in your garage from a month after she
went missing. It'll take at least two weeks before
she's steady enough to go looking for a place of her
own." Miles spoke reasonably enough.

"I'll get her household goods delivered to a new
apartment. Hell, I'll *find* an apartment for her, if
that's what it takes."

Ro and Miles stared at him. He clenched his fists,
taking a deep breath before continuing.

"I realize you two would love nothing more than
for me and Gwen to suddenly decide we made a
mistake and get back together. But it's not going

to happen, and we all know it. Why make her suffer right from the get-go? She needs to get herself squared away without being around me." And he didn't need the reminders of what had gone wrong, what they'd lost when they'd allowed themselves to drift apart.

Ro leaned over the desk. "You're all she's got, Drew. Her mother and stepdad are not who she'd pick to recuperate around. You know that as well as I. She could come stay with us, but…"

"You're still newlyweds. No way."

Ro nodded. "Right, and as much as we don't care about that, Gwen would."

"Speak for yourself." Miles smiled at Ro.

A sense of anticipation awakened in Drew. To have Gwen home, to be able to exchange simple small talk while she healed, seemed innocent enough. But it wasn't good in the long run. For either of them.

Still, his gut instinct to take care of her was hard to ignore.

"Drew, you're a physical therapist. You know that clients have to start from a baseline, work on the smaller, less challenging exercises first. Only after their strength comes back can they do the hard stuff. Like when you helped me get my hips and lower back straight after my fall." Miles gestured at his prosthetic leg. He'd survived a tough rehabilitation with the navy. He'd taken a fall several months back and had come to Drew's clinic for physical therapy.

Drew glared at him. "Being patronizing isn't your forte, pal. Your back and sacrum were easy fixes—you were already in great shape. Gwen and I haven't seen each other in over six months." And hadn't spoken, or touched or talked like a real couple in five years.

They were friends without benefits.

"This is a lot to put on you, Drew, but imagine what Gwen's going through. For her to come back to anyplace but a house she's familiar with is too much right now. She needs the easier road."

"I don't disagree with that, Ro, and you can't disagree with the fact that there aren't a lot of happy memories for Gwen in my house." It'd taken him years to call it *my* house and not *our.*

"Think about the comfort the pets will give her, Drew. You have to know it just about killed her to leave Rosie and Nappie." Ro's persistent tone grated. This was the problem with having friends who'd known you forever. They called you on your crap.

What they're saying is true.

After Gwen moved out, she'd asked to come by when he wasn't around. Said she needed to spend time with their parrot and their dog, so the pets wouldn't be traumatized by the divorce. It had evolved into a joint pet-sharing venture that rivaled the joint-custody agreements divorced parents arranged. He didn't know how much Ro knew about that, and wasn't going to volunteer it.

"Okay, fine—she needs a place, and the house is probably the best option for her. She can be with the pets. I'll take a room in town." Hell, he could camp out in his office.

Miles shook his head as he put a calming hand on Ro's shoulder. "That won't work, either, Drew. She has to be *with* someone, another adult, in the house. Hell, Drew, you know what coming home from war's like. The nightmares, the crazy crap right afterward. No one should have to do that alone."

Miles was right. He watched Ro slip a protective arm around Miles's waist. Both Miles and Ro had gone through their post-war transitions as single sailors, living on their own. They'd found each other in the midst of it.

He couldn't let Gwen suffer on her own, no matter how difficult the living arrangement was for either of them. He stared down at his closed laptop, unable to look at the happy newlyweds while contemplating the antithesis of a honeymoon with his ex-wife.

His injured, battle-fatigued ex-wife.

Shit.

He looked up at his closest friends.

"When did you say she'd be back on the island?"

DREW SHOVED THE glass-paned door wide open and strode into the parking lot behind his practice. The blustery March day was no match for the heat of his blood as it pumped through his veins with an intensity he hadn't experienced since—

Since the navy told him Gwen was dead.

He ran both hands over his head, willing the sharp, cold bite of the March air to prove he wasn't dreaming.

Gwen was alive.

Maybe there was a chance. Maybe the reason neither of them had connected with anyone else yet was— *No, never.*

She was still Gwen.

They'd never forgiven themselves for ending their marriage. They'd been too young to understand that sometimes it was okay to let a relationship go before it hurt too much.

Gwen hadn't made any attempt to say goodbye before she left on deployment. He didn't know what had possessed him to drive to the hangar to see her off that last day. He was sure she'd chalked it up to pity, as she always did whenever he expressed compassion for her.

He'd said he was seeing her off like any other friend, and thanked her for her service. Gave her a friendly hug.

What had he been trying to prove? That he could touch her without wanting to make love to her again?

Her reaction had been cool, professional. The shell she'd grown over the past several years had hardened to an impregnable wall that didn't let anyone in.

Especially him.

Living through what, by all accounts, had been hell on earth—captured by insurgents, escaping, being on the run through the Philippine jungle— must have cracked that wall in more than one place.

Didn't Ro say she'd saved a baby?

And if there *was* a chance for him to get inside Gwen's heart again, did he really want to?

He gazed at the water and shook his head.

Surviving the worst nightmare of her life wouldn't change Gwen's mind about their divorce, and it hadn't changed his. No matter what the circumstance, they'd always end up back where they'd stalled—neither willing to compromise for the relationship.

He'd worked hard to start a life without her, and she'd never sacrifice her career for a marriage.

Thoughts of what might have happened to her ripped at the shock he'd been in since he ran out of the building. If she'd been raped…

"Damn it all to hell!" He yelled at the parking lot, to the soccer fields and playgrounds that edged the perimeter of the island's shore, to the calm water of Puget Sound.

A startled seagull flapped off the waste bin Drew's practice shared with a hair salon. He registered the bird's presence but didn't try to shield himself from any potential droppings.

He dug his numbed fingers into his pockets and pulled out his car keys. He'd left everything except his keys and his wallet in the office. He'd been too crazed to grab his jacket.

Didn't matter. The car had a heater and he had to get out of here.

LOST IN THOUGHTS of Gwen's return, Drew drove up to the Koffee Hut. Drive-through-only specialty coffee shops were a common feature in the Pacific Northwest, and Whidbey was no exception. Only after he'd shifted the car into park next to the trailer window did he realize his mistake.

"Drew! What a nice surprise. In the middle of the day, too." Opal smiled at him from the serving window of her business. She'd set it up after leaving his employ; she'd been one of his assistants for the first two years he'd had the PT clinic, during which she'd earned a part-time business degree at the community college.

"Yeah, well, I needed a break. I'll have the usual."

"A large cup of drip, coming right up." Worry lines appeared between her perfectly shaped brows. With stunning blond curls and bright blue eyes, Opal looked like a cherub in an Italian painting. He watched as she plucked a cup from the tall stack and poured the coffee. Her expression reflected friendly concern.

"What's going on, Drew?"

"Nothing much." He wasn't going to confide in

Opal. It'd been hard enough convincing her that he didn't want to pursue a relationship with her. He refused to encourage her or lead her on.

The entire time she'd worked for him she'd been a worthy employee, but he never crossed the line and dated people he paid. Good thing, since she'd bought the house next to his right after he and Gwen split. It *might* have been a real-estate coincidence, but it was still awkward in those first few months after his divorce, when she'd started her new business. She'd repeatedly emphasized that she didn't work for him anymore. If he'd dated her, it would have been a disaster when they broke up.

Because they would have. Long-term relationships weren't on his agenda.

One had been enough for him.

Opal's feelings had been hurt that he wouldn't even consider a date with her. They were both single, ran their own businesses, loved the Pacific Northwest.

After several attempts to have Drew over for dinner, Opal had accepted their "friends only" status.

Maybe he *had* been crazy to turn her down. If he was involved with someone else, he wouldn't be a safe harbor for Gwen. He wouldn't feel as if he was staring down the wrong end of a weapon.

"You don't look your usual chipper self." She handed him the hot cup. As he reached to take it, she put a hand on his wrist.

"Drew, we're friends. How many times have I

told you I don't take it personally that we didn't work out? It's okay if you need an ear." *Didn't work out?* They'd never been more than friends.

Neither had he and Serena, who still worked for him so was technically off-limits. Serena was another available woman who, on paper, appeared to be a good fit for him.

Drew fought to keep a scowl off his face.

He'd had every opportunity to date other women and like a fool he hadn't. If he had, Gwen's return wouldn't be shaking him up so much.

He gently removed her hand from his arm and took his coffee, leaving the payment on the small Formica counter.

"I appreciate your concern, Opal. I'm just not ready to talk about it."

Opal's kind smile was back. "I totally understand. Let me know if you want me to bring over some dinner for you tonight."

"Oh, no, I'm fine. Did a big load of grocery shopping yesterday." He was lying and prayed she hadn't checked his refrigerator the last time she'd popped in uninvited to leave him muffins or a casserole.

He really needed to start locking the side deck door.

Until now he hadn't minded her unannounced drop-ins, since she'd accepted that they'd never be more than friends. Now that Gwen was going to be staying with him, he'd have to convince Opal to stop her visits.

Or keep his damned door locked.

DREW DROVE TO the other side of the island with his coffee in one hand, the other on the steering wheel. It used to be a favorite haunt of his during the dark days of his divorce from Gwen.

Gwen.

He gulped too much of the hot coffee, which burned his throat, but that served as a way to keep him grounded. God knew he needed *something* to keep him focused on reality. It'd be too easy, too natural, to think that he and Gwen were going to find a way to reconcile.

Never. You can't reconcile what isn't there. When there's nothing to work with.

They had nothing left of what had been their marriage. Just a run-of-the-mill friendship.

Drew didn't consider himself a stupid man. But maybe he'd screwed up by not forcing himself to date more regularly. When the divorce became final, he swore he'd never settle down again. Plus, he'd almost no time to date. He'd blamed it on the stress of his expanding practice, the stress of the adjustment.

You know why you haven't looked at another woman.

He crushed the paper cup, scalding his hand

and spilling the coffee all over the steering wheel and his lap.

"Dammit!"

Drew unzipped his gym bag, which sat on his passenger seat. His smelly workout T-shirt soaked up most of the liquid. He'd finished more than half the cup, so the damage wasn't as bad as it might have been.

He looked at his pants and frowned. The brown stain spread down his zipper, onto his right leg.

If the mere thought of Gwen coming back into his home unnerved him this much, how was he going to stay steady enough to help her while she suffered through her reentry?

Frustration was already a constant companion; with Gwen under the same roof it would be that much worse.

Drew threw the soaked shirt on the passenger-seat floor and leaned back, forcing himself to focus on the scenery.

The ebb and flow of the waves on West Beach were in stark contrast to the flat Puget Sound water he saw out of his office windows every day. The energy in each white-capped wave soaked up his anxiety, bit by bit.

He'd come here every single day after he and Gwen had agreed to separate with the intent to divorce. She'd never asked where he was going and he'd never volunteered it, even when he knew she probably thought he was meeting friends at a bar.

The first two months after she'd ditched her plane in the South Pacific, he'd been out here every chance he got. He'd never missed an appointment that first week she was MIA, but Serena and the rest of the staff had known his mind was elsewhere. Wondering what kind of torture Gwen was enduring. The local and eventually national news media reported the Pentagon's assessment that she'd been lost at sea.

Gone. Dead.

But he'd *known*. Deep down, he'd known. Gwen's heart was still beating, somewhere.

Ro's position as the wing intelligence officer gave her access he'd never get as a civilian, and she'd brought him what little intel she'd been able to gather. Miles had cornered him after a therapy session one day and told him that both he and Ro were concerned about his increasing isolation, his avoidance of them and others outside work.

Miles had convinced him that going on with his life wasn't an affront to Gwen's memory.

After Gwen had been gone six weeks, Drew allowed himself to mentally engage with the world again. He couldn't fight the facts, but he didn't have to ignore his instincts, either. He'd figured that if she were still alive after six weeks—which he'd believed even if no one else had—she'd survive whatever came her way. Somehow she'd make it out.

As she had.

He went to sip his coffee and only when his

empty hand curved around air did he shake off his thoughts. He couldn't prevent a smile. Gwen would never settle for plain drip coffee. She took hers like a lot of people native to the Pacific Northwest. Two shots of espresso, with steamed low-fat milk. Maybe a shot of almond syrup if her sweet tooth was nagging her.

Their Sunday-morning routine rushed at him with its remembered familiarity and warmth. They'd hem and haw over whose turn it was to get the pastries, their once-a-week treat from the local bakery. Gwen liked the fresh-made éclairs, while he favored the apple fritters. One of them would pick up the pastries and coffee, while whoever stayed home walked the dog, fed the bird and got the woodstove blazing if it was chilly.

It'd been so easy, so natural, their life. Their love.

Until it got hard. Their professional drive, perfectionism and insistence on each being the best at what they did took its toll. Damaged the bond between them.

Memories of their competitiveness still made him squirm. They should've seen it; two strictly trained naval officers were innately competitive at a primal level. That hadn't changed, even when he'd left the navy. Of course it had bled into their relationship and blown it to smithereens.

The event that had exploded the fissure into an impassable crevice had taken place on the night of a squadron party. He'd been there with Gwen, acting the consummate navy spouse as usual. He'd played the role willingly; anything to keep the peace, to let her see he wasn't threatened by her success. His practice was still fledgling but promising.

He'd left the celebration early—told her he'd meet her back at home. They'd taken separate cars as they'd both come from work.

Unbeknownst to him, one of Gwen's subordinates followed him home and tried to convince him to let her come in and talk to him. She was an attractive aviator, a younger version of Gwen. Except that she didn't seem to care that Drew was married. To her boss.

But Gwen had come back before he'd gotten rid of her, and assumed the worst. Hell, at that point in their marriage he would've thought the same thing if he'd found a strange guy in his house.

After he'd pummeled him.

He'd told her the truth.

Gwen, nothing happened. She came over and said she needed to talk. I let her in, told her I wasn't interested. She's just young and dumb.

I've never thrown myself at my boss's husband. You're a professional, Gwen.

She'd shaken her head. *It doesn't matter, Drew. The point is I believe you—and this doesn't surprise me. I wouldn't blame you if you* had *taken her up on her offer. Let's face it, I haven't been a great wife to you.*

She'd referred to their lack of lovemaking. Either

or both of them had been too tired over the past few months. It should've been a red flag after the way they'd burned for each other in their earlier years.

The conversation hadn't solved anything. The disbelief, hurt and anger that Gwen *should* have expressed, *should* have felt, wasn't there.

Gwen's desire to pursue her naval career, his decision to open a private practice that made him averse to further navy moves, as well as their inability to forge a solution to their failing relationship—it had all been too much for any marriage.

Gwen had moved out within the week, and their road to friendship had begun.

Five years ago. It felt more like fifty.

He turned the key in the ignition so that he could lower the windows. The salty Pacific breeze cooled his face, tugged at his hair.

Reminded him that he was alive.

Gwen's alive.

Sunlight played off the frothing waves as it slipped out from under a heavy cloud. He'd been here for over an hour; he needed to get back to the office, back to reality.

And get ready to do the one thing he dreaded most— living in close quarters with his ex-wife again.

CHAPTER TWO

THE FIRST THING Gwen noticed when she arrived in Washington State was how clean and fresh the air felt.

The second impression was that she'd developed claustrophobia. The military hospital she'd been "requested" to stay in for a complete post-trauma physical was pristine and comfortable, even spacious. But it was still a building. With solid walls. After six months on the run, most of it spent with little more than a thin barrier between her and the jungle, she felt hemmed in.

At least that was what she told the medical staff. In reality her chest hurt as if a three-ton gorilla sat on it, keeping her from freedom.

Whidbey called to her. She wanted to go home. She needed to be back on the island.

The doctor who sat across from her didn't agree. Not yet.

"I'm ready to go." She shifted in the soft-cushioned chair.

Gwen still couldn't get over the relative plushness of her psychiatrist's office compared to the way she'd been living for the past half of a year. She'd only met with him for the past few days but it felt as if he'd peeled back every layer of emotional skin she had left. She knew it was his job to determine how emotionally healthy she was after her time in the Philippines, but that didn't make it any easier.

"You will go home, Gwen. Soon, I promise. We can't send you back without some basic reentry tools. I can't underestimate the mental stress you've been under." He peered at her as if she were a biological specimen. Dr. Lucas "just call me Luke" Derringer had told her he lived out on San Juan Island but commuted into Madigan Army Hospital as needed to support returning warriors "such as yourself." He explained that he was permanently working on San Juan at the Beyond the Stars Resort, which was a counseling center for Gold Star families—families who'd lost a loved one to war.

She liked how Luke, a former SEAL, seemed to truly appreciate what she'd been through. A quick look at the walls of his office told her he'd served at Walter Reed National Medical Center, so he knew his way around the effects of PTSD.

Still, he was a psychiatrist. Gwen knew she needed help but the only assistance she craved at the moment, besides getting Pax back in her arms, was climbing into her own bed, under clean sheets, wearing soft, freshly laundered pajamas.

Dear, sweet Pax. No one would believe her when she said she was going to be a mother, was already a mother to the little boy. She hardly believed it herself.

Luke droned on about how she needed to watch for any signs of severe PTSD, including suicidal thoughts. It was a given that she'd suffer some symptoms, but it could get a lot worse before it got better.

She didn't care. She was back home.

Almost.

"If you want to go back sooner, you'll have to move in with your ex-husband for the time being."

Shock forced her head back, her spine straight.

No.

Lucas stared at her, unblinking. Gwen shook her head in an attempt to make sure she wasn't hearing things.

"What?"

"As I've just explained, you can't be alone for the first several weeks that you're back. This is nonnegotiable, if you want to be released to go to Whidbey." He paused. "If you're serious about adopting the baby, Gwen, this will give you the best chance to prove you've made every effort to heal and provide the child with a stable environment."

"But we're divorced. *I'm* divorced. I have my own apartment. Drew rents his half of the house from me—we kept it undivided in our settlement as an investment. We're divorced." How many times did she have to remind him?

The counselor looked at his file.

"The apartment you rented has been sublet to someone else. All of your finances had been put on a hold. Your ex-husband is the only one who had access to them. You'd left him as next of kin on your Page Two, and he had power of attorney when you went missing."

God, what *didn't* the navy have on file about her?

"I gave him the power of attorney for the house, for my finances, in the event of my..." She swallowed. "Oh."

"Right. Even though everyone hoped you'd made it to land and were still alive, all indications pointed to your death." Lucas leaned toward her. "This is where it's going to take some time, Gwen. You're coming back to a world that thought you were dead. Add that to the usual adjustments after six months at sea on any deployment. You've got your work cut out for you."

"I can't go back to that house."

To Drew.

Lucas looked up. "Were you abused there? Was your breakup acrimonious?"

"No, not at all." She bit her lip, still severely chapped from months of sun and primitive living. "Drew and I—we're friends, we've remained friends. He's never hurt me." No, she'd done a good job of hurting herself, thank you very much.

"Then you can manage this. You don't have a choice, Gwen, not if you want to go back to Oak

Harbor. You're not ready to live alone—you need someone there to help you reenter."

He made sense, but…

"My ex won't be expecting me."

Lucas watched her with compassionate eyes. "You're not the first GI to come back to this type of situation. Your time away has certainly been unique, but coming home to an ex—it happens. Especially when there are children involved. You haven't had kids together, but you told me you had pets, right? And now you want to adopt baby Pax. Your friend—" he glanced back at his records "—Roanna, she suggested moving back in with your ex. In fact, I know she's spoken with him." Lucas shrugged. "It's just until you're on your feet again. Nothing permanent."

"Doesn't look like I have much of a choice, does it?" She sure as hell didn't want to spend one more day in the hospital.

"Not really."

She clutched the sofa's throw pillow to her belly. He wasn't going to give her any more wiggle room.

"You told me all along that you and your ex have maintained a friendship. Since he's amenable to the arrangement, I recommend that you accept it. It'll be easier to room with someone who knows you, and having your pets with you will be helpful as you adjust."

Gwen tried to slow the thoughts that whirled like pinwheels. "What if the adoption comes through quicker than we expect? I want to bring Pax to *my* home, the place I'm going to raise him. Plus, isn't having a man around who isn't permanent, too confusing for an orphaned child?"

Luke leaned back in his chair. "Gwen, I do hope your adoption goes through. I've got no doubt that you'll make an excellent mother. But you need to learn the first lesson all mothers have to master—you give yourself the oxygen first. Adoption, overseas adoption especially, can be emotionally grueling. You have to allow yourself some mental space before you go through everything required to bring Pax home. And you need time to heal."

She refused to consider that the adoption wouldn't clear; the fact that she'd saved Pax from his burned-out village when he was two months old, and had cared for him until she'd walked out of the jungle last week, put the odds in her favor.

But living with Drew again? Didn't Doc Lucas know that it could present its own kind of torment?

You're friends.

True, her ex-husband didn't have any idea of the thoughts she'd had as she'd faced her own mortality over the past six months. No one did. She and Drew were friends, had been since their split. But her feelings for him had been magnified by her adrenaline, by the threat of imminent death.

She'd made it through shark-infested waters, a terrorist camp, unbearable living conditions.

Compared to that, living with Drew, for a few nights or even a few weeks, would be a cakewalk.

For Pax, she could do anything.

"Okay, fine."

She wasn't going to argue with a medical dude. She'd made it this far—she'd agree to whatever she had to, to get back. Drew was obviously being nice enough to go along with this, and she owed him. When she got there, she'd explain that she wasn't going to stay at the house any longer than absolutely necessary. They'd lived under the same roof without communicating for the last year of their marriage. She could manage a matter of days.

GWEN OPENED HER eyes to the small hospital room she'd lived in for the past three days, and let the thrill of being free wash over her. Her hospital bed was far more comfortable than the commercial plane seat she'd endured for the twenty-two hour flight back from the Philippines, and much cleaner than any of the night camps she'd made for herself during her six months on the run. Today was go-home day.

Drew.

The phone on her nightstand rang. The clamor startled her, and her muscles tensed painfully in her back, her legs.

"Hello?"

"Gwen, honey, it's Ro." Gwen felt a sense of warmth wash over her, and she couldn't stop tears of relief from spilling down her cheeks. Her best friend from way back when they'd been midshipmen at the Naval Academy, Ro knew her as well as Drew once had.

"I'd know your voice anywhere, sister. How are you?"

Ro laughed. "How am *I?* More like how the hell did you do what you did? First, I'm jealous as hell that you're getting all this attention for ditching and saving your crew. Now you come back alive, from conditions a lot of SEALs haven't survived. You're a hero, sweetie."

"Can you hear that flutter? It's my BS flag. I'm waving it in your face."

They both laughed.

"I'm glad to see you're not letting any of it go to your head."

"Oh, I will, trust me. You owe me at least a month's worth of almond lattes."

"Done." Ro paused, the silence scaring Gwen as much as the ringing phone had.

"What?"

"Have you talked to Drew?"

"Of course not. Why would I?" Gwen deliberately sounded obtuse. Ro had always held out hope that she and Drew would work things out. Especially since she herself was—

"Wait, Ro. You're married! I'm so sorry I missed it."

"You had other things to worry about, sweetie."

Ro paused again. "I missed you so much that day. It was so beautiful. I wish you could've seen it."

"Me, too." It was hard to imagine Ro married; she'd been so gung-ho about her career and hadn't wanted any distractions.

Gwen heard sniffles. "Are you crying?" she asked. "Don't cry, Ro. I'm fine. You'll see me soon and I'll prove it to you."

"I've missed you, Gwen. I can cry if I want." Rustling tissue and a cough or two echoed over the phone. "Listen, honey, you know you were assumed— I mean, people thought you weren't coming back?"

"I'm aware I was presumed dead—or at least as close as you can get to it, yes."

"It was horrible. We were all sick about it. I can't tell you how good it is to hear your voice, to know you made it back."

"I promise you I'm really here, Ro."

"You're okay with staying at Drew's?"

"Hmm. I hear you had something to do with it."

"Sweetie, don't be mad. I knew you wouldn't want to go to your mom's right away. You love Whidbey."

"True, but honestly, Ro, suggesting I live with Drew again?"

"Miles and I were with him when he found out you'd ditched, and again when we found out you got out. It's true, I suggested it to him."

"So I do have you to blame. I'll bet he's thrilled about me moving back in."

"He's okay with it, Gwen. He still cares for you."

"And I care for him. We'll always be friends."

She wasn't going to rehash her divorce history with her best friend. Not today.

Besides, she was so tired, exhausted, from talking.

"I have to hang up, Ro. When will I see you?"

"Later today. I'm sending a suitcase of clothes for you with the commodore's group. They'll be there soon. I'll see you when you land, okay?"

"I can't wait. Thanks for getting me some real clothes, Ro."

"Sure thing. See you. Love you."

"Love you, too."

Gwen hung up the phone and fought the urge to throw herself on the bed and have a long cry. But if she let one tear fall, there'd be so many more behind it she'd never get out of here, never get home. Ro's voice, so full of unabashed love, threatened to burst her thin layer of composure.

She wanted to get home, to sleep in her own bed.

Shivers of reality jumped on her skin. She didn't *have* a home to go to. Who knew where her bed was if the apartment had been sublet?

How had going through hell led to more torment? Being in close quarters with Drew would be nothing less than emotional torture. They hadn't lived together in too long. Awkward didn't begin to describe it.

Why did Drew have to be such a good guy, Mr. Do The Right Thing? For once, having him say "no" would have been a blessing for both of them.

She felt unease and even guilt at her lack of appreciation. Blaming Drew for being a good person wasn't going to get her very far.

He'd been the last person she'd talked to before she left on deployment.

She'd gone on a mission that had been moved up by a few weeks. The terrorist strongholds in the southern Philippine Islands had to be destroyed before they reached a point of serious threat to the nearby nations, as well as U.S. interests in the area.

Drew had come to the base, walked into the hangar and said goodbye to her. Wished her the best. They'd exchanged a friendly hug—they *were* friends, after all. She willed her mind not to go back to the beginning of her department-head tour, nearly six years ago. To the reason she and Drew had decided to end their nine-year marriage—the discovery that the spark, the romantic love, had died.

The timing had been bad. She was to assume command when she returned from deployment and the squadron spouses were all acquainted with Drew—he'd played the perfect navy spouse. He brought the right mix of concern for each person, the squadron's mission and the Oak Harbor community at large. His renowned sense of humor combined with his clean-cut good looks in a charming package. Gwen had been grateful to him, until that charm proved irresistible to one of her officers. An officer she'd pulled out of her ditched P-3.

Lizzie.

Don't. Go. There.

It could've been any other woman who'd turned out to be too interested in her husband. Their marriage had been a mess all on its own by then. She and Drew hadn't had a regular sex life in months, and when they did it'd become cursory, a matter of doing the familiar, getting the known-and-needed release. She slowly stood up from the hospital bed and let her legs bear her weight. Thinking about Drew made everything hurt all over again.

Gwen didn't fight the shame. No marriage fell apart due to one person. It always took two, and theirs had been no exception.

Her hands were still shaky. Lucas had told her it would take time for her system to settle back into a routine of regular meals, a safe place to rest, no constant need for vigilance.

Her body didn't realize that the threat she perceived today wasn't from the jungle or a terrorist insurgent. It was from her fear of not getting her baby back, the child she'd saved in the jungle. It was from the fear of having to finally face her grief over her failed marriage. She had to go and live with her ex-husband. What *wasn't* there to be afraid of?

Their marriage had been good once. Drew had been her safe harbor, giving her the chance to grow—as a woman, a naval officer, pilot and wife. But the hours of study his Physical Therapy education required, combined with Drew's need to live in Seattle for school during the week, meant they were hardly ever together. Her operational job as a department head, the last chance she had to prove she was worthy of the plum command tour billet, hadn't helped.

When Drew graduated and moved back to Whidbey they'd thrown themselves into setting up his new practice. With the onslaught of injured vets returning from Iraq and Afghanistan, his business had nearly tripled the first year.

She was happy for him, but they never had enough time alone for her to really express her pride in him. Weeknights were filled with social obligations for her and long hours in the clinic for him. Even a few words before sleep became rare.

Her record-breaking performance as the squadron operations officer made her a shoe-in for squadron command. Before she'd finished her department head tour, their marriage was over. She'd taken shore duty orders away from Whidbey, away from the emotional fallout of the divorce. It had been a tough time in Washington, D.C. She blamed it on missing Whidbey and their pets.

As expected, she was awarded her own squadron. She asked for a billet in Jacksonville, Florida, but her detailer sent her back to Whidbey as the executive officer. The promise of commanding officer in one short year took her career to a new level.

She and Drew had picked up where they'd left off—as the good friends they'd become since their divorce. Contact only when needed to facilitate her visiting the pets. A text here and there to check in, but no more than a couple of times a month, if that.

It still bothered her that she'd failed at marriage. She'd run from the vulnerability needed to maintain intimacy in the middle of everything life threw at her—her job, Drew's job, the long deployments.

Couples drifted apart all the time.

But the drift wasn't what had brought the final blow to her marriage.

The death knell to theirs hadn't been finding Lizzie with Drew that awful night. Gwen believed Drew—nothing had happened between him and Lizzie. Not then, anyhow. What had cut deep was the realization that they didn't have a relationship anymore. She didn't have a husband, she had a housemate.

"All ancient history," she grumbled to her empty room.

Just great. She'd been back only a few days and she was already talking to herself. Maybe the months in survival mode had forever changed her.

"WHICH VILLAGE WAS it, Gwen?" Navy Captain and Wing Commodore Buzz Perry, her boss on Whidbey, sat in front of her. He was the last one to question her. Yet because he was her boss, the closest in her chain of command, he thought he'd be able to ferret out what the past five days of interrogation hadn't.

"I don't know the name. I don't speak Tagalog, Commodore. I told you what I've told everyone else. Pax was the only survivor." Tears scalded her eyes at the mere mention of the baby she'd saved. The child she now considered her own. "No offense, sir, but I'm talked out. The sooner I get back to Whidbey, the sooner I can report to the squadron."

Gwen refused to tell the commodore that she was afraid she'd never feel strong enough to go back to her job. She hoped it was her weakness from lack of decent nutrition and the overwhelming stress she'd dealt with for too long.

A vulnerability that would heal with time.

She'd survived the debriefings she'd been through with the State Department, Department of Defense, Department of the Navy, and now her boss, the wing commodore. He'd been flown down from Oak Harbor on the base C-2 airplane to meet with her before he escorted her back to Whidbey Island.

"We're here to help you, Gwen. We'll help you adopt the baby you rescued, if that's what you want. But you have to see the difficult position you've put the government in. We want to reward you for all you've sacrificed but you seem to feel that nothing less than this baby will be enough. It's not so simple, Gwen. The needs of the navy and the country, not to mention diplomatic relations, have to come before any personal issues."

The commodore's eyes were steady but she knew the deal. His chain of command had put him up to this. The highest levels of government wanted to get as much information from her as possible.

Fresh intel was always a hot commodity.

She fought to keep still.

"The difficulty *I've* caused? What about the difficulty of flying a forty-year-old aircraft that wasn't fit for fair weather, let alone outmaneuvering a surface-to-air-missile during monsoon season? What about how I escaped from a terrorist training camp? What about the difficulty that serving my country has caused *me?*"

The commodore stretched his arms across the worktable in the psychiatrist's office and placed his hands over Gwen's.

"I'm not the enemy, Gwen. Neither are any of the doctors or officials who've questioned you this past week."

She sighed. Her body ached to lie down; she wanted to sleep for hours, days. Pax hadn't been the only weight she'd carried through mile after mile of jungle. She needed a safe place to shelve her emotions before they got the better of her.

"Then stop acting like one." She clasped her hands and stared at the floor.

Buzz shifted in his seat. This wasn't easy on him,

either, but she didn't have the energy to muster any compassion.

"Gwen, if I could've changed anything, I would have. That airframe would've been recalled before you left on deployment, and you would have had one of the new P-8s. Our funding's been short-changed by my predecessor's actions."

Commodore Perry referred to the criminal deeds of the previous commodore, who'd falsfied the aircraft maintenance books. He was now doing jail time in Fort Leavenworth military prison. As a result, it was taking longer for the newer airframes to come on line in the wing and her squadrons. The plane Gwen had ditched in the Pacific Ocean hadn't been up to the rigors of a deployment, much less being shot at by a modern missile. The crew would've had much more of a chance in one of the new P-8s. The former commodore's crimes also included murder, but his punishment hadn't helped the crews flying the aging planes.

He'd indirectly put aircrews like Gwen's in danger.

"The old frame was part of the problem, but we both know a surface-to-air missile brought her down, the same as it would have a brand-new P-8." Not to mention the fact that the plane had checked out okay before deployment.

Fatigue blew out her anger.

"Face it, Commodore, it goes back to pilot error,

doesn't it? I should have abandoned the mission earlier." Five minutes would have saved the navy an old plane, protected her crew from trauma and avoided her jungle adventure.

"Gwen, *you* brought her down safely. You saved every life on that bird. The intel your mission captured prevented what would've been a massacre of tens of thousands of people in a sports stadium two weeks later. To top it off, you rescued a newborn from a burned-out village. You're a hero to me, to the whole damned country, Gwen. But it would help everyone if you could remember more details about your captors. We want to prevent future terrorist attacks."

"Don't you think it would help *me* to remember, too? Then our interview would be over. I'm lucky I made it ashore, Commodore. I was so afraid of the sharks in that warm water. The prison camp wasn't fun, either." She leaned her head back. The soft leather of the office chair was like cashmere compared to the old material that covered the P-3's she was used to.

Would her arms always feel this empty without Pax in them?

As long as her baby remained eleven thousand miles away in the Philippines, yes. There was a possibility she might never see him again—slight but a possibility nonetheless. Still, her heart would never let go of him, of his smile, the way he clung to her through their struggles. If that happened, she'd have to accept it, as she'd had to accept her failed marriage.

Drew.

Friends. We're friends with a unique history together.

GWEN DRESSED WITH care in the outfit Ro had sent her—dressy black jeans and a soft flowing grey cardigan. Her cream-colored Italian wool coat set off the ensemble. Leave it to Ro to understand that she needed to feel pretty again, more like the woman she'd been when she left Whidbey.

This wasn't a usual homecoming. No navy band would play upon her arrival; she wouldn't be dressed in her uniform or flight suit. The squadron, at her request, wouldn't be there. She wasn't up to it yet.

As she shakily applied the makeup Ro had included with the clothes, she ignored how pale her reflection in the mirror was, how chapped her skin, her lips. Whidbey was the best place for a sailor to do reentry. She wouldn't be alone in her struggles, if and when they came. Other survivors were doing just fine, whether they were still on active duty like her or had transitioned to civilian life.

A lot of the vets *weren't* fine—they continued to suffer immeasurably. Would she be one of them?

It felt odd to put on makeup again. What would Drew think when he saw her?

"Nothing," she muttered. "He's going to think the same thing he did when Miles, Ro or any of our other friends came back." Anger at her uncontrollable emotions sucked away the last of her energy, and she leaned against the hospital room's sink.

Where was the tough streak she'd always been able to rely on?

She had no control over what she'd been through, or the fact that she'd returned from the dead, virtually homeless. Gwen slapped some blush on her cheeks. She didn't have to *look* as if she'd been through hell, at any rate.

They'd all thought she'd died, out on that ocean. So had she.

Miracles still happened.

THE FLIGHT HOME TO Naval Air Station Oak Harbor was thirty minutes, tops, but Gwen felt as though she was on another endless journey.

After a quick drive from Madigan Army Hospital, they'd taken off from McCord Air Force Base in a C-12, the twin-engine turboprop owned by NAS Whidbey. She hadn't been so keen to get on another plane after the long trip back from Manila, but at heart she remained a pilot, and a practical one at that. Twenty-five minutes in the air versus more than two hours in a car, longer if there was typical Seattle traffic, was worth any anxiety.

Once her feet hit the tarmac on Whidbey, her healing could start.

She closed her eyes and tried to imagine the feel of Pax's little body as she'd held him, carried him through miles of jungle and through the crowded streets of Manila. His baby scent… These memories sustained Gwen in her hope that she'd be his legal mother soon. She'd gotten through the jungle, the journey to the American embassy and all she had left was this flight home to Oak Harbor.

The experience of having the medical team poke, prod and question her to determine the extent of her injuries was over.

The only hurt she continued to suffer was remembering the excruciating goodbye to Pax as she'd turned him over to the Philippine social service workers. He had to live in an orphanage pending his adoption.

She squeezed her eyes shut against the vision of row upon row of tiny cribs, Pax one of dozens of babies.

"Mama's getting you out, baby."

The drone of the engines kept her words inaudible to the others. She opened her eyes and looked around. The commodore and his few staff members were reading, napping or staring out the windows. They'd be exchanging knowing glances if any of them had noticed her talking to herself.

Heck, did Drew realize what he'd signed up for when he'd agreed to help her transition?

He'd never believe she'd had a change of heart about her priorities, even when he found out she wanted to adopt a baby. He'd assume the worst of her as he always had those last fractured months of their life together. He'd assume she was in it for herself.

You survived a ditch, war-torn terrorist country, turning over the baby you love. You can do this.

When her life was threatened, it'd been clear that, of all her accomplishments, the one that mattered most was her marriage. A marriage that had failed. Gwen didn't kid herself—she knew she was far from perfect.

So she'd thought of her marriage during those long, traumatic days and nights. As she ditched her P-3C, as she floated at the whim of the ocean's harsh currents, her thoughts had gone back to Drew and to the love they'd once shared. She was only human.

CHAPTER THREE

GWEN SAW HIM as soon as the plane stopped taxiing and pulled up to the hangar.

Drew.

He was the tall one with the sure stance, waiting for her with a small group of other people. Relief eased some of the tightness in her chest. She'd specifically told the commodore that she wasn't ready to meet and greet her squadron. Not yet, not like this.

Unstable.

How did she go from constantly being "on" while in survival mode, to feeling like such a complete emotional wreck?

"Gwen." The commodore's hand was on her shoulder. It took every ounce of energy she had left to take her gaze from Drew, to unbuckle and get out of the small plane. The squadron XO carried her bags. He'd had to fill in for her, be the CO, until she came back. Yet now he deferred to her.

"Thanks, Bradley."

"No problem."

Both men looked at her, waiting. They wanted her to be the first off the plane.

Gwen tried to grin but it wasn't much of a success. She turned and walked to the main cabin door. The airman who'd opened the door stood back after he'd let the ladder down.

"It's all yours, ma'am." He motioned for her to leave.

She took a deep breath and ignored the immediate sharp pain that lanced through her left side. Her ribs were still bruised from the last fall she'd taken, tripping over a tree root on her way out of the jungle with Pax in her arms. Thankfully he hadn't been injured.

The day was bright and she squinted at the light as she grasped the railing and took the four steps down to the tarmac.

As soon as her feet hit the deck she bent her knees, then sank to the ground and kissed the concrete. To hell with her fancy dress pants or what anyone else thought.

There'd been many nights when she'd believed she'd never be on Whidbey's tarmac again.

She straightened and walked to the hangar. The open doors and the welcoming group were at least a hundred feet away, but Drew's features were as sharp as if he stood six inches from her.

His sunglasses hid his eyes so she only had his facial features and posture by which to judge his demeanor. He looked taller, his face more defined, more mature. Not as young as she'd remembered him for six long months.

She'd fought to come back here alive.

Her independence was still intact even though she had to accept help from the last person she ever wanted to depend on—Drew. It was only temporary.

At least she'd be able to make amends to him, to tell him she finally understood that neither of them was more to blame than the other for their divorce. She'd played a big part by not recognizing her own need for independence sooner and wanted him to know she didn't hold any ill will toward him. She truly only wanted his happiness.

This would be a new start, a chance for both of them to move on like they should have done years ago.

Before she could finish her train of thought Drew stood in front of her. She hesitated. Was he angry he'd been coerced to take her in?

"Gwen." He closed the distance between them and embraced her. She smelled Ivory soap and the hint of black licorice, his favorite snack. Licorice was Drew's go-to stress reliever. He'd devoured it from big plastic bins after his return from the war, and again during his final dissertation and exams for his doctorate.

He kept his arms tightly around her, and she relished the feel of his winter jacket against her cheek. By keeping her eyes closed she could almost convince herself she still had him to come home to. That this was real.

She felt an urge to pull back, to look him in the eye and tell him she'd realized what really mattered in life.

If she did, he'd think she was crazy, suffering from PTSD, that she didn't mean any of it. She had no way to convince him of her sincerity.

Her epiphany—that love and relationships were the only important things in life—was too late. He didn't deserve to be harangued with revelations that might have served them better four years ago, maybe even earlier.

Homecomings weren't good times for surprises or emotional breakdowns.

Instead, she clung to his shoulders and leaned heavily against him. It beat collapsing on the tarmac in front of onlookers.

She would have stayed in his arms for hours if he'd allowed it. The longer she could soak up his strength, the longer she could put off facing the reality that she had to go home with him and play at being friends.

Drew made the decision for both of them as he pulled back and bent his head to hers, taking the sunglasses off. "I'm so glad you made it, Gwen."

His eyes were unnaturally bright and she wanted desperately to believe it was from relief that she was alive.

"I am, too. And I'm doing great. I won't be in

your way for long. I appreciate your taking me in, though."

His instant frown removed the shine from his eyes and his mouth formed a straight line. An all-too-familiar expression from the last months of their marriage. His body stiffened next to hers but he kept his arms loosely around her waist.

"It's going to take a while to recover from everything you've been through, Gwen."

"Do I look that bad?"

He had the decency to appear chagrined.

"You've been to hell and back. Ro told me you were living in the jungle for most of your time on the ground."

"I was. But I've been trained to do that. I went to SERE school, remember?" Graduating from the navy's Survival, Evasion, Resistance and Escape training had been one of her proudest accomplishments.

Until she'd carried Pax through one of the more dangerous places on the planet and lived to tell about it.

"Speaking of Ro…" She peered over his shoulder to where her best friend stood next to the ridiculously handsome Miles.

"Ro!" She stepped away from Drew, holding her arms open. Ro ran up to her and gave her a big hug.

"Welcome home, sis."

Gwen couldn't say anything past the burning in her throat.

DID HE *REMEMBER* her going to SERE school?

Drew shoved down a distinct, primal need to growl as he watched Ro and Gwen reunite.

How could he *forget?* When Gwen arrived back from SERE she'd sported several scrapes and bruises. The large bruise over her kidney had given him pause—and been the start of a long battle to convince Gwen that she belonged somewhere other than the navy.

He ignored the tension in his stomach. He'd been young and fiercely protective of his new wife. She'd been just as intense, determined to prove she'd make a good officer.

Gwen had never understood that of course he supported her career and her talents. But to him she'd been his wife first. And he'd wanted to protect her, to keep her from the horrors she'd witnessed in the war in Afghanistan.

Now she'd survived the wilds in the southern Philippines. She'd evaded terrorist camps and again, death.

No wonder she hardly spared him a glance. He couldn't stand to look at himself, either.

Because in the end he hadn't been able to protect her—from anything.

He waited until she was done with the brief greetings from Ro and Miles. They'd agreed before she landed to keep it short. Ro would visit Gwen soon enough, at home.

As soon as possible without being rude, he

walked back to her side and slipped his arm around her waist. She stiffened for a moment before she relaxed, no, *leaned* into him.

He noted that Ro and Miles discreetly moved away as she turned her head into his shoulder. Fear raced through him. This exhausted, drained Gwen was not the proud woman who'd left on deployment eight months ago. Not the good friend he'd had on island over the past several years, the one he'd split the vet bills with.

"I never doubted that you'd survive this, Gwen." He couldn't resist planting a kiss on her head before he lifted her chin to let her see he meant it.

"Liar." Her mouth tilted up in its lopsided grin. God, he'd missed her. He couldn't stop himself from stroking her cheek before he stepped back. He still kept his arm around her, in case she needed the support. His fingers tingled. Her skin, even after months on the run and recovering from the brutal conditions she'd endured, was still the softest thing he'd ever touched, at least in the places the sun hadn't reached.

"Maybe I was scared you'd been killed, but I knew if anyone could get out of that hellhole alive, it was you. I never gave up hope, Gwen."

Her gaze measured him and he had no doubt he didn't make the grade. How could he? He'd begged her to leave the navy during her department head tour, the ticket to her XO/CO tour.

Back off. You're friends.

"Homecomings always stir up emotions. Once you're back on your feet this will feel like a dream."

The spark in her eye extinguished and she looked exhausted. "You're right, of course."

Guilt ran a knife through him, leaving another invisible wound. He'd been safe and warm in his bed, working in his office, living on the island Gwen loved so much while she'd battled a monsoon, a missile, terrorists. Yet she'd come back. And she'd saved the lives of her crew, and—

"The baby. When will you get to see the baby again?"

"You know?" Her eyes were wide, her mouth open. Her soft, sexy mouth.

"Of course I do, Gwen."

"I'm not sure when. It may be a long while. I can't believe you already found out about him."

He sighed. "I was still listed as next of kin on your Page Two. Because everyone knew we're still friends, the command kept me informed pretty much every step of the way. Ro gave me any information I wasn't officially cleared for." He nodded in Ro's direction. "Without her I wouldn't have known you were safe until a day or so later."

He also knew that she'd told Ro she didn't want any visitors at the Madigan Army Hospital, not even her best friend. Certainly not her ex-husband, no matter how solid their friendship was. She'd requested that everyone wait to see her until she got back to the island.

It had nearly killed him to wait, not to drive down on his own and burst into her hospital room.

He had a lot of ground to cover if he was going to make things right with her. Although it was nothing like the horrors Gwen must have gone through, during the past six months he'd lived in his own kind of hell. Trying to persuade her to get out of the navy and settle down into *his* idea of the perfect life had been his biggest mistake. He'd paid for it with their broken marriage. But at this point all of that was inconsequential. Except for his deep desire to make it up to her, to be anything but the pain in the ass he'd been for too long. Gwen's independence was so important to her that she'd left their marriage rather than rely on him to meet her emotional needs. Needs he hadn't been capable of meeting, not then.

The least he could do now was be a real friend— with no expectations.

"Drew, thanks so much for coming today." She put her hand on his forearm. "I'm sorry I didn't want anyone to visit right away, but I thought it was best. I was looking pretty rough when I first got back."

He shook his head. As if he'd ever thought she was anything less than beautiful! "Don't you remember how awful I looked when I got back from downrange ten years ago?"

"You were tired. And the nightmares weren't

exactly fun for you." A glimmer of fear flickered in her expression.

"Gwen, you're going to be okay. You'll get through it—I did."

"I don't want you to think you have to take care of me just because of that time, Drew. We're not married anymore. I'm not your responsibility. About the baby—yes, I found a baby while I was on the run." She faltered, her eyes downcast and her shoulders slumped. "I want to go home, um, to the house, and talk about it there. Not here."

"You're free to leave, Gwen. No one's going to ask any more of you than you want them to." He glanced over at the commodore, Ro and Miles. They were huddled in a group several feet away, trying to look as though they weren't studying every aspect of their reunion.

Some reunion. He hoped they hadn't expected a passionate embrace. He and Gwen hadn't kissed that way since they were both younger, still married, still in love.

God help them both get through the next few days.

THEY DIDN'T TALK on the drive to the house. Gwen couldn't get past the weight of exhaustion that pressed on her bones, and thankfully Drew didn't attempt conversation.

You're going home. You're almost home!

As much as she told herself the house would

never be home again, not with Drew, it was how she felt as he pulled into their driveway. As if she were returning from a regular deployment, home to the safety of their marriage. She'd always felt safe with Drew, regardless of how ugly it got between them.

"Here, I've got your bags."

Drew grabbed the two small overnight bags—one she had from the embassy in Manila and the one Ro had sent stuffed with new clothes and cosmetics.

"Ro went overboard—she bought me so many outfits and girly stuff. I need to thank her and pay her back."

"You know she'll never take any money from you. She was worried that you were living in Madigan Army Hospital gowns and sweatpants from the embassy store in Manila."

Gwen laughed as she climbed the wooden steps to the front door. "It was pretty bad, at first, but the embassy staff found clothes that fit me, and as you know, there are some wonderful markets in the PI. They outfitted me with all kinds of summer clothing."

"It's a little too chilly for that here."

"Yes." Actually, she hadn't paid much attention to the weather or the temperature—she'd been focused on Drew. Early spring on Whidbey was typically windy and chilly. Today the air was still and the sun shone, making the grass sparkle. She'd missed the deep emerald-green unique of the Pacific Northwest. Gwen soaked up the scenery, let it lift her spirits.

"The door's unlocked."

Of course it was. Drew didn't see the need to lock the door, ever. It'd always bothered her, his view that if thieves wanted in, they'd get in.

"So Nappie's still guarding the place?" They'd shared the dog, a hound mix, along with the parrot, when she'd moved out.

"Rosie's helping. Nappie's hearing isn't as good as it used to be when she was a pup."

Sure enough, as soon as Gwen stepped foot inside, the bird belted out "Mommy's home!"

Rosie said "Mommy's home!" whenever anyone came into the house, male or female, acquaintance or stranger. Still, it made Gwen smile and she had to wipe away a few tears of gratitude.

"You all right?" Drew's hand was on her shoulder and no, she wasn't all right—not considering the way she'd reacted to his touch.

"Fine, fine. Like you said, I'm going to be overly emotional for a bit. The docs told me the same thing. It's not personal, just part of my recovery process."

Drew dropped his arm and motioned for her to go up the stairs.

"Let's get you settled."

"Wait—I need to say hi to my girls." She bent down and accepted wet sloppy kisses from Nappie, the long-eared rescue who'd been their first pet.

After she was certain Nappie had received enough affection, she walked over to Rosie, the Indian Ring-Necked parrot who hadn't stopped talking.

"Whatcha doing?" Rosie cocked her head at the angle that always made Gwen laugh.

"Rosie's a pretty bird, aren't you, girl?" Gwen crooned. Rosie bent her head forward, exposing her nape for Gwen to scratch. It was the ultimate show of trust from a winged creature. More burning tears pushed at Gwen's eyes.

Was she going to see everything through a lens of grateful tears from now on?

"Good bird." She gave Rosie a kiss on her beak and turned back to Drew.

"Where to?"

She thought he'd take her to the guest room, where she'd lived for months before she'd moved out, but followed him to the master bedroom.

"I made this up for you. I wasn't sure how you felt about coming back. Wait—let me rephrase that. I know you didn't want to come back here, that you'd want your apartment. I'm sorry it got rented out from underneath you, Gwen."

Gwen watched Drew put her small travel case on their bed. What *had* been their bed, in the master bedroom, which was oddly devoid of any hint of Drew's presence. Neat stacks of her clothes and favorite books were on the bureaus, where Drew had placed them; *she* never folded her clothes so meticulously.

That was why he'd always done the laundry.

"Losing an apartment is part of the deal when you're considered dead, I suppose." Her attempt at humor was weak, and she knew it.

"This is not going to be easy for you, Gwen, and I want you to promise you'll tell me immediately if you think you're down too far."

They both knew what the *down too far* could lead to. Friends had attempted suicide at such points in their post-war return to "normal" life.

"I'm not one of your PT clients, Drew." She held up her hand. "Wait, that came out way too harsh. Can you tell I haven't had regular conversations for a long time?" She referred to not having to use gestures the way she had with Mia, the woman who gave her and Pax shelter in a remote village, or using the very few words of Tagalog she knew.

He smiled. "Does it seem weird to be talking to people who all speak English again? Other than doctors and navy personnel, I mean."

"Yes and no. I had to communicate with Pax, of course, but that was mommy-baby stuff. All physical. Hugs, kisses, tickles. When I settled in with a village woman, Mia, she and I communicated mostly through sign language. It's not like I was in solitary confinement or anything."

Except in her thoughts of him…and the mental and emotional review of her life those months away from civilization had granted her.

"Like I said, you need anything, you tell me."

"Sure."

"I'm in the guest room. As you can see, I've brought in some of your stuff— the rest is in the garage." The gruff edge of apology surprised her. It wasn't his fault she was here, that he'd had to go through her household goods.

She tried to smile, tried to look as if she knew how to handle a multisentence conversation anymore. He was right; she hadn't talked to a lot of people for the past six months, not until the past two weeks during which she'd been quizzed and downright interrogated by every embassy and military official who needed information from her.

How did you survive, Commander? Were you raped? Were you hungry much of the time? Where is the baby from? Why did you decide to take a baby with you? Do you really think you can leave the country with that child? How can you prove you didn't kidnap him?

"Gwen? You okay?"

"I'm fine." She couldn't, wouldn't, have him waiting for her to explode with PTSD symptoms. "Don't worry, Drew, I haven't shown any signs of PTSD yet. I've had one or two nightmares, but that's to be expected."

His expression softened. "Of course it is. It's like being downrange, Gwen, but probably worse. You were without your crew, your team. You were all alone out there for a lot of the time, weren't you?"

"Yes, at least the first month and a half. Shortly

after I found Pax I made some friends I could trust among the locals." Heat rushed to her face. "You've heard all this, haven't you?"

"Not all of it." He shifted on his feet. "I know you're not ready to talk about it. Once you decide you are, I'm probably not the person you'll want to share everything with. But I'm here, Gwen. Ro's here. You're not alone. And your mother wanted to be here with her husband when you landed, but I convinced them to wait at least a week or two. She'd appreciate a call that you're here—later, when you're ready."

"I AM SO sorry you got saddled with taking me in, Drew."

He shrugged. "It's not a problem." He shot her a lopsided grin. "You never changed that Page Two, you know."

Ah, her Page Two—the second page in any sailor's service record, but the most important in the event of his or her death. It listed next of kin and who their Service Group Life Insurance was going to.

"No, I didn't change it."

"You've had a busy few years. Your Page Two was an easy thing to forget, although I'm surprised your admin chief didn't ask you about it."

Admin *had* reminded her, but she'd purposefully kept Drew as the primary beneficiary on her policy after the divorce. She would never have made it this far in her career without him. He deserved it all if she was killed in the line of duty, legal husband or not. Her mother and stepfather were financially secure; they wouldn't need the money.

And even if they had, she would've kept Drew as her beneficiary. It wasn't his fault he'd married a woman who was never meant to be married.

They'd been so young.

She couldn't say it. Not again. Not now.

"If anything happened to me, it would take care of my share of the house. Plus, it'd keep Nappie and Rosie fed and in great toys for the rest of their lives."

Drew's silence proved how crazy she sounded.

"I've changed, Drew. I'm not who I was six months ago."

Should she tell him about those thoughts? The visions of them when they'd been in love? Making love.

Oh, no.

"You've been through a lot, Gwen, and yes, it's changed you, changed your outlook on things. But trust me, it's like life on Whidbey. New restaurants pop up, coffee shops switch owners, but the water, the mountains—all the fundamentals are still there. Same as always."

"The snow cap on Mt. Baker is shrinking."

He grinned. "Well, yeah, there's that."

Standing next to Drew, feeling his warmth,

smelling that familiar scent…her head was so heavy and his shoulders would feel so good to lean on.

It wouldn't be fair to either of them if she took advantage of the situation.

"Yeah." Her voice cracked.

She couldn't find the words, didn't have the energy to explain that she'd changed from the inside out. She'd forfeited any right to accept comfort from Drew the day she'd signed their divorce papers. The things she'd found boring before her ordeal—a safe home, a good meal, time to simply relax—meant the world to her now. She wished she could explain this to him without the risk that he'd think it was PTSD or related emotional upset.

You're the only one who needs to know you've changed.

Why did she care whether or not Drew understood she'd turned into a mother, a family woman?

"I'll leave you for a while. Take your time. Have a long hot shower if you need it. When you're ready, I'll put together some dinner." He left the room and shut the door behind him.

The instant quiet scared her. After the incessant humming of bugs, birds and animals she never identified, the silence of the bedroom made her uneasy. At least the hospital had a constant *whirr* of activity and air systems serving as white noise.

You're safe.

As she'd done these past two weeks of freedom, she forced herself to focus on the next obvious task.

A hot shower.

The novelty of readily available water hadn't worn off yet. She'd never take hot running water for granted again.

Before she walked into the master bathroom, she tiptoed to the bedroom door and silently turned the handle to open it. Just a crack.

It was silly and stupid and maybe superstitious, but it made her feel connected to Drew.

An invisible link could save your life.

DREW FIRED UP the gas grill and used the few minutes outside on the deck to calm down.

"Damn it." He spoke under his breath to the trees, the earth, the fates that had blessed him with Gwen's survival while cursing him with her nearness.

He really needed a cold shower. Gwen had never stopped turning him on, difficult though it'd been that last year they'd lived together. As the friends they'd become, he knew she was off-limits. That didn't change his initial reaction to her each time she came over to see the pets, or whenever he ran into her in town. Sexual compatibility had never been a problem for them.

It was emotional maturity they'd lacked. Apparently, he still hadn't grown up. He felt lower than a caterpillar, getting turned on by her when she was clearly so fragile. When they both knew where it would all end.

They'd still be divorced.

If he was going to be the friend she needed right now, he had to ignore the sexual thoughts that had started the minute he saw her again.

He had to let go of the way his arms ached to haul her against him. The way he wanted to kiss her. To make love to her until she forgot about the world and everything she'd endured.

Double damn it.

When he went back in, he found her sitting at the long kitchen counter that divided the great room. She looked so waifish, all bundled in sweats and perched on the bar stool.

"You've kept the place clean, I'll give you that." Wet hair and chapped lips, and she still had her sense of humor.

"I have help. After you left on deployment my business picked up. I couldn't keep the house anything close to hygienic on my own." He offered her a grin. "My talents are limited to folding clean laundry."

"You, Mr. I-Can-Do-It-All, hired a housecleaner?"

"It was a long fall, but I'm tough that way. I can handle it."

She giggled, and it was like a blast of tropical wind as his ego reacted to her small sign of pleasure.

He needed to make sure he kept his distance over these next few weeks or he'd start misinterpreting every little thing she did.

Gwen had often told him that his sarcasm and arrogance had endeared him to her at first, but grown tedious as the years went by.

His self-recrimination had passed, though. There was no point in wondering why the heck he'd waited so long to grow up.

"I'm grilling veggies and chicken—that sound good?"

"Wonderful." She gazed around the kitchen as she absentmindedly rubbed the top of Nappie's head. "I don't expect you to wait on me, Drew. Let me do something."

"I'm not going to be your slave, believe me. But today's your big day. You're finally back from deployment."

"Yes, I am. Only two months late, right?"

Her squadron had returned two months ago, after six months in Japan. She'd deployed with them, but gone missing during their second month, on her ill-fated mission.

"Your XO has been acting as the CO since the change of command. He's kept me informed."

"How much did he know?"

"Not much, at least not based on what he shared with me. Like I said, Ro filled in the holes, plus she learned stuff ahead of the squadron. She didn't keep anything from me, even though I'm a mere civilian." He stopped himself from adding "and an ex-husband." He'd been read out of his clearances over seven years ago when he'd resigned his commission.

He watched her while he sliced zucchini and red onions for the grilling basket. To his immense relief, he could still recognize the real Gwen beneath her pallor and extreme thinness. But the shadows in her eyes worried him. What horrors had she faced?

"Look, let's save this conversation for later. For now, we'll eat and celebrate that you're back."

And I'll do my best to keep my hands to myself.

DETECTIVE COLE RAMSEY knew this wasn't the time to bother Anita Perez. It was the end of her workday, and her twelve-hour night shifts at Coupeville General Hospital left her tired and needing to sleep while her kids were in school. Her parents had moved in with her after her husband died, enabling her to take the graveyard shift. She had a boy and a girl, both in elementary school, two years apart.

They were adorable, like their mother.

Anita would be tired and in no mood to deal with the likes of him.

Too bad.

He'd read the island paper this morning and the news of his good friend Drew's ex-wife, Navy Commander Gwendolyn Brett, coming back from the dead was the big headline. The feel-good ending to what everyone had assumed would be a tragic story was the kick in the pants he needed.

It reminded him that miracles happened, even on Whidbey where he saw the worst of the community up close and personal each day.

Ramsey balanced the paper coffee carrier that held two steaming-hot cups of local brew, and a bag of fresh cinnamon donuts. If Anita wouldn't talk to him, he'd bribe her. When he'd conducted the investigation into her estranged husband's murder last year he'd discovered she had a wicked sweet tooth.

Her tall, slim figure exited the side door of the hospital and she made a beeline for her old station wagon. He pushed back the uncertainty that tightened his chest.

"Good morning, Anita."

She abruptly paused and her cool blue eyes sparked recognition before her professional nurse's mask fell back in place.

"Ramsey."

They studied each other for a full minute. He'd bet his paycheck, admittedly never enough, that she felt the attraction, too.

"Coffee?"

Anita was at eye level with him, but only because she wore flat working shoes. In the slightest of heels, she'd be taller than him.

He didn't care. In fact, it turned him on.

"Thanks." She reluctantly took the paper cup he offered. "I have to get home, Ramsey."

She started walking toward her car.

"I know you do. And this isn't a date." She'd declined the two other times he'd asked her.

She had the longest stride. He almost had to jog to keep up with her.

"Who said anything about a date?" she asked. She stopped at her car and looked up at the sky. He saw the raindrops hit her skin before he felt the *splats* on his sleeves.

She sighed, looking back at him. Resignation, maybe an acceptance that they should give it a try?

She nodded at the passenger side. "Get in."

Ramsey wasn't going to argue. If a beautiful woman told him to get in her car, he did it.

The interior smelled of sugar, coffee, her. Crumpled snack wrappers littered the back with its two booster seats. They sat in the comfortable quiet of the rainfall, the companionable silence completely different from the manner in which they'd met and their encounters until now.

"Mmm." The froth of her cappuccino stuck to her upper lip and he watched her tongue lick it off, her eyes closed.

"How was your shift?"

She sent Cole a sidelong glance, giving him a quick glimpse of arctic blue, before she returned her gaze to the windshield.

"The usual, but not as busy. Quiet." She sipped. "I prefer to have more to do. Not that I wish anyone ill. It's just that when it's quiet, I have too much time to…think."

"I know." Ramsey felt the same way when his days held nothing but paperwork.

"Yes, I suppose you do. Our jobs aren't really that different."

He took a gulp of his black coffee. He hadn't come here to talk about himself.

"How are your kids doing?"

"Fine." Which meant she wasn't going to allow him to step one inch into her life, much less her children's. She hadn't in the year since her husband was murdered by an overzealous senior naval officer who had stopped at nothing to secure his own career success. Why would she let him in now?

"Eventually you have to open up to somebody, Anita."

"Who says I haven't?"

"I saw enough of you last year to see that we operate in much the same way. You're not going to let anyone in who wasn't already there, who doesn't already know your story, at least that part of it. It's too much to put on anyone else."

"You haven't answered my question, Detective. For all you know, I took a lover and confided in him. But for the sake of argument, let's say I didn't. Why do you think I'd ever want to open up to anyone else again? To risk changing the family life I've built with my kids by bringing in someone new?"

He saw tears glistening in her eyes, turning them a bright aquamarine. They weren't tears of self-pity or even sadness. They were there because she was speaking her truth, revealing herself.

To him.

"You're a beautiful woman with two smart children. You're talented, hardworking, a doer. You're going to crave companionship again, if you haven't already."

Anita's gaze remained on him a split second after he'd finished, until she looked away. She stared at the steering wheel, her cheeks the exact shade of the red turtleneck she'd worn when he'd met her last year.

Crap. He'd said too much.

"You think I'm beautiful, huh?" She lifted one side of her mouth in a smile, producing a dimple his tongue wanted to explore.

Relieved, he returned the grin.

"Just the facts, ma'am."

He couldn't show her how damned attractive he found her. She'd have to make the first move if he was ever going to have a chance.

GWEN WATCHED DREW as he took a salad out of the refrigerator.

"You've got veggies on the grill."

"I saw fresh beets at the store and remembered that it's one of your favorites."

A delicious shiver of appreciation went through her. She didn't miss this proof that he'd been thinking about her, as she had him.

Worse, however, was her sense of anticipation. This was too much like other homecomings— where they'd enjoyed the day, ate a gourmet meal, made love…

Don't think about that.

Her unexpected desire and resultant frustration at knowing she wouldn't be acting on it anytime soon had to be a byproduct of being alone for so long. She was too tired to be thinking about sex. It had to be the stress, the chaotic emotions. Drew could be any other guy and she'd feel the same.

You fooling yourself with that line?

His shoulders stretched under his shirt as he turned back to the refrigerator and her unwanted need increased.

"Gwen?"

"What?"

"Iced tea or soda?" His raised eyebrows indicated that he'd had to ask her twice.

"Iced tea's fine."

She hoped he hadn't seen the desire on her face. What was she, fifteen and on a date with the rock star of her dreams?

Close enough, she supposed.

"Let me help, will you?" She stood up from the bar stool.

"Not today. I thought we'd sit inside at the table instead of the counter. Here." He handed her a glass of iced tea. "Take your drink and I'll be there in a sec."

She slid into a dining chair and looked around.

He'd changed virtually nothing since she'd left.

"All I'm doing lately is sleeping or sitting." She sipped her drink and nearly groaned with pleasure. He'd made it exactly the way she loved it—strong, with extra lemon.

"You've earned it." He placed the last of the lunch in front of her and took the chair across from her.

"Hmm."

They were quiet as they ate. Gwen couldn't remember when simple vegetables and grilled chicken breasts had tasted so good.

Eventually, she looked up. Drew was wearing a wide grin.

"What?"

"Nothing. It's great to see you enjoying your food. I don't know the last time I saw anyone attack their plate like that."

Gwen swallowed the veggies in her mouth and laughed.

"I keep thinking I'm not hungry, but the minute food hits my tongue, I can't stop eating."

His gaze dropped to her mouth and she wished she'd used any word other than *tongue*.

"I had to pretend I wasn't hungry to get through those early days out in the bush."

"I'll bet you did." Finally, after several excruciating seconds, he quit staring at her mouth.

Not before her lips tingled and white-hot heat shot to the sweet spot between her legs. Even her nipples were hard—she felt the lacy bra Ro had sent her brush against them.

She silently damned Ro for picking out such sexy underwear for her. It gave her body too much to remember.

All the wonderful sex she and Drew used to have…

"I didn't starve, not once I made it to the safe village, anyhow." But she'd suffered from fevers and depression, and during those times she didn't eat. Only the broth Mia spooned into her mouth had sustained her. That, and seeing Pax in Mia's arms. Wanting to be strong enough to hold him herself. Drew didn't need to know about that—no one did.

It was over.

"It takes time to start absorbing nutrients again. You'll probably feel better with simple meals for now."

"This is sheer magic." She spoke around a mouthful of the beet-quinoa salad.

Drew laughed. "Not quite. You know I'm a very basic cook."

"You're a great griller. I can bake my way through anything, but when it comes to the grill, I suck and you know it."

"Speaking of baking, Ro left you a treat."

"Oh, yeah?"

"What's your favorite dessert?"

His eyes sparkled and if she wanted to she could

pretend they were still married, still happy, still in love.

Cruel thing, imagination.

"I don't know—chocolate cake?"

"Her three-layer cake with that fancy frosting you like."

"Her ganache?" Besides knitting, baking was one of Ro's talents. She'd taken it up in earnest once she and Miles got together. Ro's deep-dark-chocolate cake with ganache was a specialty.

"That's it."

Gwen studied his face and found herself lost in his eyes. Was he remembering their personal history with chocolate cake, too?

Like the time they'd eaten it in bed after a long Saturday morning of lovemaking, only to break the dirty plates when their sheets fell to the floor as they went after each other again?

His eyes showed the same heat she felt.

"Drew, I had a lot of time to think out there."

He blinked. "I had time to think here, too. We'll talk about all of it, but not today."

"Okay, but I want you to know I'm all right. I'm not as badly off as you might think. I wasn't raped, you know." Unlike too many female POWs who'd had to deal with the after-effects of sexual assault, heaped on top of whatever conditions they'd survived.

Relief flashed in his eyes. She was glad she'd told him this much.

The rest would wait. It was too soon, her soul too raw.

CHAPTER FOUR

GWEN AWOKE TO the muted colors of their bedroom. She allowed herself to lie there and relish the warmth of the comforter, the familiarity of the mattress.

Reality crept in, inevitably. This wasn't her room anymore; it wasn't their bed, their life.

It was all Drew's.

She turned her face into the pillow and inhaled. Under the aroma of fabric softener and cotton, she could smell Drew's clean scent. Regret over all she'd lost seeped into her mind, and her morning lassitude disintegrated.

Getting up and dressed was still something she had to think about, but the promise of seeing Rosie and Nappie again, having a cup of coffee, spurred her on. She could dress later. For now she threw on her plush, pink, terry robe. It felt like heaven after wearing the same clothes for months on end. Her skin was still pretty red and scabbed over in some places where the filthy fabric had rubbed away the surface layers. Yet after only a matter of a week on antibiotics and special prescription ointments, it already felt so much better.

She headed for the kitchen, perhaps her favorite place in the house. Memories of meals she'd eaten here with Drew seemed to cling to the backsplash tiles they'd set themselves, and to the oak-stained cabinets they'd made a mess of until they'd found a rhythm, figured out how to work together on their new home. They hadn't been able to afford all the optional extras offered with the house when it was built. Lucky to get into the exclusive development with its priceless view of the surrounding area, they'd happily taken on the finishing touches themselves.

Somehow, between Drew's studying and her deployments, they'd done it. They'd made the barebone house a comfortable if not luxurious home, complete with modern conveniences that included a small cedar-lined sauna in their basement.

It was the house they were supposed to bring babies home to, not break in two during a divorce settlement.

At least they still both owned it. Drew rented her half, giving her a nice amount to invest each month. When he eventually sold the house, they'd split the profits.

The image of Drew with a new wife, moving into a different home, wasn't something she cared to dwell on. Friends or not.

She found the coffee and filters where they'd always been and started a pot.

The hardwood floor was warm under her bare feet. She stood in the spot where a sunbeam danced across the kitchen, the very spot Nappie wanted to claim.

"I know this is yours, but we can share it." Gwen sat down beside Nappie and looked into the dog's droopy, sad eyes before she hugged her. Gwen burrowed her face into Nappie's fur. The once-rich chestnut of her coat was peppered with gray, noticeably more than eight months ago. It was at once endearing and alarming to see the brown muzzle turning snowy white.

They'd named her after the second honeymoon they took to Napa Valley, California. While doing a bike tour of the valley, stopping at wineries whenever they wanted, they'd come upon an abandoned dog and her litter of puppies. Gwen had wanted to save all of them but practicality dictated that even one dog might be too much with their schedules. They took the mother and pups to a local vet, and ended up adopting Nappie, the runt of the litter.

Their friends had teased them, saying a dog was the "tester child," the step before the babies came.

No babies had happened for them. They'd never tried for kids because she'd never felt ready. Still, there'd been a few scares along the way, as in most marriages.

Once they were divorced, she'd known it had all worked out for the best.

"You're getting too old too fast, girl." Gwen rubbed Nappie behind the ears and the dog sighed her contentment before she released a noisy blast of gas.

"Lovely, Nappie."

"Helloooooo." Rosie the ring-necked parakeet sang her jealousy. She was in fact a parrot, but small compared to the kind normally associated with pirates. It didn't stop the spirited bird from talking all day long. Drew had surprised Gwen with Rosie when he'd gotten out of the navy—his way of telling her he was going to be their anchor and keep the home fires burning while she finished out her time.

"Don't be so jealous, Rosie. Nappie was here first." Gwen stroked Nappie's velvet-soft ears. "She's a jealous bird, isn't she, Nappie?"

Oh, noooooo. Rosie was as opinionated as she was loud.

Living on the run with nothing but dirt and jungle humus under her battered flight boots made this ordinary morning feel like paradise—one she'd never thought she'd have again. It helped ease the ache in her heart where it was broken from having to leave Pax behind.

"Lie down, lie down!" Rosie chanted at Nappie. The old hound ignored the nagging bird, used to her chatter and hypnotized by Gwen's strokes.

Gwen laughed. "I missed you, too, crazy bird."

"They both missed you." Drew's voice reached down from the upstairs loft.

Gwen jolted in shock. "I thought you were at work already."

"Obviously," he grumbled as he came down the open-backed stairs. The floor plan was everything they'd hoped their marriage and their life together would be. Bright, designed to let in the maximum amount of light. On the top level they had views of water, mountains and fir-tree forests. The window over the kitchen sink offered a spectacular view of Mount Baker when the skies were clear.

Unfortunately, the stunning house couldn't make up for the effects of the mutual neglect they'd heaped on their marriage. Not to mention the hard truth they'd reached, too late. They were more concerned about their careers than each other. "Are you going in late?" Her skin broke out in gooseflesh as he walked up next to her. No matter how long they'd been divorced, she'd never lost her physical awareness of him.

Even in those last painful months of their marriage.

She'd hated herself for her continued attraction to him. Wished she was more in control of her reaction to Drew. But after the last months of sifting through her life, self-loathing became an unaffordable pastime.

"The office thought I could use a couple days off.

They've threatened to beat me off with a weight bar if I show up before tomorrow."

"Oh." Of course they were protective of him. He'd been through so much. First an unsuccessful marriage, followed by a divorce. Then his ex-wife went missing, presumed dead, only to return six months later. To stay with him. While her career demands hadn't allowed the time necessary for her to know the staff well, she'd always enjoyed Drew's company picnics and holiday get-togethers. His staff's respect for him was reflected in their joking banter.

"This has to be an awful shock for you. Don't think for a minute that I'm foolish enough to think my reappearance is stressful only on me."

He rubbed his eyes and poured himself some of the coffee she'd brewed.

He didn't speak until he'd swallowed half of it.

"Not really, Gwen. I knew you were still alive."

"You don't have to do this, Drew. There's nothing wrong with believing I was dead. It's not your job to make me feel better about the fact that people accepted I was gone for job."

"I'm not." His eyes smoldered as he kept his gaze on her a heartbeat too long. "We have a connection. Maybe it's because we met so young, knew each other so well and remained friends after the divorce. Just because our romance died, our marriage ended, doesn't mean the entire thing, the bond, is shot."

She wished she'd picked one of the oversize

hand-thrown pottery mugs from the cupboard for her coffee instead of the small Japanese porcelain cup between her hands. She had nothing to hide behind.

"Didn't they *tell* you I was dead? How could you think I was still alive when I didn't come back with the aircrew? I never made it to a life raft, and the waters there—"

She didn't have to tell him. He knew the odds as well as she had.

"Yeah, everyone thought you'd died, from the commodore to your aft observer. They said navy intel and other 'sources' all pointed to the fact that you'd been lost at sea. Ro admitted that even though she wanted to believe you were still alive, her professional training forced her to accept that you were gone." He stared at her. "Did you ever attempt to launch a flare?"

"I couldn't. From the moment I felt solid sand under my boots I had to stay on the move." She shook her head. "Do you know, even as I was celebrating that I'd made it to shore, that I was going to live, I saw my first sign of insurgents. They'd left a makeshift base camp near the beach, on the edge of the jungle. There wasn't time to come back and try to contact anyone. I lost my radio, but I still had a map and the compass on the watch you gave me."

He'd given her an aviator's watch for Christmas seven years ago, complete with a minibarometer and compass.

"You still have that?"

"Thank God for navy training, right?" She smiled at him.

He didn't smile back. "I never believed you'd do anything but survive, Gwen. Of course, it didn't hurt when Scott stopped by—he let me know he had some other info that indicated you probably made it to shore alive."

Scott Stauffer was a colleague they'd met when they'd all been junior officers in their first P-3 tour. He'd gone on to work for a "corporation," which they assumed was the CIA, though he never told them as much. All they knew was that he remained single and was often gone for months at a time. He'd surface every year or two, blowing into town and having dinner with them.

Maybe Scott had experienced similar situations to her six months of survival in the Philippine jungle.

"If Scott knew so much, why didn't someone come and get me?" She heard the slam of her mug on the counter, saw the shards of the porcelain fly across the granite, before she realized she'd smashed it.

"Whoa."

Warm breath, the musky scent of male—pure Drew. He grabbed her hand and put it under the faucet and ran cool water over the three small cuts.

Shame heated her face, and tears welled in her eyes. The drops mingled with her blood and the water as she leaned over the sink. It was simultaneously heaven and hell to be so close to Drew.

"I didn't mean to—" She stopped at the trembling in her voice.

"It's okay, Gwen. You're allowed to be pissed off. You *should've* been saved sooner. No GI should go through what you did."

"There aren't any guarantees." They'd both known that when they'd raised their right hands and taken their oath of office. It was what she'd still known when she'd accepted her command tour, and what they'd both known when Drew got out and she stayed in. At any moment she could be called on a dangerous mission she wouldn't return from.

"No, no promises about what you'll be asked to do. But if you think I haven't had a few angry outbursts of my own, you're kidding yourself."

She removed her hand from his and shut off the water. Reaching for a kitchen towel and wrapping it around her fingers, she looked at him.

His skin was paler, his cheekbones more pronounced.

He'd lost weight.

"Wasn't it a relief? You wouldn't have to worry about keeping up our friendship. Face it, Drew, it's not easy to be buds with your ex. Especially on Whidbey. We kept running into each other. There'd be no more pet-sharing to worry about, either."

"That's your reentry uglies talking, Gwen."

"You're not denying it. You never contested the

divorce, never stopped to ask if we were making a mistake."

They'd quietly filed for divorce two weeks before she'd gone out on a deployment five years ago. With neither of them willing to compromise their individual careers for a relationship that had died, it was best. The divorce was final by the time she'd returned.

"Wait, it's the SGLI, isn't it?" She jestingly referred to the life-insurance policy that every active duty person in the military was entitled to. She'd signed hers over to Drew when he'd been her spouse.

"Do you think so little of me?" His tone was scarily even as his eyes burned with anger.

"I'm just kidding, Drew. You have to admit it's kind of funny."

She desperately wanted to believe that he'd spoken with sincerity—that he'd always believed she'd come back alive.

"Your death is nothing to joke about. If I was after the money, I would've pushed for you to be declared KIA instead of MIA, don't you think?" There was a menacing edge to his voice she'd never heard before. She knew she wasn't the woman who'd left Whidbey for deployment almost eight months ago. The past six months had irrevocably changed her.

Had Drew changed, too?

Her chest and neck itched; the plush fabric of the robe suddenly became a straitjacket.

"I need to get out of here. This isn't going to work."

"Holy hell, Gwen!"

She held up her hands.

"I agreed to do what the psychiatrist suggested, and you were kind to pick me up at the hangar, to keep me last night. But—" Her gaze drifted to their wall calendar.

It was still on the month she'd left for deployment.

His gaze followed hers.

He swallowed. His face reddened. "I've had a lot on my hands with the office."

"And with your ex-wife disappearing and showing up again?"

His wary expression made her feel like a fly in a spider's web.

"Something like that."

That tiny glimpse into his soul warded off the impending anxiety attack. Nervous energy swirled into the sexual energy that always existed between them. Her toes curled. Lust mixed with compassion, and she moved toward him. She let her hand smooth the lines on his forehead.

"I'm so sorry, Drew. Thank you for stepping up to the plate."

"That's what you think this is, *stepping up to the plate?*"

His tortured stare turned bold in the same instant she realized what he was thinking about.

"Drew, wait a minute…" But she let him draw her close to him, right up against him.

"Waiting gets old, Gwen."

CHAPTER FIVE

HIS LIPS WERE firm and decisive as he kissed her. Classic Drew, once he made up his mind to do something, he went for it.

Gwen couldn't figure out if it was exhaustion from her ordeal, jet lag, the sudden unexpected nearness of Drew after being without him for so long or all of the above. It didn't matter, but at some point in the past twenty-four hours she'd decided she wanted one last time in Drew's arms.

Why not now?

She kissed him back with months of pent-up sexual frustration and longing. Her tongue fought with his, she nipped at his lips. He untied the belt on her robe and his hands roamed confidently up and down her back, her butt, her breasts. It was surreal to watch as Drew—*Drew*—bent to her breast. She loved the feel of his hair as much as the anticipation of his sucking on her. Gwen was stunned by the quickening of her desire; she went from needing his touch to downright greedy and on fire for him in the breath it took him to lick her nipple before he devoured it.

"My God, Drew, it feels so good."

"The couch, Gwen."

They were five easy steps from the long, wide, leather sofa but it felt more like running through jungle overgrowth. She would lie down on the kitchen floor for him if he asked her.

She dropped her robe off her shoulders and lay back naked on the sofa.

"No," she said. "Take your clothes off before you come one step closer."

Drew complied and as much as she'd always enjoyed watching him undress, all she cared about in this moment was seeing that he needed her as much as she did him.

As his jeans and underwear dropped to the floor, she was rewarded with the sight of his erection.

"Come here."

HE WANTED TO drive into her before they ever hit the couch, but she looked so thin, more fragile than an eggshell. And God, the bruises on her body were enough to make him weep. Quickly he knelt between her legs and supported his weight on his forearms. He wanted to kiss every inch of her but she had her hands on his ass and her wet center was hot with the same need he had.

"I don't want to crush you, sweetheart."

"Crush away." She grasped his face and pulled it to hers. Their tongues met before their lips, and Drew was lost to her.

It was as good as it ever had been and perhaps more. They weren't strangers to homecoming sex—it was one of the perks of the long navy deployments. But this was different. They weren't celebrating a simple reunion.

He pressed his pelvis against Gwen's and her moan sent gratifying shudders through him.

"Your skin, baby. I don't want to hurt you."

"You're not. I need you now. *Now.*"

She wriggled her hips under his in the way she knew drove him mad.

"No, let me please you first, honey."

"This pleases me." She wrapped her hand around him.

"Wait." He reached over to the drawer of the end table and pulled out a condom.

Gwen took the packet from him and put it on him. His erection swelled.

"Now," she said again.

Drew's last shred of restraint disappeared and he thrust into her. He cried out at the sheer sensuality of their joining. Then his need and Gwen's murmured urging drove him to push into her again and again. He managed to hold on until her first cry. He climaxed with her pulsing around him.

IT TOOK SEVERAL minutes before either of them moved or spoke. Drew lay atop her, still inside her, still connected.

Oh, God, what had she just done?

Besides have the best sex of her life.

It's the homecoming magic. It's not real.

But Drew's chest, crushing her breasts, was very real. So was the heat of her response to him, slowly being replaced by the warmth of her embarrassment.

"Um, you're heavy." She shifted beneath him.

He immediately slid off her. "I'm sorry, Gwen. Are you okay?"

She kept her head turned to the side, looking at the back of the couch.

"I'm fine."

More than fine, as far as her sexual satisfaction was concerned. The last vestige of her sanity, however, was hanging by a thread thinner than a cobweb.

He maneuvered until he sat on the edge of the sofa cushion, leaning with his arm on the back of the couch. His breath fanned her bare breasts, her neck. She couldn't move her head but he did it for her, his fingers on her chin.

"Look at me, Gwen."

Her lids were heavier than a hundred-pound bench press as she opened her eyes.

Drew's revealed nothing but male forthrightness. "Did I hurt you?" he murmured. "Be honest."

"No."

He smiled with a hint of satisfaction. "Did you—?" His raised his left brow. He'd always been the most polite lover. Even if she'd screamed to hell and back with her orgasm, he always asked if she'd come.

"Yes. You know I did." Her face felt hot with self-recrimination.

"Don't regret this, Gwen, and don't feel bad about it."

His chest rose with a determined sigh. A girl could get lost looking at all that muscle, the sprinkling of hair over his pecs.

"Can we get dressed before we have this discussion?"

"Sure." He eased away from her and she shivered.

They dressed in silence, which involved her pulling on her robe.

"I'm going to get some real clothes on." She got herself another cup of coffee before she went upstairs.

SON OF A BITCH.

He hadn't been able to keep his dick in his jeans for more than five minutes once he was alone with Gwen.

As remarkable as their sex always was, it came with a price. Either it drew them closer, the way it had in the earlier years of their marriage, or it made Gwen angry, blaming him for using their sexual attraction as a weapon.

He wasn't in the mood for her blame, but neither was he prepared for his own disgust with himself.

What had gotten into him? He'd promised himself he'd do right by her, give her a wide berth, a chance to heal. Sure, he knew he was still attracted to her, yet he'd thought he'd be able to handle it.

"Good morning, sailor!"

"Shut up, Rosie."

Rosie replied with several grunts and a scream that was distinctly Gwen's. Damn bird had learned their sex sounds early on, and there was no stopping her when she heard them. What used to be a private joke between him, Gwen and the damned bird was now plain cruelty.

He went about preparing buckwheat pancakes, Gwen's favorite. They both needed the soothing rush of carbs. Maybe it would keep their post-sex, aka The Big Mistake, conversation less emotional.

"Woof!" Nappie was at the sliding door, asking to go out. Drew turned off the stove burner and stepped out onto the deck as he let the dog out. She raced down the steps to the grassy area below. More like waddled—she was aging faster with every month.

The passage of years hit Drew in the gut. He still remembered the first time he and Gwen had made love. They'd been fresh out of college, both in flight training. It'd been after a long night of first sharing drinks at a pub in downtown Pensacola, then talking on the beach.

Life had been simpler then. So had their lovemaking.

What just happened this morning was beyond any expectation his younger self had regarding sex. Life was changing. Maybe even transcendent.

Complicated.

He scratched his head. There was only one way to deal with this.

GWEN WAS GORGEOUS in her simple white zippered sweatshirt and blue jeans when she joined him at the dining-room table after her shower.

"You look good. Feeling better?" Crap, he sounded as if he was fourteen.

She didn't flinch. "Yes." Sitting down, she picked up a fork. "We need to talk."

"Yes, we do."

"That can't happen again. We're friends. Friends don't, don't…"

He nodded.

"I mean it, Drew. I don't know what came over us."

"I'm sorry, Gwen, and I agree. We won't do that again. Before you go blaming yourself or me, however, take a step back. Don't you think it's only natural after what you've been through?" He bit his tongue. He sounded like a doctor speaking to a reticent patient.

"What I've *been* through? What makes you think that living through terrorist hell made me want to come back and screw your brains out?" Tears made her eyes glitter and he'd be damned if he'd cause any more of her sadness.

"You know I don't think that. But…we never said goodbye."

She stared at him. "Goodbye?"

He shrugged. "Most couples have goodbye sex at the end of a relationship. It's not uncommon for divorcing spouses to have a round or two under the sheets before it's all over."

"And your source on this is?"

He wanted to laugh at her haughty tone.

"Just observation. Here, have some syrup." He passed her a bottle of marionberry syrup, her favorite. He'd seen it at the local produce stand when he picked up the fresh beets and other produce for her first few days back. He'd never been the cook during their marriage, and he'd looked forward to showing her what he'd learned.

Bullshit. You just want to make her happy.

"Well, this is a heck of a time to check that off the list." She bit into the fluffy pancakes and he waited to see if they'd turned out okay.

"Mmm, these are delicious."

Phew.

"Glad you like them."

She pinned him with her hazel eyes. "Back to what you said. If that's true, then we just had a major farewell party."

He laughed. "I'd say so, yes."

"Now we can move on, and still be friends. Is

that the idea?" She eyed him with a sharpness he'd missed. No one challenged him like Gwen did. No one else pushed him to his limits, made him want to be the best man he could be.

"So I'm told." He wished he could enjoy the meal a fraction as much as Gwen appeared to. It all tasted like paper in his mouth. Even his coffee tasted burnt.

"I need one last favor from you, Drew."

"Whatever you want. Shoot." *Whatever she wanted.* Whatever it took to let her walk away without feeling diminished by it.

Her stare forced him to see the truth in himself. He had to get out of this with some semblance of himself intact, too, or he'd die another death like he did when they'd divorced. And again when she'd been lost at sea...

It was simple. He couldn't go through losing her again. The only way to prevent her loss was not to open up to her.

"What is it, Gwen?"

"I may need you to vouch for my mental and emotional stability until the adoption clears."

SHE WATCHED HIM as he rubbed his hand over his face.

"Why wouldn't I?" He sighed, leaned back in his chair and looked at her. She ignored the sizzle she got from staring into his eyes. "I admit I feel like a complete shit. You've been through hell and back.

You're not on your home turf for twenty-four hours and I jump you like a horny dog."

She swallowed. It wasn't a lump in her throat; she was just tired.

"You didn't force me to do anything I didn't want, Drew." He was apologizing for that sex? It had been earth-shattering. "It's crazy—I'm like a ghost. When's the last time you could say you screwed a ghost?"

Her one-liners needed work.

She wanted to squeeze his shoulder reassuringly, make him see that she was fine, it was all fine, their lovemaking didn't mean anything more to her than an expression of confused emotion.

Touching Drew was off-limits.

She stayed in the oak chair.

"You still try to get in the last word, Gwen. That's a sure sign the jungle didn't take everything from you."

"No, it didn't."

"And now you think you want to adopt a kid?"

"Not a *kid,* Drew. A little baby named Pax. I rescued him from a burned-out village. His mother saved him by covering her body with his."

"I know. It's been all over CNN. That you rescued a baby, not that you want to adopt him, though."

Trepidation roiled her insides. "What else did the news reports say?"

"That you escaped an insurgent camp, were taken in by a friendly villager after you found the baby."

"I wish Pax wasn't involved in the story at all. If—" she swallowed a sob "—if I don't get to adopt him, he deserves a fair start without this history."

"They didn't show any photos, Gwen. The stories have revolved around you and the survival of other women in combat POW camps."

His unspoken question hung between them.

"I told you the truth. I wasn't raped, Drew."

His expression remained neutral except for the emotion in his eyes. Of course a good friend would be relieved. "I'm glad."

"It was going to happen—but I got out before they figured out what do to with me. I imagine the media already has me raped, tortured, you name it."

"Not really. But they do mention it happens more often than it doesn't. I knew you'd get out of there, Gwen, but I feared the worst, too."

She hadn't so much as turned on a television since she'd crawled out of the jungle with Pax. There hadn't been an opportunity at the embassy in the PI, and by the time she'd been left alone in her hospital room at Madigan, she'd been too exhausted to do anything but curl up under the covers.

"You have no idea what an impression you've made on people, Gwen. You've become a national hero."

"It'll die down soon enough." They both knew that as soon as an unfortunate natural or terrorist disaster occurred, her story would be relegated from national media to the local paper until all interest died.

"Don't be so sure. The point being that with the popularity of your survival story, you have the support of the American people for your adoption. Contact your congressman—you won't have a problem getting whatever you want."

"Now who's treating Pax like a prize, a thing? It's not so simple, Drew. It's nice that people think they know me from a few sound bites but public opinion has nothing to do with a very private family matter like adoption. The State Department has weighed in, and that helps, but if it turns out that Pax has any living relatives, I'm out. Philippine law would place him with his family before me."

"You'd still have options, wouldn't you? If he has any living family, wouldn't they agree to allow you to adopt him, to give him a life they could never afford?"

She shook her head. She'd asked the diplomats the same questions, gone through every possibility concerning her chances of adopting Pax.

"They probably wouldn't, and it's not something I can risk thinking about. I have to make my case as strong as possible and pray that the legalities go through before anyone shows up claiming to be his relative."

"You know people can start coming out of the woodwork."

"For the money? I know. It's why State is trying

to keep it quiet, to prevent an avalanche of false relative claims."

She watched him. Her senses were still hyperalert, and she didn't want to think how long it might take them to ease up, for the urge to jump out of her skin to vanish, if ever.

His face remained drawn, and his head rested on the back of the chair. His arms were folded across his chest and it didn't take a trained psychologist to know he was keeping her out, keeping up his defenses against the enemy.

She'd become his enemy. She knew him better than anyone, or at least she once had, and she was in his sanctuary, under his roof.

Asking him to vouch for her, to verify that she hadn't lost her mind.

The brief intimacy they'd shared on the sofa disintegrated, and she'd never felt more awkward, more unsure of where she stood with him.

Had it been this bad before she'd left?

You never talked about real stuff—you'd been living separate lives for years.

He raised his head and sat up, leaning forward with his elbows on the heavy oak table.

She met his gaze and knew what he was going to say before he said it.

"I won't lie to the doctors or social workers if I don't think you're physically or emotionally ready to adopt a baby, Gwen."

CHAPTER SIX

"YOU CAN'T TELL me in the same breath that you'll be my friend, my support, as I enter my real life, and then shut me down so quickly. I'm only asking you for one thing!"

Her shaky expression didn't match her angry words.

God, she didn't get it. Didn't get that he'd been through hell, too. Every day she was missing he'd lived alongside her in his mind, his heart. He saw the look of disappointment and betrayal in her eyes.

"A baby's not a puppy, Gwen. How are you going to raise a kid when you can hardly take care of yourself yet? And what about commanding your squadron?"

"Who said I'm going to command a squadron? Let's be real. It's not *my* squadron anymore." There were tears glistening in her eyes again, the amber flecks in stark contrast to her green irises. Gwen, the steely warrior who'd rarely cried in all the years they'd been together, was about to shed a waterfall.

"Why wouldn't you?"

She played with the marble eggs on their mantel.

They'd bought them in Carrera, Italy, from the same quarry where Michelangelo had excavated the marble for his *David*. Drew couldn't watch the way her long, pale fingers played across the smooth surfaces. Those fingers could make him hard in an instant, had always exerted the right amount of pressure....

"The XO's been doing my job just fine. He's been the acting CO for over six months. No one expected me to come back, as you've so politely pointed out. As it is, there are only about six months left in my command, all on shore." Her tired voice lacked her usual level of annoyance with him. He'd do anything to have the once-familiar tough Gwen back, no matter what the cost to him.

His fists ached to take out the terrorists who'd captured her, beaten her. If he could erase whatever had broken her like this, he'd do it, regardless of the cost.

All the more reason to help her get well.

"You're a freakin' hero, Gwen. They're not going to keep you from finishing out your command. In style!"

"Maybe I don't want it anymore." It was the merest whisper. Her hands shook and she shoved them in the pockets of her favorite hoodie. The one he'd bought her at an alumni reunion at the Naval Academy in Annapolis, Maryland. When all her classmates had congratulated her war-proven pilot skills, years before she faced her destiny in the jungle.

A bark of laughter escaped his chest. "Were you smoking something I'm not aware of while you were in the jungle?" This wasn't the Gwen he'd come to know in the past few years.

She looked like the little girl he'd caught glimpses of whenever they'd gone back to her hometown. Twice in the entire time they'd been together. Once for her father's suicide, once more when her mother remarried.

"I don't want my career anymore, Drew. Not like I did before."

"Before what?"

Her eyes widened and in an instant the hard Gwen was back. Ice dripped from her voice as she replied. "Before I spent the last six months fighting for my life, praying I'd make it back here. The last four months of my time there, Pax was the only thing that kept me going, kept my sanity."

Not Drew, not hope for reconciliation.

But why should her survival have had anything to do with him? They'd secretly lived as no more than roommates, in separate rooms, with separate lives, for a year before the divorce. That made six years of no intimacy, no confiding in each other.

"Let's take it as it comes," he said with finality. He'd put too much pressure on her by giving in to his baser instincts.

She nodded, as if in understanding.

He knew her, knew her so very well. She'd be assuming he had to think about it because he couldn't wait to get rid of her, to finally be on his own again.

In fact, he needed to get his heart back where it belonged—without crushing it. He needed to be her friend.

THEY PUSSYFOOTED AROUND each other for the rest of the day, keeping conversation light and mostly about Nappie and Rosie. Gwen seemed restless, and he'd suggested a walk, but the way the wind howled and the house creaked they both agreed she'd probably be blown away. Instead, she napped and read the books Drew had left in the master bedroom.

Neither spoke much during dinner, but she made sure to compliment him on the chili and rice he'd prepared.

"The cornbread was good, Drew. I never knew you could bake like this."

He grinned. "Yeah, baking was your arena—as you've reminded me."

The woodstove crackled as they sat across from each other in the great room. She watched his face but his expression remained unreadable. He obviously wasn't going to resume their earlier conversation, so she dived in.

"I never meant to suggest that I wanted you to lie about my mental state, Drew."

His silence brought back the anxiety that had plagued her since she'd handed Pax over to the Philippine social worker in Manila. The only thing keeping her from full-fledged panic was her belief that deep down, below the constant tension between her and Drew, they still had some type of bond. That Drew was a good guy and would go the extra mile because it was the right thing to do.

"I know."

His scrutiny was more unbearable than hiding under leaves on a bug-infested forest floor. His eyes still revealed nothing, but she knew him well enough to understand that he was judging her.

White-hot anger mixed with humiliation at having to beg him for this one last favor, especially after he'd been all but forced to take her in. She searched for a safer place to rest her gaze and locked on to the phalaenopsis orchid that grew from the hand-painted ceramic pot he'd given her for their eighth anniversary. The creamy white vessel was sprayed with brilliant orange, red and yellow tulips. They were reminiscent of Washington State's Skagit Valley Tulip Festival, where they'd gone that year. They'd delighted in taking photos of each other in every pose imaginable, their backdrop the acres upon acres of tulips.

"So now what, we wait to see if I'm crazy? Or if I'll keep getting better?" She dragged her focus back to him. A jolt of awareness made her blink. There was no denying he was the handsomest man she'd ever known.

He's your ex-husband.

"I need a chance to adjust, Gwen. I believed you

were still alive—but I was so scared you were dead. *Dead.* Gone, never to be seen again." He shook his head. "I imagined you'd been eaten by sharks. No one thought you'd survive the monsoon, much less months on the run through some of the most remote areas on the planet." He paused. "And yet… It was like I believed two things simultaneously—that you were alive and that you were dead."

His revelation twisted his face into a mask of confusion.

"It's not my fault, Drew. I didn't purposely disappear for six months. I didn't choose to find a baby in a pile of burned-out huts, either, but I did."

"Why do you think it's your job to save this kid?"

"It's not a job, Drew. It's fate."

DREW WENT BACK to work on the third day after Gwen's return. They needed distance, he knew, but it was still hard to pull out of the driveway before she woke up. What if she had a nightmare? In three short days his Gwen radar was pinging as though it'd never stopped.

"Hi, Serena." He entered the clinic and walked to the receptionist's desk.

"Nice to have you back, Drew. You okay?"

Serena was a true beauty, with her dark, shiny hair and luminous brown eyes. She'd proved to be a superb single parent to her young son. She'd lost her army husband to the war a couple of years ago. They'd been stationed in Texas, and she'd used the tragedy as a reason to start over and come west. She fortuitously landed on Drew's doorstep—he'd needed a receptionist/assistant when Opal quit and Serena had worked in a PT office near Fort Hood, Texas, for three years.

"I'm great, glad to be back. Do we have a busy schedule today?"

They went over the clients, discussed where they'd need to coordinate with his other assistant, Terri.

"Terri won't be in until a bit later, when we start the aquatracker schedule. Dottie Forsyth's the first of six clients for the tracker today. Terri and I will be able to manage the schedule between us."

Drew nodded. The aquatracker was his clinic's pièce de résistance. A rectangular water tank, it housed a small but powerful treadmill that allowed his clients to walk and run under water. There were various levels of power for the treadmill, as well as jets that could be employed to provide resistance for the more advanced athletes he often treated.

"If Terri's not in when Dottie arrives, I'll need you to stay with her during her session, as usual." Drew mandated that a staff member be in the room or nearby with any client on the aquatracker. His insurance did, too.

"Of course." Serena smiled as she went over the schedule with him. "How's Gwen?"

Drew paused. Serena had been supportive of him

throughout the ordeal. She, of all people, knew what it was like to lose a military spouse.

"She's okay, thanks for asking. It's going to be a long road to recovery for her." Even as he said it, he felt horrible for not saying everything was perfect. What Serena's husband would have given to come home to his family....

"I'm sure it will be. But her time here isn't up yet. She came back for a reason." Serena said the words as if she were simply stating a fact.

"You may be right."

Drew believed in something greater than himself, or so he thought, but he didn't have the faith Serena did. There might be a divine reason Gwen had survived, but it wasn't to come back to him.

Fate was a bitch.

IT WASN'T FAIR. She'd put in her time, learned Drew's every need. She knew what he wanted before he did. It was only two days after his wife was back, barely two weeks since she'd returned after miraculously surviving that crash, and Drew was completely distracted by Gwen. He'd almost been over the bitch but then she'd gone missing. Because he was such a wonderful man he'd had survivor's guilt.

They'd been so close to taking the next step in their relationship.

As usual with Drew, she was going to have to give him a little push in the right direction. Something to shake him up and out of the rut he was in over Gwen.

Honestly, when would Gwen get it? Drew didn't love her anymore.

It didn't take her long to figure out what to do, how to work it so that Drew's attention would be off Gwen and he'd be turning to *her* to lean on.

It was almost too easy. The idiots in the front office didn't realize anyone else was back here.

She didn't even try to suppress the nasty, whiny voices in her head. She was tired of having to rein them in, tired of having to play by society's rules.

Drew was a fool, but she forgave him. He didn't understand how manipulative Gwen was. Gwen didn't love him, not like she did. No one could love him like she did.

Damn Gwen, that bitch. If she hadn't fought her way back from being lost at sea, things would be smooth sailing with Drew. She would be Mrs. Drew Brett by now, and Gwen would be a fading memory.

She'd worry about her later. If Gwen wasn't careful, she'd pay dearly for keeping Drew from her.

It was sad, really, that Mrs. Forsyth turned out to be her ticket to Drew. Dottie didn't deserve to go through any more trouble than getting old was already causing her. But Dottie was a tough old broad. And all she needed to do was give the clinic a little scare.

"Hello, Dottie. How's it going?"

Dottie Forsyth lifted her wrinkled face. Her short

blueish-white hair was damp at the neck, her skin saggy where it was exposed by a bathing suit that looked as if it had seen better days. In the last century.

"I'm fine, thanks. I didn't realize more than one of you was working today." Dottie knew the voice was different but she'd never be able to identify; Dottie's eyes were bad. Without her glasses she was as blind as a newborn rat.

"You know how busy it gets in here. We have to hop around the stations. Drew asked me to check on you."

"I'm almost done." Dottie paced along the underwater treadmill in the aquatracker, Drew's prime piece of real estate on Whidbey Island. He'd been the first physical therapist to purchase one, and it had become a real boon to the business. Drew was so smart. They were a great team.

Doubt clouded her intentions for a moment. Would this make Drew suffer? Would he lose business if Dottie had an "accident" on the aquatracker?

No. Dottie would be fine. And no one would ever blame Drew for anything. He was the perfect man. All she needed was a chance to get Drew's attention. Make him see that *she* was the woman for him.

Gwen.

That bitch was supposed to be dead.

"I haven't seen you in a while." Dottie was nearing eighty years old, panting like a dog, submerged in water to her chest. Her long-term memory was reasonable, but short-term was starting to go, which would be a nice benefit when she had to talk about her accident to the staff.

"We're always switching up the schedule. You usually come in on my day off. Drew's business is doing so well he's had to hire new people. It's spread out the schedule more evenly."

She faced Dottie as she spoke to the old bag, so Dottie didn't hear her lock the door to the main therapy room.

Dottie squinted at the digital readout.

"Damn these cataracts. Without my glasses I can't see as clear as I used to. How much time do I have left?"

"Five more minutes. You can get your eyes fixed, Dottie."

As long as it's after today.

She walked up to the water tank, her body separated from Dottie's by thick plate of glass and hundreds of gallons of water. "Insurance usually covers cataract surgery for seniors."

She maintained eye contact with Dottie until Dottie turned away, face pointed forward as she kept walking at the speed of an ancient turtle.

Do it. Without hesitation she reached for the rpm dial and turned it up several notches. Next, she flipped on the hydro jets, which forced water at Dottie's bird legs. The jets were great for injured athletes, giving them enough resistance to help build muscle mass more quickly. But an old lady like Dottie would never be able to keep her head up, not with the strength of the jets working against her.

She wouldn't be alone for long, though. Just long enough to cause a commotion.

"Hey, did you—" A splash. Drops sprinkled the floor as Dottie's hand hit the water. There was a thud. The treadmill whipped Dottie back against the fiberglass shell of the aquatracker's water tank.

She looked over the rim at Dottie. The hag's face was barely above water as her terrified, unfocused gaze sought her out.

She smiled at Dottie. "You okay?"

Dottie opened her mouth to scream but the sound was no more than a gurgle as her head submerged.

She had to wait a few minutes to make certain Dottie was staying under, for the time being. As she waited she reopened the door to the main therapy room, just a crack.

Drew and his stupid staff had never noticed anything amiss.

"Drew, that call's on line two," The female voice carried into the aquatracker room. Time to duck out.

She left the water-therapy room the way she'd entered—through the door that exited onto the main corridor. Within minutes she was back in her regular life, no one the wiser.

Drew would be hers. She'd just assured it.

GWEN WASN'T SURE if she was more relieved or reluctant to be alone in the big house.

It helped that Ro called in the morning and promised to bring lunch. As she showered she planned to have a simple breakfast and maybe surf Ravelry, a social media site for knitters and crocheters, for a knitting project Ro could do with her. Sitting around waiting to get healthier wasn't going to be easy, especially while she was expecting word on Pax's adoption.

Drew hadn't promised her any help yet, either. Could she blame him? The dry taste of regret clung to her. He'd have every right to think she was trying to manipulate him through sex. Her feelings for Drew were anything but simple, and she'd only compounded the conflict between them.

"Way to go." She spoke to the empty room as she threw on sweatpants and a cozy hoodie. No sense in brooding; Drew had started work again today and she had the entire house to relax in. Gwen couldn't get over how the upstairs hallway blissfully cushioned her bare feet. The varnished wood railing was familiar and sturdy under her fingers as she looked out at the great room. From her perspective she saw that Drew's chair, the oversize leather recliner she'd given him on their tenth anniversary, showed no indentations, no signs of regular use.

The sofa, however, looked as if it had been through the jungle with her. The bourbon-colored leather had wrinkles and scars she didn't recall. As she continued to stare at the cushions, she recognized the indentation, the shape—of Drew. Where his head would be, his back, his legs.

As if he'd slept on the sofa the entire time she'd been gone.

Where they'd made love yesterday.

Love? More like goodbye sex, just as Drew had said.

Tears spilled onto her cheeks.

He'd slept on the couch when they'd first started fighting a year or so before their divorce. The occasional one-night couch foray turned more permanent as their fighting cooled into its more sinister cousin—indifference.

When Drew had moved out of their bedroom and into the guest room on the other side of the house, it had been the death knell of their marriage.

It'd taken them several painful months to face up to that reality.

She'd been able to ignore the pain of it all by throwing herself into her work.

Nappie's growl surprised her out of her thoughts. The sound of the side kitchen door shutting frightened her. Drew wouldn't come back this early, and Ro wasn't due for several hours.

"Grrrrr." Rosie's imitation of Nappie's growl validated Gwen's fear.

Gwen watched from the balcony as Nappie struggled up from her bed near the bottom of the stairs and headed for the kitchen.

She stayed on the landing, wondering if Drew still kept the baseball bat next to the bed.

A petite figure emerged into the great room.

Opal.

Opal?

She has a key.

Was Drew seeing her? He never said he *wasn't* seeing anyone.

The tiny blonde looked up before Gwen could slip back behind a column. Because of the open architecture, Opal saw Gwen as soon as Gwen saw her.

"Gwen! I'm so sorry. I thought you'd be out at the base."

Gwen was excruciatingly aware of how disheveled she was in her sweats. She wished she'd put on real clothes.

"Hi, Opal." She started down the stairs.

"Gosh, I hope I didn't scare you. I'm only looking for Drew." Opal's eyes were wide. She seemed as shocked as Gwen felt.

"He's at work." Gwen took in Opal's tight black jeans, her inky blue turtleneck accentuating her perky breasts.

This is still your house.

Kind of.

She was not going to be made to feel like Frumperella in her own home, for God's sake!

"He's never too tired to miss a day, is he?" Opal smiled.

"I didn't realize you had a key." Drew always left

the doors unlocked but even so, Opal acted as if she'd been walking in here regularly for a long time.

"Oh, well." Opal had the grace to appear embarrassed.

Gwen wished she could have grabbed the words back.

You've been gone for eight months.

Who was welcome in Drew's place, who did or didn't have a key, was none of her business.

"No need to explain. Can I help you? Is there anything you need?"

"Gee, this is awkward." Opal grimaced, but in a friendly way that reflected her discomfort.

"I'm sorry, Opal, this isn't anyone's fault. It's hard on everybody, me showing up alive and all." Gwen heard the sarcasm in her own voice but Opal took the words at face value.

"It is, isn't it? I mean, I'm so relieved to know you're okay, and so is Drew. He's such a sweetheart. When you were reported missing, he felt so bad for you."

"Oh?" Gwen gritted her teeth and shoved her hands into the deep pockets of the hoodie. Opal didn't need to see her clenched fists.

"I tried to tell him he wasn't responsible, but you know, you two are still friends, and his natural instinct is to protect you like a big brother would."

"Right. Don't worry about it, Opal." Gwen sighed. How could she be angry at Opal? Opal was all girl. From her curly blond locks down to her tiny feet, always in spiked heels, she was the antithesis of Gwen's taller stature and athletic build.

Gwen had often wished Opal was a dumb ass, too. It would have been easier to dispel her jealousy, a jealousy she hated admitting she felt toward any other woman, especially one Drew worked with. Opal wasn't only attractive, she was bright. She'd bought a failing business and turned it into a profit-making venture in under a year.

"Are you still going to school?"

"Oh, no, I got my business degree last month. I'm working my tail off at the coffee shack, but I love it, you know?" Opal laughed. "Drew's complained that he had to hire two people to replace me."

"He probably did." Drew had praised Opal up and down when he'd hired her as a temporary assistant. She was a gem of a worker and reliable. As soon as she had the funds for her business, however, she'd quit the clinic.

"How's Brady?"

Opal frowned. "His daddy has him for the rest of the school year. I'll get to have him this summer."

"I'm so sorry, Opal." And she was. They were close in age, but Gwen was extremely aware of the advantages that going to the Naval Academy had given her, compared to the hardship Opal endured as a single parent, especially during the years she was struggling to earn a degree on a part-time basis.

"I'm sad and I miss him, but a boy needs his father. Drew—"

Opal cut off whatever she was going to say.

Drew always wanted to be a dad... Gwen's cheeks ached from forcing a relaxed, noncommittal expression. Her head started to pound behind her eyes.

"I have to get some coffee, Opal. Would you like some?"

"Oh, no, I've had enough this morning." Opal smiled. "If I'd realized you were here, I would've brought you your favorite latte."

"You're sweet—thank you. Is there something I can do for you?" Gwen knew she wasn't being the best hostess, but it wasn't as though she'd *invited* Opal.

Besides, she'd never been the hostess type. Give her a ready-room with suited-up aviators eager to execute a mission over social pleasantries any day.

"No, no, thanks. I have to get back to the Koffee Hut. I ran home to get my laptop, so I can keep up with my supply orders. I only came by to see if Drew needs anything." Opal looked wistfully toward the upper deck. "He doesn't get enough sleep."

Opal knows his sleep patterns.

Which meant they'd slept together?

None of your business.

"I'll let myself out. I hope you feel better soon, Gwen."

"Thanks."

Opal left through the kitchen door. Her shape cast a shadow on the lowered shades as she walked along the side of the house to the deck stairs that would take her down to street level.

Gwen went to the coffeepot and poured herself a cup from the half pot Drew must have brewed. The coffee was bitter but the heat comforted her. Her body still thought she was in the jungle, and she shivered against the chill of the house.

Gwen stared at the kitchen door for a full minute before she walked over and threw the dead bolt.

LUNCH WITH RO was a relief after dealing with Opal. Ro sat next to Gwen on the couch in the living room, asking benign questions about her time in the PI.

"You haven't touched your lunch." Ro looked at Gwen's plate on the coffee table, laden with take-out barbecue that Ro had brought, then back at her.

"I haven't been able to eat a lot at one time, and I had a big breakfast."

"Are you sure?"

Gwen sighed. "To be honest, my appetite for pork isn't back yet."

"Oh?"

"Let's just say I had more than my share of pig over the past six months."

Ro laughed, and Gwen loved her for it.

"Kind of like trying to have ramen noodles after the academy?"

"Exactly!"

While living in Bancroft Hall, the Naval Academy's dormitory, late-night study sessions were often fueled by easy snacks like soup and noodles in a disposable cup.

"You know, I still can't eat any kind of instant or freeze-dried anything." Ro smiled and her whole face lit up.

Gwen stared at the woman who'd been her best friend for the better part of two decades. Ro was brunette with short-cropped hair that emphasized her feminine features. They'd met at the academy and Gwen considered her more of a sister than a friend.

"I can't believe you're getting out of the navy, Ro." She'd always been as gung-ho career navy as Gwen.

"I can't believe *you're* alive." Ro reached across the sofa and gave Gwen a bone-crushing hug.

Gwen hugged her back. And was very aware that six months ago she would have shied away from such a demonstrative gesture, even from Ro.

Gwen pulled back before more tears could flood her already swollen eyes. Between the painful conversations with Drew, not to mention impulsively making love to him after so many years apart, she was emotionally spent.

"You've become awfully touchy-feely, Ro. Where's the lifer I knew?" She referred to Ro's determination to make the navy a lifetime career—twenty years of active duty, minimum.

"Yeah, the West Coast's definitely been good for

me. I've reevaluated my priorities." Ro's eyes sparkled with an enthusiasm Gwen couldn't remember ever having.

Yes, she had—a long time ago.

When she'd believed that Drew had hung the moon…

Ro's expression sobered. "I know you've been through a lot, honey, and if you need me anytime, for anything, all you have to do is call. Is there something you want or need to talk about now?"

Gwen laughed. "I want you to enjoy your happiness, Ro. You've deserved a great relationship in, like, forever." Which made Ro the last person she wanted to burden with her joy-smothering tales of survival. "Of course I'll call you—I already have! If it wasn't for you, I would've had to come home in scrubs from Madigan Army Hospital."

"I'm glad the clothes fit, although I'll bet they were too big, but I know you'll put the weight back on soon enough." She paused. "What else happened over there? Or aren't you ready to talk about it?"

Gwen snorted. "All I've been doing is talking, Ro. I'm talked out. I had to tell the State Department folks at the embassy in Manila the whole story at least three times. They had an on-staff psychiatrist who talked to me, as well. Once I was back stateside, I had to do it all over again with the docs at Madigan. Even the commodore wanted his cut of the interviews."

Ro rolled her eyes. "He's harmless. Ever since

the last one went to the brig, and he stepped in, everyone's been a little testy, shall we say."

"It wasn't easy when we found out Commodore Sanders had turned out to be a murderer." The previous spring the entire wing had gone through chaos with a sailor's assumed suicide that was actually murder. All hell had broken loose when further investigation revealed it was the commodore, who'd then tried to eliminate the two people who got too close to the truth—Ro and her now-husband, Miles.

"Yeah, that was ugly. But nothing like what you've been through."

"I don't know about that, Ro. You and Miles faced the reality of dying out in Deception Pass. The only difference is that I was in the PI."

"We've all faced it, downrange." Ro spoke quietly. She was right—all four of them, both couples—had individually deployed to either Iraq or Afghanistan. Miles had physically sacrificed the most; he'd lost his leg to the war against terrorism.

"And that's why what I've been through shouldn't merit any more attention than the experience of every other vet coming back from deployment."

"Spare me, Gwen. You were totally on your own, in the midst of who knows how many insurgent groups, without any outside support. You must've figured out that you were assumed KIA."

Ro bit her lip after she'd used the acronym for Killed In Action.

Gwen grasped her hand. "After what I counted

as thirty days on the run with no sign of an extraction team, yes, I assumed that no one was coming in for me." She shook her head. "I lost it yesterday, with Drew. I didn't even realize I was still pissed off that there weren't any rescue attempts. I never heard one damn U.S. aircraft overhead." Of course she'd been assumed lost at sea, and since she'd had to take cover in the jungle, rescue attempts were all but pointless due to the dense foliage.

"You have every right to be angry. You were up against it."

They sat in the kind of silence only close friends can share.

Gwen finally spoke.

"I'm not having any of the post-war type of dreams you told me you had when you got back from Afghanistan."

"Good. But if things change, don't be a hero—go get help. No one goes through what you did and comes out unscathed."

"I suppose not."

They sat together quietly once more.

"I wish we could keep the focus on your newlywed status. Tell me what you and Miles do together—besides the obvious!"

Ro giggled before she started talking about how much fun she was having with her husband, and how absolutely blissful she found married life.

"Blissful, eh?"

"I don't know another word to describe it."

"Hmm."

Ro turned to Gwen. "Are you going to tell me about the baby?"

"Drew told you?"

Ro shook her head.

"Of course not. I read some of the message traffic that was sent to the commodore from the State Department, but your heroic acts were also on CNN. Miles and I were watching television one night and *bam!* There you were, holding a kid, being rushed into the embassy."

There it was again—the light in Ro's eyes that appeared whenever she mentioned Miles.

"I came up on a village that the insurgents had burned out. There was nothing left, and the smell—" She couldn't go on. She couldn't tell anyone where she'd found her baby.

Under a burned-down hut.

Under a dirt floor.

Beneath his mother's corpse.

"That's where the baby was?" Ro prompted. Ro and Gwen had a connection normally reserved for sisters, a connection they'd never lost. They knew each other's moods, all their "tells." The nuances in expression that meant nothing to anyone but the other.

"Yes. He's perfect, Ro. So sweet, a little bear of a guy. When I first found him he was so helpless." Gwen wiped away the tears that had fallen. "I had to save him. If I could've nursed him, I would have. I know, strange coming from the career gal, right?"

"No, not strange. Not at all."

"I am so damn lucky I stumbled on a safe village, a safe place to hide out. I was able to live with Pax—that's what I named him—and there was a family who helped me get formula. Sometimes it was just sugar water, I think, but he's alive, healthy and— Oh, Ro, what if the adoption doesn't go through?"

"It'll go through if it's supposed to, honey. Are you sure you want to be a single mother, Gwen?"

"I don't have a choice. I love that little boy and I'm the only mother he has now."

"You're being obtuse. You know what I mean."

"Drew and I are beyond reconciliation, Ro. You of all people understand that. You saw what we went through, how immature we were. We had no business getting married so young. Not with both of us such diehard career people."

"You've remained good friends. You seem comfortable enough here, for now, anyway. Are you?"

"Not really," Gwen said with a shrug. "I need to leave as soon as I can. I appreciate all he's doing for me, but he's got his own life now. Just this morning his former assistant, Opal—you know, the woman who runs Koffee Hut? She let herself in and I think we scared the hell out of each other."

Gwen looked at Ro and smiled. "Drew's moved on, and I'm happy for him."

"No way, Gwen, you're wrong. I've never seen a hint of anything between them other than the fact that they're friends and neighbors."

Gwen rubbed her eyes. "Face it, Ro, Drew and I aren't getting back together. Five years is a long time, and we were fighting so much by the end of our marriage, I never want to risk going through that again." She jumped up from the sofa and walked around the great room, needing to get outside, away from the house.

"You aren't your mother, Gwen. Brenda's life has nothing to do with yours. She chose to remarry and you thought she didn't need to. It doesn't mean that needing a life partner is a weakness."

Gwen heard the note in Ro's voice and sighed. There was no talking sense to her while she was in the midst of marital bliss. Ro still held out hope for her and Drew.

"We've been over this before, Ro. I'm a born career girl and no man should have to give up his life because of mine. Even if I decide to leave the navy, quit flying, I'd still work. It's in my blood after all these years. Drew deserves to be happy. We all do. Speaking of which, I've asked him to help me with the adoption. It'll go much more smoothly if he can vouch for my mental health."

"What did he say?"

"It was as if he was more worried about whether or not I've thought it all through. I know it's hard for you all to believe but I'm not who I was when

I left on deployment. I'd never put anything ahead of my child, and that includes my career. That's why I'm thinking about all my navy options here."

Ro sipped her tea. "I've never doubted you'd make a wonderful mother, Gwen. So it took you a few near-death scrapes to realize it. Just don't ignore any other lessons you might have learned over there."

CHAPTER SEVEN

AFTER RO WENT back to work, Gwen hoped to get some of her things out of the storage boxes in the garage before Drew came home. Her mother was planning to visit with her husband within the next few days and Gwen wanted to have some of her own clothes to wear, her own things around. She loved her mother dearly, but also dreaded the inevitable cross-examination she'd get regarding her time in the PI, and her temporary living situation with her ex-husband.

The garage door rose smoothly after she hit the electronic button. Nappie wagged her tail against Gwen's legs.

"Okay, you can stay out here with me, but don't go far." Nappie promptly headed to the carnation bushes Gwen had planted with Drew six years ago.

Right before everything started going downhill.

Her cell phone, in her rear pocket, buzzed, and she pulled it out.

"Hello?" She couldn't read the caller ID in the bright daylight.

"Gwen, it's Ro. Where are you?"

Gwen looked at the boxes stacked on and beside the steel storage shelves Drew had set up when they'd moved in. Was that her box of knitting stuff up on the highest one?

"Where I've been since you left, and where I'll be for the next few days—or weeks. In this house, wondering why I can't go back to the squadron yet. Actually, I'm in the garage." She was surprised Ro had called again so soon but she supposed her reappearance affected everyone differently. Maybe Ro needed reassurance.

"You're feeling okay?" The urgent note in Ro's voice hit Gwen's solar plexus.

"Yes, yes. What's going on?"

"Do you think you're up to driving? You need to go to the PT clinic. Drew needs you."

"For what?"

"There's too much to explain—just go there."

Ro clicked off before Gwen could respond.

Was this a sick attempt of Ro's to get her and Drew back together? Ro wasn't an alarmist by nature, and although she'd continually expressed hope for Gwen and Drew's marriage, even at its worst, Gwen *knew* Ro, knew she wouldn't pull matchmaking crap this soon after Gwen's return.

The feeling she'd had all morning—an inexplicable dread she'd attributed to her overall anxiety at the transition back home—caved in on her. She'd tried to blame it on Opal's unexpected visit, but those anxieties had been soothed by her conversation with Ro.

Something was wrong, and it wasn't her post-PI trauma. Drew needed her.

Gwen pocketed her phone and coaxed Nappie inside. She hadn't driven in the three days since she'd returned to Whidbey. The doctors had warned her to ease into everything, especially driving. It was the same protocol all sailors followed when they came back. What she'd practiced after every deployment downrange.

This wasn't the time to worry about the pace of her transition, however. She looked over at her small fuel-efficient sedan, parked where Drew must have left it. As long as she could get it started, she was good to go.

GWEN DROVE INTO town, marveling at how the five-minute trip to the clinic seemed more like five miles. Being behind the wheel felt strange, but her concern over Drew after Ro's scary call distracted her from her driving fears. It allowed her subconscious to make the physical decisions.

When she'd tried to call him on his cell or the clinic phone, she'd been put through to voice mail.

Several police cars were parked in front of Drew's physical therapy clinic, either the Oak Harbor City Police crest or the Island County Sheriff's emblem on their doors.

Her anxiety roared, and her muscles grew tight.

She scanned the scene as she walked up to the cordoned-off area, the yellow police tape separating her from Drew.

"Ma'am, I'm going to have to ask you to keep back, please."

"But I'm a friend of the owner."

"Drew Brett?" The officer looked at her a little too sharply.

"Yes—he's my…my ex-husband."

Was she going to find out she was a widow?

You can't be a widow if you're divorced.

Where the hell was her command voice when she needed it?

The police officer kept his gaze on her while he spoke into his transmitter. "I have a woman here who says she's Drew Brett's ex-wife." Gwen stared at the officer as he listened to his earpiece. He was with Oak Harbor, not the Sheriff's Department, and his last name was Joseph. Officer Joseph was Drew's height, about six-feet two inches, but with a bit of a slimmer build. She knew it was her military training that had her noticing and filing away all these details; it prevented her from succumbing to complete and utter panic.

Officer Joseph's eyebrows rose. "What's your first name?"

"Gwen. Gwendolyn." Oh, God, were they checking his next-of-kin notifications? Was he injured, or worse? Had he kept her on his list, as she had his?

"Right. I'll walk her in." Officer Joseph gestured

to a colleague who leaned against his patrol car. "Hey, Billy, watch my area, will you? I'm doing escort."

The other cop straightened and waved at his coworker. "I've got it."

"Okay, let's go." He held up the yellow tape for Gwen to duck under. The image of crawling under thorny vines in the jungle flashed through her mind.

Stay here. You're on Whidbey, not in the PI.

Gwen followed the police officer as they entered the clinic from the street. The sunlight faded to a dark, heavy atmosphere that shrouded the usually bright space.

There were small clusters of people humming about the clinic. Police and other unidentified workers with latex gloves took photos, put objects in clear plastic bags and took notes. Gwen's gaze passed over them all and didn't stop until she found Drew.

Alive. He was alive.

His golden skin was pale and it pulled around his eyes, making it look as if he'd been up all night.

Yet he'd left the house only hours earlier.

He stood with his back against the far clinic wall, near the water cooler and the pulley apparatus that aided clients recovering from rotator-cuff injury. The clinic usually felt like a second home to her, even after the divorce. It had been one of the few topics of conversation besides the pets that she and Drew were able to manage. It'd cemented their friendship.

A tall man in a suit jacket and jeans spoke with him. From the way he kept writing notes on an electronic tablet, Gwen figured he must be an insurance agent or such. Until she got closer and realized it was Detective Cole Ramsey from the Island County Sheriff's Department. He'd become friends with Drew after Drew treated Cole for a torn Achilles tendon he'd suffered during a brutal criminal takedown years ago.

Drew's eyes met hers briefly as he noted her arrival with Officer Joseph. She saw a spark of—gratitude?—then total dread in his glance.

"Detective Ramsey, Mr. Brett's ex-wife asked to come in."

"Gwen." Cole nodded at her.

"Hi." She looked at Drew. "What happened?"

"I lost a client." Flat. Expressionless.

"What do you mean *lost?*"

"A client. Died. Here, in the clinic." Drew's voice was low and she detected the note of despair she'd heard only when they were at the end of their marriage, when they'd decided to call it quits.

When he'd accepted that she'd be happier without him.

"A heart attack?" Drew had so many senior clients. This wouldn't be the first to require a 9-1-1 emergency call.

But it would be the first death.

Drew shook his head. "No. The aquatracker."

"Someone had a heart attack in the aquatracker?" She'd helped him do an emergency drill with the staff when he'd first acquired the equipment. It took three people to get an immobile body out of the tank while it was full of water. But it could be done quickly, and the entire staff was CPR trained. Drew always had a minimum of two staff members present, including himself, but usually three with the receptionist and a therapy assistant.

"We don't know if it was a heart attack. It could have been, but we found her already under—"

Gwen didn't miss the fact that Cole Ramsey stood there, unmoving, taking in everything about their conversation. Of course he did—it was his job. He was their friend; she could trust him. She knew this but still wanted to shove him aside and speak to Drew privately. The urge to console Drew was visceral.

"Okay, but why all the police?" Accidents happened. Usually not in a PT clinic that was as expertly run as Drew's, but still. What wasn't he telling her? What was she missing?

"You don't understand, Gwen. A client died— because she was left unattended for too long. None of us heard her call for help."

"Oh."

Drew might as well have punched her with his fist instead of the potent words. She struggled to think clearly.

"You never leave your clients unattended in the aquatracker," Ramsey said.

"I know. But the phone rang, and I'd asked Serena to make sure she didn't miss any calls this morning—I was waiting for an important one. I was on my cell phone with Gwen at the time." Drew ran his fingers through his hair, then along his jawbone. "It couldn't have been more than a few minutes, and the door to the main clinic was open. We never heard a call for help."

"Which is why you think it was a heart attack or other sudden event." Gwen thought it should be clear to Ramsey that Drew was no criminal. Why did she feel they were treating him like one?

"I don't know, Gwen."

"Who found her?"

"Serena." Oh, God.

"Wait. Serena, the same one who lost her husband?"

"Yes."

"Crap." Gwen grimaced. Serena was a beautiful woman whose sorrow at losing her husband to an IED in Afghanistan was eclipsed only by watching her young son grieve for his dad by going inward, refusing to talk to anyone.

Drew had said the boy, probably six or seven, was doing much better since Serena had taken him to Beyond the Stars, the same place Gwen's psychiatrist at Madigan Army Hospital worked. BTS was a kind of resort for Gold Star Families. Military families who'd paid the dearest sacrifice—they'd lost their loved one in the war. Drew volunteered at BTS, out on San Juan Island, whenever he had the chance. She'd always admired his generosity. No matter how busy he'd been as a doctoral student, or now as a clinician, he made time to reach out to the community.

Now, just when things had improved for Serena, she was faced with yet another tragedy. Pepe had started talking more since Serena had taken him to BTS. That was last summer, before Gwen went on deployment.

Serena had been through enough, and yet she'd found a dead client in what was supposed to be a safe place.

Drew's haggard expression confirmed that he'd already been through the same depressing chain of thought.

Gwen walked over to him and put her hand on his arm, ignoring the instant reaction her fingers had to his warmth.

"Drew, this *wasn't* your fault. You have so many elderly clients."

"Of course I do, Gwen, but she was found submerged. And we're not going to know how long she was alone in there until the autopsy results come back."

"Gwen, I have to ask Drew a few more questions. You're welcome to stay, of course, as a friend. Also I'll need you to sign a release so my staff can get your phone records. Drew's already signed for both his phones." Cole's voice was kind but his expression remained impassive.

"Of course. No problem."

Drew needed her. He'd stood by her these past few days; the least she could do was be here with him in this horrible moment. At the very least, the phone records would provide an alibi, evidence of how long he'd been in his office, away from the aquatracker.

"I'm not going anywhere." She looked at Drew. She saw a definite flicker of gratitude in his eyes before he turned back to Cole.

"Where were you when you heard your assistant shout for help?" Cole asked.

"I've already told you, I was in my office over there." Drew motioned to the room farthest from the aquatracker. "I was printing off instructions for my client, Will Hartz, who's getting ready to go out of town for a week. He needed instructions for his stretch band exercises."

"Where was Mr. Hartz while you were doing this?"

"He was lying there." Drew pointed to the row of therapy tables. "Doing his usual routine of exercises for his rotator cuff."

"Why weren't you in the room with Mrs. Forsyth?"

"I don't spend time in the aquatracker room once the client is accustomed to the machine and his or her particular exercise routine. I rely on Serena or Terri to handle it."

"Have you ever trained anyone else on the aqua-tracker?"

"You mean another assistant? Yes. Actually, I've trained several other people. There have been six assistants who don't work here anymore who've gone through the training. Gwen learned how to use it when we were still married. But Gwen only learned enough to be able to help in our emergency drills when I first opened."

He'd referred to their previously married status without missing a beat.

Guilt flushed Gwen's cheeks. Drew was going through hell and she was obsessing over petty crap. Personal crap.

Cole Ramsey fired what seemed like the most inane queries at Drew. Gwen was proud of Drew as he answered each and every question without hesitation or any sense of discomfort, other than his obvious distress at having lost a client.

The shock of seeing him in such a traumatic situation compelled her to stay at his side.

"I'll need to speak with you, too, Gwen. Not right now, but sometime soon. What's the best number to reach you at?" Cole was practically in her face. He seemed innocuous, but she knew better. He wasn't going to antagonize her, not if there was a chance she'd have some dirt on Drew. She knew how the interrogation process went. SERE school had taught her well, as had her experience in the PI and afterward, back in the U.S.

Cole Ramsey might be a good friend of Drew's, but he was one hundred percent Detective Ramsey as far as this scenario went.

"I'm home all day." She let out a shaky laugh. "This is the first time I've been out since I landed on the island a few days ago. I'm not cleared to go back to work yet."

Ramsey gave a curt nod. "Welcome home. I'm sorry you're involved in something like this so soon after your return."

"I'm not really involved in it." As Cole continued to look at her she rolled her eyes. "Come on, Cole, you know what I mean."

She thought the death of Mrs. Forsyth was awful, yes, but didn't see how it affected her, except for Cole Ramsey's need to question her because of her relationship to Drew. Fact was, Cole had remained Drew's friend when they'd stopped seeing other couples together. Drew and Cole had still gone golfing or bike riding, and they were in the same Friday-night poker club.

"Accidents happen."

"Why do you say accident?" Cole's head tilted a little.

"I mean that no one was in the room with her." She glanced over at Drew, whose pained expression begged her to shut up. "No one could have prevented her from having a heart attack, right?"

"We don't know the cause of death yet, Gwen." Ramsey spoke succinctly and with no emotion. He turned to Drew again.

"You may want to consider getting a lawyer, at least until we've determined the exact cause."

"In addition to the insurance litigator?" Drew's brows drew together, his anger simmering. Gwen knew that look; she'd lived with it aimed at her for the better part of the past two years.

"Yes."

Drew stared at Cole Ramsey.

Gwen stepped back next to Drew and placed her arm around him, her hand on his lower back. They'd avoided physical touch, except for his hugs goodbye and then hello, and their frenzied sex the first day she was back. Still, touching him, being a silent support, didn't feel awkward. More startling yet, Drew didn't withdraw from her gesture. He leaned into it.

"Am I a suspect, Detective?" His voice vibrated through her fingers.

"Until we have conclusive autopsy results, you're at minimum a person of interest."

"You've got to be kidding me! You know me, Cole. And Dottie—Dottie Forsyth —has been my client since I opened seven years ago. She's a regular in the clinic. Everyone loves her."

"I don't doubt that, Cole. But I've got a dead body with no probable cause. She was an octogenarian, yes, but from all reports a very healthy one. Wasn't she in here for sciatica she'd developed doing a Zumba class?"

"Yes, I told you that. You have her file. No one here wanted her to die."

"Let's hope the autopsy report backs up your story, Drew. Until it does, I need you to stay in town. Will that be a problem?"

"No." Drew shook his head in exasperation. "I take full responsibility for her being in the room alone, *Detective Ramsey,* but no one here, including myself, did anything deliberate to harm Dottie Forsyth."

"Okay. Sit tight, Drew. I'll be in touch." Cole nodded and left without further comment.

Drew remained leaning against the wall, against Gwen, her arm around his waist. She didn't like the way his skin looked. Clammy. Pasty.

"You need to sit down."

"I need more than that." He allowed her to steer him to his office, where he sagged into his chair. Gwen perched on the desk.

"You didn't do anything wrong, Drew."

"How do you know, Gwen? You don't work here."

She sighed. "We have to stay focused on today, Drew. One thing I've learned in the short time I've been home is that I can't look back at my months on the run with Pax. I don't know if I'll ever hold him again, and it kills me to imagine that I won't. But if I stay in the present, I can take comfort in the fact that there's a chance I'll have Pax and be able to raise him as my own."

She squeezed his shoulder. "You have to stay in *today* to keep it together, Drew. You can't bring Dottie Forsyth back, no matter how much you beat yourself up over telling Serena she had to answer the phone. She slipped up and was out of the room at the wrong time, for a little too long."

He had his head on his arms, and she reached over to run her fingers over his hair, but stopped and rested them on his shoulders, instead. She'd lost the right to touch him like a wife long ago. But a friend would rub a beaten-down guy's shoulders.

His muscles were knots of tension. "The autopsy is going to show that Dottie had a heart attack or stroke. It was her time. No one can change that."

He raised his head and she steeled herself to take his glare.

"I am accountable, Gwen. Someone should have been in there with her. She shouldn't have had to die alone."

"You're not God, Drew."

He pushed back from the desk and she let her arms drop. Drew paced. Even in the throes of their dying marriage, she'd never seen him like this. Cornered. Trapped. As if he'd never get out of the hell he saw himself in right now. She understood. It'd been her life for six months in a hot, merciless jungle where she'd fought like hell to come back, if only to tell Drew a heartfelt "sorry" for all the misery she'd brought down on both of them. For not letting go sooner. For selfishly clinging to their marriage when it was so clear it wasn't working for either of them. She'd been too focused on her career.

She wasn't going to abandon Drew to the depths of despair she'd fought through herself, with Pax in her arms.

CHAPTER EIGHT

GWEN TOLD HERSELF she wasn't listening for the automatic garage door opener, wasn't counting the minutes until Drew came home.

She wasn't allowed to report back to work for another three weeks. Her military medical team had said it was standard practice, to give her time to decompress and allow her body and psyche to heal.

None of it mattered now, not with the crisis Drew had on his hands. She had to be here for him, whether he thought he needed her or not.

"Crazy, isn't it?" She spoke to Rosie and Nappie.

Nappie slowly wagged her tail, and Rosie uttered her usual greeting, "Hello, sailor."

"Did you miss me, sweetie?" Gwen put down her mug of tea and held out one hand. Rosie climbed on, as if months of separation hadn't happened. As if Drew and Gwen had never ruined their marriage.

Then Rosie bit Gwen's finger.

"Ouch!" Gwen winced. "Dammit, Rosie, I don't need that today."

"Aww, are you okay?" Rosie cocked her head and started to whistle at Gwen.

Gwen laughed. "You're lucky you didn't draw blood, you green chicken." She put the bird back on her perch and walked to the back kitchen window.

Puget Sound had whitecaps on it. Typical for April, when the winds still blew like winter.

There'd been whitecaps when she'd ditched the P-3. They'd damned near made her food for the ocean's bottom dwellers.

Her initial elation at still being alive when she'd finally hit solid sand on the southern Philippine shore had been crushed by her almost immediate capture. Lucky for her, her captors hadn't been well trained by their leaders. She'd been able to escape and make a run for it.

She'd thought of Drew the entire time. About forgiveness. About how, in the big picture of life, maybe nothing was impossible. Even an impossible marriage.

Her gaze shifted to the side kitchen door and she remembered Opal's visit. She'd meant to tell Drew, but it could wait.

"I can't worry about it now, right?"

"Pretty bird." Rosie seemed to agree.

The creak and rumble of the garage door as it opened brought a sense of anticipation.

She had to stay firm for Drew. It was the least she owed him.

He walked through the door and Gwen looked over from her water view and offered him a smile, which drooped into a frown as she studied Drew's appearance. His hair was wild, his skin white and clammy and his shirttails weren't tucked in. Drew never looked less than completely put together when he was going to or coming from work.

"I thought I was the survivor here," she said lightly.

"I can't joke about this, Gwen." His voice sounded as shaky as he looked.

"I'm sorry. Here." She walked to the cabinet where they kept their glasses. "Let me pour you a strong drink."

"Nothing fancy. Just the Makers Mark."

"I know." Of course she remembered his go-to drink in times of stress. He wasn't a big drinker; neither of them were. They'd enjoyed wine together with delicious meals when they'd still been married, or rather, when their marriage was real. She'd watched him throw back a shot or two as they went through the death of their relationship, or when they'd lost another friend to the war.

"Here you go." She handed him the whiskey and reclaimed her large mug of half-drunk tea. "I'd join you but I'm still feeling a little shaky. I'll have a glass of red later." In truth, she hadn't felt her usual, solid, know-it-all self since she'd floated on the Philippine Sea for two days, praying a shark wouldn't find her. It was a miracle she made it out of the ocean. She wanted to laugh bitterly as she recalled that she'd thought her hardest times were behind her.

Until she heard the rapid automatic gunfire from the first of many insurgent takeovers.

None of it compared to watching Drew's life fall apart in front of him.

This isn't about you—it's about him.

"Do you want to sit outside?" she asked.

"Sure." He sighed and walked to the sliding glass door, waiting for her to pass through first.

Even in his despair, Drew was a gentleman. She'd hated him for this particular trait when they'd been fighting for, and then accepting the failure of, their marriage. She'd wanted him to crack, to just be a bastard so she could feel better about letting him go.

Letting *them* go.

She sat in the lime-colored Adirondack chair farthest from the door, while Drew sank into its royal blue twin.

The yard looked like spring on Whidbey. The small patch of grass was green, but come summer it would turn brown and dormant. Brambles threatened to take over the back part of their lot, but the blackberries were worth the creeping tangle. She used to love making blackberry pie for Drew. She gazed down at Nappie, who, loyal even when it had to pain her arthritic bones, was curled up at Drew's feet.

Gwen waited. The silence wasn't fraught with the usual tension between them, but with a certain dread that life as Drew had known it was over.

She'd witnessed enough of his business to under-stand the dire mess he was in.

He was no longer the best, the most reputable physical therapist on Whidbey. A death in the very piece of equipment that had set him apart from the other therapists and rehab clinics was an impossible tragedy to come back from.

"Aren't you going to ask?" His harsh query cut the late afternoon like the sunbeams that streaked across the western side of the lawn.

"Ask what?" She tightened her grip on the mug.

"If I did it."

Compassion squeezed her throat. "Of course you didn't do it! Why would you expect me to ask that, Drew? To think it for even a second. We both have our dark sides, but nothing *criminal.* You're a healer, for God's sake. That's why this is affecting you worse than it would someone like me."

"Bullshit. You care more about people than I ever have."

"You're confusing my drive to motivate sailors with your own compassion. You're more natural at it." He also didn't know what she'd learned about herself while she'd held Pax in her arms, constantly aware that an insurgent could take the baby's life in a single shot.

She'd kill for someone she loved.

He turned away and hit his head against the back of the chair.

"I just can't believe we didn't hear her." He closed his eyes for a brief moment before he sat back up.

"Someone could have killed her, Gwen. A murderer may have been in my clinic this afternoon. A *murderer,* for God's sake."

He leaned back again.

"Don't even go there, Drew. It's an unfortunate accident, but maybe it was her time. She happened to be in the aquatracker when it happened, that's all."

He shook his head. "Do you really believe that?"

"Yes. Yes, I do. I think we all have a certain amount of time here. Otherwise, why would I have lived when someone like Serena's husband died over in Afghanistan?"

Drew stared up at the sky, unseeing. "Serena knows that equipment as well as I do. She's emptied the tank, cleaned it inside and out on her own. She would never have set the dials to the settings they had to be at to force Dottie under."

"Right. Just another reason to believe it was her time." Gwen bit her tongue; she'd almost called him "honey." Between her transition back to her real life and Dottie Forsyth's death, her brain acted like a soggy sponge. She couldn't hold on to the reasons she'd hated Drew, the reasons she'd been certain divorce was the only way out.

It's not your brain.

But dammit, her *heart* wasn't part of this dis-

cussion. Her heart belonged to Pax now. Being a
mother was what mattered.

What about a father for Pax?

She was a lot of things but she wasn't a user.
She'd never stay with Drew just so Pax could have
a father in his life. Drew wasn't interested in the
position, either; she was certain of it.

Not when she'd refused to start a family with
him.

Drew tapped his drink on the wide arm of the
wooden chair.

"I've been through some rough shit in my life,
but this has to be the worst."

As HE SAID the words, Drew knew she'd assume that
her disappearance hadn't affected him.

It had, more deeply than she'd ever know. More
than he'd ever be willing to tell.

"I'm going to lose it all, Gwen. If the authorities
don't charge me with murder or negligent homicide,
the family will. Her granddaughter sat in the waiting area while her grandmother drowned."

She put her hand on his and he hated himself
for the immediate sexual response he had to her
touch. What kind of monster was he that he thought
about making love to Gwen when he'd just lost
a client? All the possibilities he'd been afraid to
examine—his feelings for Gwen, hers for him, if
she'd consider involving him in the adoption—none
of it mattered anymore.

Someone had died on his watch. Dottie was dead. So was his career.

"You're exhausted and in shock, Drew. Let me get you another drink and then you need to go sit in the hot tub and let your muscles relax."

"Like Dottie did?"

Her sharp hiss warned him a second before her words cut him to the marrow.

"Knock it off, Drew. You've never been one for self-pity. Why start now? You have a long road ahead of you and you need to keep yourself in shape for it. Beating yourself up will not bring Dottie back."

"Gwen, her body's not even cold yet! Can't you cut me a break?"

Apparently, his words could still hurt, too. Her open expression shut down, and the smug face he'd learned to live with as they'd shared the house, but never their bed, fell back into place. As though the moments of comfort she'd given him today had never existed.

Without a word, Gwen picked up her mug and went back into the house. Nappie raised her head, gray snout sniffing the air. She groaned as she pulled her heavy body up onto her short, little legs and followed Gwen back into the house through the doggie door he'd installed when Nappie was still an energetic pup.

Even his dog knew he was done for.

"You don't understand."

GERI KROTOW   177

He had nothing to offer Gwen. He'd almost convinced himself he did—that he'd be able to help
ease her way back into her old life, and let her go
when the time came.

But then she'd come back more fragile than he'd
ever seen her. And she wanted to adopt a baby.

He actually thought he could help her adjust,
vouch for her stability to the social workers, then
let her go.

Again.

But now… "Tell me, Drew. Tell me what I don't
understand," Gwen said from the side door.

"This isn't something that can ever heal. It can't
be fixed, Gwen. Regardless of the reason, the
cause—my clinic is done. I'll lose my license to
practice. It's over."

DREW SANK INTO the bubbling hot water and Gwen
didn't try to look away. He'd worn baggy old swim
trunks, but instead of distracting from his physical attributes, they only accentuated his muscu-
lar frame. The dark brown hair covering his chest
narrowed into its familiar sexy line down his abdomen, past his belly button. Desire, sure and life
affirming, stirred. She hadn't seen him naked, except for their unplanned sex three days ago, since
well before the divorce.

"You've been kind to me since I've been back,"
she said. She sat on the edge of the tub, her feet submerged. She wasn't in a bathing suit and it wasn't

because she couldn't find hers in the boxes in the garage. She'd had enough wet heat in the jungle to last her a lifetime. Maybe one day when it was snowing and she was older with arthritis from her years of navy training, she'd be tempted back into a hot tub or sauna. Not yet.

You'd go in if Drew asked you to.

Not a good idea. She'd successfully put any thoughts of Drew and his sexy body out of her mind for *years.* She wasn't going to let sex jeopardize the truce they'd found.

You already did that.

He kept his eyes closed, his head resting on the back of the fiberglass rim. "Yeah, well, you earned it. You had more than your share of hardship in the last half year."

"I have and I got through it, and that's why I know you'll get through this, Drew." She flexed her feet against one of the water jets. The surge of air massaged her arches and she wanted to groan with pleasure. But groaning wasn't something she needed to be doing in front of a man she was desperately trying to stay away from.

"There's no way I want to invalidate what you've been through, Gwen. I'll never grasp the sheer evil you faced in the jungle. And you had a baby with you, to boot." He rolled his head from side to side, slowly, stretching his neck.

She'd watched him do it hundreds of times before their separation. Maybe he'd always turned her on this much, but her skin felt as though a backdraft from a forest fire was hitting it. It wasn't from the heat of the water in the pool, either.

This isn't about you being horny.

"It's done. If that's what I had to do to save myself and Pax, then so be it."

"What if you don't get him back, Gwen?"

She hugged her folded legs to her chest. "Then I'll have to deal with it like a grown-up, won't I?"

"Like I am?" His eyes were open but he still didn't look at her. She gritted her teeth for a moment before she became conscious of what she was doing and forcibly relaxed her jaw.

"We always lose when we compete with each other, Drew. It never worked in flight school or on active duty." When they'd met, in flight school in Pensacola, they'd started flirting by comparing their training flight grades.

"One-upmanship won't work now, either. We need to be friends."

His gaze slammed into her. "We don't *need* anything, Gwen. It's about what we *want*. I wanted to have a marriage that lasted forever, a family with noisy kids running around, a job I loved to go to every day and a woman I loved to come home to at night. You and I blew most of those things out of the water, but through it all I've had my career. I've been able to make a difference to my clients. Until today."

She sighed and let her feet dangle in the water

again. He needed to vent, and she refused to take it personally.

"Like I said, it's over for me, Gwen. No one's going to come to a clinic where a client died due to negligence. Dottie should never have been alone."

"We're all human. Serena must have felt Dottie was doing fine, or she wouldn't have stepped out to take the call."

He ran his hands over his face, drove his fingers through his thick hair.

"I keep seeing the look on Serena's face when I told her I couldn't get Dottie to breathe. I gave her CPR until the EMTs arrived but she was gone, Gwen. She was gone when we pulled her out of the water."

"I'm sorry, Drew."

She *was* sorry. Sorry they'd messed things up so badly that she couldn't even give him comfort in his hour of need. He'd certainly comforted her throughout her ordeal, but he didn't know it.

She'd never tell him, either. It was Drew who'd saved her life. She'd thought of him every day, every hour, every long, scary night in the jungle.

CHAPTER NINE

NIGHTS WERE OFTEN long for a career detective, especially one who was worried about a friend. Cole Ramsey felt for his friend Drew. But Cole had to stay impartial, friend or not.

Cole looked at his kitchen clock. Only half past eleven, and he hadn't made much headway with the case. There's wasn't anything more he could do until he had the autopsy results, but Drew... Cole couldn't, didn't, get involved with the subjects of his cases. Until Anita.

She'd been a murder suspect in the death of her estranged husband, which made her a potential felon. He hadn't allowed himself to get involved, not until she was cleared of any wrongdoing.

He wasn't sure what attracted him first—her sexy bombshell body, or the inner core of strength that had kept her steady through her husband's death and the small community's suspicion of her as his murderer.

Oak Harbor and the Whidbey Island towns around it were tight-knit and gossip was rampant, especially during a murder investigation. Working for the Island County Sheriff for the past twelve years had taught him that much.

Anita had been exonerated and Cole had found the real murderer, a navy commodore who was locked up for life.

Yet the community had prejudged Anita, and her trust in others had been broken.

Shattered.

Because of him.

He could blame the base NCIS for not being as forthcoming as he'd needed. They'd held their evidence against the commodore tight to their vests until the last possible moment. He could blame the sheer fact that most murders were domestic crimes, perpetrated by a relative. Anita certainly had motive, considering her soon-to-be-ex's philandering and financial irresponsibility. Her husband had risked not only Anita's security but that of their two young children, as well.

She was a warrior. She'd fought for her kids and herself, never gave up on her nursing degree and was now the best ER trauma nurse on the island. She'd been awarded the Community Cares award as healthcare professional of the year last December.

Cole liked a woman with drive; he could relate to it.

His cell phone vibrated and he braced himself for the next crime as he answered. "Ramsey."

"Cole? It's Anita."

She'd never called him anything but "Ramsey."

"How are you today?"

"Can you meet me for coffee?" Her voice, always strong and decisive, cracked.

"Where are you?"

"At home. I stayed home."

"Give me ten minutes."

The drive from his office in Coupeville up to Oak Harbor was twenty-three minutes following the speed limit and with no traffic.

Cole was going to do it in half that time. Anita needed him.

HE MADE THE drive in fifteen minutes. The route to Anita's was burned in his mind. From the first time he'd met her, right after her estranged husband's body had been discovered on West Beach, he'd known she was unlike any other woman he knew.

He walked up to her front door and it opened before he could ring the bell. Her eyes were swollen and her hair mussed. She wore Hello Kitty pajamas. He'd never seen her in anything but yoga clothes or her nursing uniform. The pajamas were baggy and didn't reveal much of her knockout body, but on her they were sexier than anything from Victoria's Secret.

"Come on in." She stood back to hold the door open for him.

"Where are the kids?"

"With my parents." She closed the door and turned to him. "I'm sorry to call you at night."

"You know you can call me anytime. What's bothering you?"

She stood there without moving, her gaze on his as though she was weighing how much to tell him.

"I just found out that one of my patients died."

"At the hospital?"

She shook her head, her tangled blond hair moving with her like a mop.

"No, at a physical therapy clinic here in Oak Harbor."

Cole's stomach dropped.

"Who was it?" He already knew but he couldn't reveal details of the investigation. Anita had to say the name first.

"Dottie. Dottie Forsyth. I took care of her whenever she came in for blood sugar spikes. She had a GP and endocrinologist but her diabetes was still pretty unmanageable. She's been in the ER at least three times in the last month."

"When was the last time you saw her?"

"This morning, shortly before she died." Anita put her hand on his forearm. "Oh, Cole, what if I sent her away when I should've had her admitted? What if she died because of her diabetes?"

"Come here." He took her in his arms. To his great surprise and equal delight, she melted against him.

She smelled like vanilla and cinnamon. Cole closed his eyes and breathed in her scent. Finally, the moment he'd wished for—but not under these circumstances.

"Shh. It had nothing to do with you."

"She was the sweetest lady." Her words were muffled against his chest.

He nodded. Anita pulled back and looked at him. "You knew her, too?"

"Not before I was called to the scene today."

"Oh, no!" Anita stepped back. "I shouldn't have told you what I did, should I? You're in charge of the case?"

"It's fine, Anita. You did not kill her nor were you the cause of Dottie Forsyth's death. I can't talk about all the details, obviously, but she most likely died from natural causes—a stroke or a heart attack. Even if it was connected to her blood sugar, you're not responsible. She was eighty, sweetheart. Nobody gets out of this world alive."

God, he hoped what he was telling her was the truth. But even if the autopsy showed that she'd been having a diabetic episode, it wouldn't have been enough to kill her.

"You know you can't tell me that with certainty, Cole." She shuddered. "There's going to be an autopsy, right?"

"Yes. Can we sit down?"

Anita gave her head a little shake as if clearing away mental cobwebs.

"Let's go into the living room. I'm sorry I didn't offer right away—"

"Stop." He steered her to the sofa with his hand on her lower back. Once they were seated next to each other, he turned toward her and took her hands.

"I've seen a lot of death, Anita, as have you. You're right. I can't promise that her diabetes didn't make Dottie pass out and slip under the water. But I *can* say that you had nothing to do with it. From the medical report we've received from her GP, she's been battling diabetes for over forty years. She looked and acted a lot younger than eighty, by all accounts, but the fact is we can't predict when our time will be up. You know that better than I do."

Anita nodded. "Yes." She smiled as tears pooled in her eyes. "She was so alive, Cole. So happy and full of energy. Did you know she still lived alone and kept up a beautiful garden? If it wasn't her grandkids and the great-grandkids she was talking about, it was how she met some cute guy at the coffee stand at the senior center." Anita's eyes shone with admiration and bemusement.

"Can you believe that, Cole? Thinking about hooking up with someone when you're eighty?"

"Yes, I can." He hadn't meant for his tone to be so somber, but the truth found its way out of his mouth.

Anita didn't miss his tone, and her smile faded as the air between them grew hot and still.

"Cole, I don't want you to get the wrong idea. I'm not interested in a hookup."

"Neither am I, Anita. I'm a battered cop who's seen the worst in human nature. Just look at these lines." He pointed at his face. "So tell me why you make me feel like a rookie."

Anita smiled. "The same reason you make me feel like I'm back in high school?"

Cole looked at her a moment longer before he leaned in and kissed the woman he'd been dreaming about for the past year.

"You still don't think you're at all responsible for Dottie Forsyth's death, do you?" Cole stroked Anita's hair back from her face as they lay together on her leather sofa. He desperately wanted to make love with her, but she'd told him she needed to take it slow.

He loved the way her lips were swollen from his kisses, and how her cheeks were flushed with her desire for him....

"No. You talked me down off the ledge. I can't thank you enough."

"I only told you the truth."

She frowned and he smoothed the lines on her forehead with his fingertips.

"Do you know for sure if it was an accident yet? Or can't you tell me?"

He sighed. "I was at the physical therapist's clinic for most of the day. I had to tell him that the autopsy will have to prove his innocence. The evidence points to an accident but we can't rule out homicide. It'll be in the paper tomorrow, so I'm not giving away any secrets here."

"Do you think he, or anyone else, did it?"

"No, I don't. What's tough is that Drew is my friend. Plus, my boss and the prosecuting attorney may not agree with me. Drew doesn't have a motive. But something's not adding up here and I can't put my finger on it."

"Does she have any family members who are going to get rich because of her death?"

Cole kissed her. Her lips were so full, so lush. God, how had he managed to fight this as long as he had?

"I'm working all the angles. Don't worry."

"I'm not worried." The seriousness of her gaze stopped him from going in for another smooch.

"What?"

"Maybe I misjudged the situation here."

Damn it.

He sat up straight. He'd ruined it. He'd pushed for too much, too soon.

"Okay, shoot."

"Forget what I said about taking it slow. I'm ready to make love to you, Cole. Now."

IT TOOK GWEN'S mother two more weeks before she visited, but true to her nature she showed up dressed to the nines, accompanied by her husband. They drove up from Seattle after flying in from San Francisco. Both were corporate lawyers and their schedules rivaled those of attorneys several decades younger.

"You look good, Mom."

"It's not about me, honey." Brenda McDill had been the consummate career woman Gwen's entire life. Her husband of twelve years and Gwen's stepfather, George, was in the kitchen cooking with Drew.

"I'm fine, Mom. I *will* be fine, even if I'm not all there yet." Tears rushed to her eyes and she ignored the urge to cross the few steps to where her mother sat in the large, cushioned club chair. She stayed on the couch, her lap covered by a blanket she'd knit with Ro several years earlier, when they'd gone on a ski trip together. The memory of sitting with Ro in the hotel room at night, knitting away while they talked and drank wine, made her smile. Ro was always trying to get Gwen to take up knitting as avidly as she had.

"It'll take you some time, yes. Are you all right with being back here?" Brenda smoothed her silver bob. She was always perfectly coiffed, a tendency Gwen hadn't inherited. When she wasn't in a flight suit or her uniform, Gwen preferred the casual style common in the Pacific Northwest. Her blond hair was usually down.

Gwen knew that by "back here", her mother didn't mean Whidbey Island. She meant back in the house she'd built with her ex-husband with hopes of a lifetime here.

Dreams that had included children… "It's okay. Besides, I didn't have anywhere else to go right away, other than a hotel, and this still does feel like home to me." Excruciatingly so, but Mom didn't need to know that. She also didn't want Brenda to realize that the navy would have released Gwen to go home to her and George. That would've been less than desirable. Brenda couldn't take care of a pet, much less an adult daughter who might fall into a PTSD anxiety attack with no warning.

"George and I aren't going to stay any longer than tomorrow. I'll come back whenever you want me to, but you need time to recover without people intruding on your quiet."

"You're not *people,* Mom. And it's a hell of a trip if you're only staying a night or two."

"Like I said, you need rest. And Drew's got enough to deal with, especially given that awful accident at his clinic."

Gwen didn't want to discuss it with her mother.

Brenda was as bad as Ro; she harbored hopes that Gwen and Drew would somehow miraculously work out their "issues" and reunite. At least Brenda had eased up on her hints about it.

Brenda and Ro didn't understand what Gwen had come to understand over the past several months. She and Drew had been kids when they'd married. Neither of them could have foreseen the harsh stresses of a dual-military marriage. Their divorce had forced them each to grow up and take responsibility for what they both wanted most—their careers.

She glanced past her mother to the kitchen, where Drew stood next to George at the counter, talking and preparing a meal. Drew looked the most relaxed he'd been since Dottie died nearly two weeks ago.

There was still no news about the autopsy report, no word from Dottie's family about whether they were going to sue. Dottie had been buried last week. Drew hadn't attended the funeral, which Gwen thought was smart under the circumstances. But she wished he could have said a proper goodbye to Dottie. She'd been one of his favorite clients. Gwen *knew* he hadn't done anything to harm Dottie.

Drew was a kind, generous man. He poured all those good qualities into his vocation—as a healer. He was lucky. He'd found his calling.

She wasn't as fortunate; being in the jungle for months, bonding with a baby when she didn't think she'd ever want kids, had turned her understanding of herself on its head.

Reality was cruel.

Brenda's eyes followed Gwen's.

"Honey, I have to ask. Are you staying with your ex-husband for the wrong reasons?"

Brenda-speak for "Are you still in love with Drew?"

"Mom, Drew and I have always stayed friends."

"So you *are* still carrying a torch for him. Finally you admit it."

"No, not at all, Mom. Did you hear what I just said?"

"Now look, honey, I've been around the block. I know the deal."

Of course she did. She'd lost her first husband to suicide, and it had taken years to get past her grief. Brenda thought there was nothing more important on earth than a good marriage. She'd given up on love until she met George fifteen years ago.

"Mom, I hear you. And if I was healing from a broken leg, I'd agree. I should get a new place today. But that's not what this is. Drew knows me well enough to give me what I need without being obtrusive. The only other person I could go to would be Ro, but she recently got married."

Besides, she'd never leave Drew when he was so vulnerable. Not until the case was resolved.

"I don't want your heart broken again. You can come home with George and me. It sounds like Drew has enough to cope with, clearing his name and trying to keep the clinic viable." Brenda lowered her voice. "I'm not a criminal defense lawyer, but if Drew needs a good one, I have contacts."

"I appreciate that, Mom."

"If you come back with me, you might heal more quickly. Then you could return here to help Drew through this mess without risking your feelings."

"There's nothing to risk, Mother. I know where

I stand with Drew—we're friends. He's going to come through it, with or without me. He's a victim of circumstance, and I have every confidence that any criminal impressions will be cleared up. Either way, Mom, I need to be on the island. I'm going back to work sooner rather than later, and everything I need is here. I have a set of doctors who are specifically trained to help me with my reentry issues. Between Drew, Ro and the squadron, there are enough people to provide the support I need. Besides, you're in the middle of a big case." Which Brenda had dropped to come and see Gwen, but Gwen knew her mother well. She was probably itching to check her phone for text updates. Brenda's career was a large part of her drive and youthful vitality.

It hasn't cost your mother her love life.

"I HAVE A challenging client at the moment, true. But I'm your mother, Gwen. I know you best. Like me, you're tough on the outside. You want the world to see that nothing upsets you, nothing hurts. As if you don't have any feelings." Brenda played with the large glass beads that hung around her neck, setting off her casual-chic outfit. "It's okay to be vulnerable, honey. It's what makes us human."

Where had this compassionate woman been when Gwen was growing up? All she remembered was her mother being engrossed in work, not to be bothered as she studied her files late into the night. It had given them a kind of shared community once Gwen was in high school and bringing home a backpack full of assignments each afternoon. But when she was a little girl, her mother was often a lawyer first.

"I didn't learn it myself until after your dad died. George has taught me what's important."

"You two are lucky, Mom."

"Lucky, sure. But we both work at it. And I've given up always having to be the best at what I do. Sometimes I hand a case over to one of the partners. Or I don't take it on in the first place."

"I don't have the option to pass on a mission in the navy, Mom."

"I realize that. But you have a choice about where you go next. What you want out of your life. There's more than the navy, you know."

"Thanks, Mom. You may be right."

When Brenda stayed quiet, Gwen wanted to pump her fist in the air. She'd learned the line *you may be right* from the psychiatrist at Madigan, who said that if anyone started giving their opinions on how she could have handled her in-flight emergency, her ditch or her time in the PI differently, all she needed to do was smile and say "You may be right." It shut up the offending speaker and helped her keep her sanity.

Maybe her mother had learned that a career wasn't the be-all and end-all. Gwen didn't even feel the usual resentment that her mother hadn't always been there for her. Gwen had made her own choices with the navy long ago, and had a commitment to finish out at least the minimal retirement option, twenty years. That meant two more tours after the command tour.

They went back to watching the movie they'd rented on the cable box. For once Gwen was happy to be the patient, begging off heavy conversation with her mother via the remote control.

She wondered if her mother was actually paying attention to the romantic comedy, because Gwen wasn't. Her mind wandered to hell and back several times a day. What Dr. Luke had told her was proving true; she still felt the fear, the sense of constant alertness and often the despair that had threatened each step of her months evading her captors. But the dark feelings were lessening. She wasn't going into the pit as often, and when she did, it wasn't for as long.

She also wasn't looking over her shoulder as much as she'd done when she'd first emerged from the wilderness. Civilization was starting to feel more normal.

What didn't feel normal was the fact that she wasn't clinging as tightly to her identity as a naval officer. She'd been stripped emotionally bare in the jungle, which made worry about her next promotion, the right career option or her rank among her peers, seem inconsequential now. She'd thought the apathy would pass the longer she was home on

Whidbey, but instead it continued, a slow, steady beat of truth.

Because of Pax.

Was this what becoming a mother meant? Was it normal for her not to take her job as seriously? To want to drop everything for her son?

He's not your son yet.

Drew understood how she felt and what she'd been through better than anyone else in this room, but he wasn't a parent.

Brenda sat next to Gwen on the sofa, her familiar profile a comfort despite the strain that sometimes existed between them. Gwen's mother had done the best she could when she was raising her. Gwen's father had been a wonderful, fun-loving, affectionate man who filled in the gaps that Brenda's career focus had left in their lives. Until his drinking got the better of him and he ended up killing himself after discovering he had liver failure.

Her mother was a formidable woman who could out-talk and out-do anyone half her age in a courtroom. George's intelligence was tempered by his endless compassion; he saved everyone he could and never complained. They'd both be great people to lean on if her trauma had been caused by anything other than a combat experience.

But they'd never been in the military. They didn't understand the breadth of her fight for survival.

Drew did.

CHAPTER TEN

AFTER THE MOVIE Gwen and Brenda moved outside to enjoy the meal Drew and George had prepared.

"Brenda and I were so worried, punkin." George looked at her over the picnic table where they'd enjoyed baked beans and hot dogs on the deck. He'd married Brenda after they'd met at a legal convention in Dallas. George was pure Texan but had moved to Northern California to be with Brenda.

"I know, and I'm sorry for the hell you both must've gone through."

Drew didn't like the pallor of Gwen's face. He was finally getting her to talk more, eat more and at least appear more relaxed. Admittedly, he hadn't been as free to take care of her since Dottie's death. But with her folks here, she'd tightened back up.

They showed no sign of calling it an early night, either. He understood why Brenda and George wanted to squeeze as much togetherness as possible into their short visit, but Gwen needed her rest.

Brenda was a beautiful woman and it was clear where Gwen got her stunning looks. Brenda and George were still vital in their careers and physically active to boot—everything Drew hoped he'd be as he approached seventy.

Except for their losses. Both had lost spouses before they'd found each other. Spouses they'd thought they'd spend their entire lives with.

He was going through a major loss at the moment. And Gwen might be facing her own huge loss if the adoption didn't go through.

As much as Gwen had her mother's strength, Drew understood that six months of living in a jungle had pushed her to her limits.

"You're back, Gwen. That's all that matters." If they wouldn't say anything, he'd do it for them.

One side of her mouth lifted as she looked down at her food, still untouched. He knew she thought about her father. She'd had a special bond with him that Brenda had never been able to replicate. "Drew's right, sweetheart." Brenda's reply was whispered as she grabbed her daughter's hand and squeezed.

Drew wanted to slam his fist into the table. Gwen's family had been through so dammed much and they still couldn't let the needed tears fall, couldn't give each other a hug.

"I'm really tired. Do you all mind if I go up for a short nap?" Gwen pushed back from the table. He felt a surge of protective pride. Good for her.

"Hell, no, sweetie. Take all the time you need. Go to bed for the night if you feel like it." George had that big-ass grin on his face as if Gwen were a child and he was simply appeasing her.

They didn't get it.

He didn't say a word as he cleared his and Gwen's plates from the table and followed several steps behind her into the house.

As soon as he knew she was in her room— what used to be their room—he went upstairs and knocked on the door. She still left it ajar, but he didn't make the mistake of thinking that was an invitation. "Gwen, can I come in?"

"Sure."

She lay on the bed, bundled to her chin, her eyes round like a doll's and just as blank.

He sat on the bed and reached for one of her hands, which clutched the edge of the blanket.

"Do you want me to call the clinic for you? Do you need more meds?"

She shook her head. "No, I'm okay. It's just a little anxiety, left over from all the—" she waved her hand "—you know."

"Yeah, I sure do."

Her eyes focused on him instead of the ceiling and his chest relaxed.

"I know you do. You've been here. I remember."

He had been, after his time in the war. He'd seen more action on the ground than Gwen had, purely a matter of circumstance and timing. It'd taken months to shake the constant sense that he needed to look over his shoulder or hit the ground or run to the nearest air-raid shelter. Gwen had conducted most of her wartime missions from the seat of a P-3. She'd had her share of scary events, but nothing like the ditch she'd executed, and the horrors in the bush. Horrors she'd had to deal with on her own.

"I was, but I did climb out of it after a month or so. Remember that part?"

"I don't want to be feeling like this in a month." One big tear rolled down her cheek and again he was relieved. If she could cry, that was good.

"You're going to be okay, Gwen, but you do have to work with the docs, and believe them when they tell you to slow down and be patient with yourself. This is bigger than you, bigger than anything you ever trained for. It's one thing to survive what you did and come back whole. Then add in the fact that you have to adjust to being home, plus you're trying to adopt a child. That's a lot." He shut his mouth. She didn't need him grilling her like a bad boss.

Or a controlling husband.

"Coming back here—it's not what I expected would happen."

"I'm sorry about that, Gwen. I hoped I'd be of more help to you…." He'd tried to keep his mental and emotional distance from her, but it hadn't been enough.

"I'm not sorry about being here, Drew. This is the best place for me, I know that, as much as I fought it." She squeezed his hand. "It's not such a good deal for you, but I'm grateful for all you've done. I'm so sorry about what you're going through at the clinic."

"Gwen, we may have made a mess of our marriage, but I'd like to think we've kept a basic friendship. I'm proud of that, in fact."

Her expression closed, and she pulled her hand from his as if she thought she'd made a mistake in letting him hold it. Damn it, wasn't there *anything* he could say that wouldn't upset her?

"This isn't the time to worry about any of it, Gwen. I meant what I said. It hurts like hell, and it may do so for a while yet, but this too shall pass. Remember?"

"Yes."

He stood up and immediately missed the warmth of her body next to his leg, even if it was under layers of blankets.

"If you need anything, I'm here. I do think a call to your doc is in order. You're still taking the meds they gave you, right?"

"I'm not a fool, Drew. Of course I'm taking my prescription."

He'd had to ask. They both knew that sometimes brain chemistry needed help, be it temporarily or for the rest of their lives. It didn't matter either way. As long as her body got what it needed to heal.

Her eyes drifted shut. For that, he was grateful. Sleep was the best healer of all.

His hand was on the doorknob when he heard her whispered thanks.

"IT'S AWFULLY NICE of you to take her back in, Drew."
Brenda sipped her remaining wine. Brenda's facial
expression was so similar to Gwen's. As hard as it
was to imagine Gwen as anything but the younger
woman she was now, he knew he was looking at a
future image of her. Beautiful, classy, still sexy…

"I didn't take her back in, Brenda. This is her
home."

"Legally."

"Ever the lawyer." He tilted his glass of water
toward her in a mock toast. He needed sleep and a
sharp mind more than staying up for aperitifs with
Brenda and George.

"You know why I married Brenda, Drew? It was
for that sharp look she's throwing you right now."
George laughed and Drew couldn't keep his lips
from tugging into a grin.

"Stop making me out to be a bitch." Brenda
smiled at them both.

"Go easy, darling." George was the smooth honey
to Brenda's molasses. Brenda represented one of the
pharmaceutical giants, while George represented
non-profit organizations. Both corporate attorneys,
yet each had very different job descriptions and interests.

"Relax, George. Drew knows me well enough by
now. I'm never going to stop being Gwen's mom."
And I've never stopped being her husband.
Sweat broke out on Drew's forehead. The timing

was a bitch. His emotions were roiling because of the terrible accident at his clinic.

Living with Gwen again wasn't helping, either. *She needs me.*

"I know what you mean, Brenda. Trust me—Gwen's well-being is my top priority."

"Mmm." She took another sip. "How can it be when a client just died at your clinic?"

"I'm managing."

He knew Brenda trusted him—for the most part. Yet the part of her that didn't, the part that insinuated he'd use Gwen's vulnerability for his own purposes, pissed him off. He'd never do anything to hurt Gwen.

The fact that he'd made love to her weighed heavily on his conscience. His pure selfishness appalled him.

None of that, however, was Brenda's concern.

"I've got an early start in the morning. You know where everything is, so please make yourselves at home. I'll take the dog out and be on my way to bed." He stopped by Rosie's cage and took a minute to scratch the bird's neck before he put her on her perch and covered her cage with its custom blanket that had ROSIE embroidered on the front.

"That bird's been awfully quiet since we got here. Remember when she used to talk up a storm, George?"

"Sure do. She still have Gwen's laugh?"

"Yes, she does." And Rosie still liked to scream

out like Gwen did when she came, a sound she'd learned as a baby bird when they first adopted her. They'd made love in their living room one too many times, and Rosie had stealthily listened to each sound and perfected it.

He and Gwen used to laugh whenever the bird mimicked Gwen's lusty words.

It broke Drew's heart when Rosie did that.

"DO YOUR BUSINESS, Nappie." Drew looked up at the stars while the dog sniffed the lawn. There was no rushing Nappie; she marched to her own beat.

The lights from the living room glowed out from the sliding doors upstairs on the deck. He used to enjoy Brenda and George's company, but tonight his hackles were up.

You're too damned protective of Gwen.

But Gwen had come back. She wasn't his Amelia Earhart, after all. *She didn't come back for you.*

"Nappie, come on, get it done, gal." The dog kept sniffing. Drew wondered if she was starting to go deaf. She'd passed her prime a while ago, but still bounced around like a younger dog when motivated.

Between Gwen's return and Dottie's death, Drew's world had imploded in a matter of days. No wonder his heart was raw. It was natural for him to seek comfort with the one woman, hell, the *only* woman, who'd ever soothed him as much as she'd driven him to the limits of his sanity.

Drew looked up toward their bedroom window. Her window now, he reminded himself once again. It wasn't *their* room, hadn't been for half a decade. He stared at the curtains, lit from behind, until she turned off the light. If things had played out differently at his clinic, he might have been tempted to join her in the darkened room.

THE DAY AFTER Brenda and George left, the cloud-covered island was windy, typical of this time of year. Instead of the mountains Gwen noticed the whitecaps on the surface of Puget Sound as she drove down the road into town.

It was too easy to stay in their house as a way to protect herself from the inevitable anxiety triggered by a trip into the real world. Brenda had told her to get out more, and she was right.

When she'd driven to Drew's clinic on the day of Dottie's death she'd been able to look past her own fears and get there with little fuss. Today was different; it was the first time she was venturing out on her own, for no reason other than to browse in a department store. She'd promised to meet Ro for coffee later so that she wouldn't be tempted to stay home.

She didn't tell Drew she was going out when he left for work. It was on the tip of her tongue to ask him why he was bothering to go in at this point. His stress was evident in the droop of his shoulders and the gray tint of his skin.

Gwen turned off the main route into town and pulled into the large shopping area. She passed the coffee shop where she'd meet Ro later and headed straight for the big-store parking lot. Her target was the garden center. She'd found comfort in her flowers and vegetables in the past and had decided to buy supplies for the window boxes that decorated the front of the house. Drew had helped her install them when they'd bought the house nine years ago.

Staying in the garden center was imperative; she couldn't bear to see baby toys or clothes. Not without Pax in her arms.

The remembered scent of his hair rushed at her, and she halted midaisle between the weed killer and the grass seed. Closing her eyes, she took deep breaths and said a silent prayer. There was nothing she could do about Pax until she heard from the adoption agency that was handling it, together with the State Department. The State Department councilor handling the case said she'd call when they were closer to resolution. In the meantime, Gwen had received emails and a couple of written updates via FedEx.

The plastic handle of the shopping cart was cool and solid beneath her clenched hands. Combined with the harsh smells of garden chemicals, that sensation grounded her in the present. In the here and now, where she could hope that Pax would eventually come home to her.

"Gwen?"

She opened her eyes and inwardly groaned.

"Hi, Opal." She forced a smile and a relaxed stance. How did the woman always manage to show up at the worst times?

"I'm taking a long lunch break." Opal smiled in response. "I'm so sorry to hear what's happening in Drew's clinic. It's been all over the paper and the TV news."

"Thank you. I'm sure he'll appreciate hearing it from you."

"Oh, I already told him." Opal swiped at her blond bangs. "He drives through for his coffee every morning and confides in me." Opal peered at Gwen as though Gwen was a gnat. "How's it been going for you?" she went on. "It can't be very comfortable to be back under the same roof as your ex-husband, especially when he has such big problems of his own."

"You may be right."

"I'm sorry. I shouldn't have said anything. It's none of my business. I totally trust Drew."

"Oh?" Trusted Drew about what? Gwen wanted to be anywhere but here, having a conversation with a woman who was so hot for Drew she leaked pheromones at the mere mention of his name.

"Well, Drew and I are definitely *friends*." Opal's tone insinuated more.

"Hmm."

"I don't mean to be intrusive, Gwen, but how long do you think you'll be in the house? Don't get me wrong—" Opal covered her chest with her hand "—I don't want to interfere with your adjustment back to regular life."

"I haven't come up with a definite schedule yet, but as soon as I do, I'll let you know." It was Gwen's turn to smile, even though she inexplicably wanted to grab one of the hand rakes and claw out Opal's eyes with it.

It wasn't as if Drew's relationships with other women were any of her business.

Opal didn't take the hint. "What are you looking for?" she asked.

"Nothing in particular. Just browsing."

"I wish I had time in my schedule to do that. I'm here on a quick run to get some extra supplies for my business. I ran out of napkins this morning. I need to get back before the afternoon rush."

"Oh, well, I'd better let you go, then. See you." Gwen pushed her cart around the end of the aisle and stared down at her hands. She was clenching the handle again, this time to keep her hands from shaking, from betraying her anger.

She hated having to face her deepest fears.

Her heart had made a fatal mistake, misjudging Drew's natural inclination toward kindness as an indication that they might become more than friends again. More than confidants.

It's just the PTSD, the reentry anxiety.

Searching for an escape from her thoughts, Gwen shoved her cart into the outdoor area of the nursery. Row upon row of blooming flowers greeted her. She grabbed containers of primroses, gerbera daisies and dianthus. Then she tossed in a couple of contrasting low-growing grasses, and found two more window boxes to add to the house. As she bent to lift a bag of potting soil onto the bottom of the cart, she heard a woman's voice carry over the aisle partition.

"Don't worry, sweetheart. I understand. It'll take time. You're going through so much. I'll wait." Opal's voice was distinct as she obviously talked on her cell phone.

Goose bumps broke out on Gwen's forearms.

She straightened and carefully brushed her hands free of the dirt.

So what if Opal and Drew were seeing each other? She had flowers to plant.

DREW STARED UNSEEING at his computer screen. It was pointless to try to get any work done in his office. Yet since the accident, he'd needed to be here more than ever.

Out of respect for Dottie, he'd canceled his appointments for a week after her death.

He didn't expect any of his clients to come back once they heard. Most of them had tried to make new appointments, but then his insurance had backed out, with no indication of reinstatement.

It'd been three weeks since Dottie Forsyth had

died in his clinic. Three weeks and two days since Gwen had returned home.

To the house.

Drew knew more than ever that Gwen, of all people, wasn't the one he should be leaning on to get through this ordeal.

She wasn't out of the woods herself, between healing from six months of deprivation and survival existence and her PTSD. He heard her cry out at night and waited in the hallway outside her door until she fell back asleep. He fought the urge to go in and comfort her every time. She'd be embarrassed if she knew he'd heard her nightmares.

Damn his stupid emotions. He'd allowed hope to light a flame when she'd asked him to help her with the adoption—to prove she was mentally stable.

Full reconciliation with Gwen wasn't an option—at least not right now. Neither of them was on solid enough ground in their individual lives, so remarriage was another complication. A huge one. But he'd been optimistic about the possibilities of a solid friendship.

Who was he kidding?

None of it mattered anymore. The tiniest sliver of hope for building a bridge of friendship, one that might even lead to future reconciliation, vanished the moment Serena found Dottie in the aquatracker.

He'd never drag Gwen into this mess. She needed to heal.

Yet all day his thoughts went back to the past

weeks when she'd sat by him as he'd soaked in the hot tub or joined him at the dining-room table. She made breakfast and dinner, the first meals she'd cooked for him since their marriage ended.

He shut down the computer and headed home.

SHE WAS SITTING in his chair, the comfy recliner she'd despised and begged him to throw to the curb for years. He'd never told her, but he didn't want to get rid of it because he had memories of some of the best sex of his life in that chair.

Sex with Gwen.

God, he missed those days. He could blame it on the stress he was going through with the Forsyth case, but he knew that wasn't fair. He'd never stopped wanting Gwen, even when they'd despised each other.

"Hey." She looked up briefly. He registered a ball of yarn and long, pointy needles but it was her expression that caught his attention.

Trusting. She trusted that she could heal in this house, trusted he'd be willing to help her adopt the kid.

"Hi."

"Another bad day, huh?" Her eyes were wide with concern and she'd dropped her yarn on her lap.

"There won't be any other kind from now on." He went into the kitchen, grabbed a highball glass from the cupboard and filled it with ice.

"Are you hungry?" Her soft voice and the

warmth of her nearness startled him. He jerked his hand back from the automatic ice dispenser and ice spewed across the kitchen floor.

"Shit, Gwen."

"I'm sorry. I didn't mean to scare you." She backed up and leaned against the granite counter.

"You didn't scare me." Anger and frustration melded with pure need. Even now, during some of the worst days of his life, he was still aware of her.

He wanted to take her on the kitchen floor. No matter what happened between them—or, more likely, didn't—she'd always be the most attractive woman he'd ever known. He sighed. "I'm on edge all the time, waiting for a lawyer representing the Forsyth family to serve me papers." He bent down and started to pick up the ice cubes before they melted. Nappie had come into the kitchen and was scooping up cubes as quickly as she could, crunching the frozen treats.

"Here, let me do that." Gwen knelt down and her hair fell over her face.

"Helloooo!" Rosie yelled from the family area. She hated when people were home but out of sight.

"Hey, Nappie, cut it out," Gwen shouldered the dog out of her way as she picked up the last ice cube. Nappie licked Gwen's face and tried to take the cube from her hand before she tossed it in the sink. Gwen laughed and allowed herself to get knocked onto her bottom, Nappie's face in hers, tail wagging furiously.

Gwen's yoga pants were snug in all the right places. Despite the weight she'd lost, it was obvious that she still had all her curvy woman parts.

Drew stood up, intending to get the hell out of the kitchen.

"Give me a hand, will you?" Gwen reached up for him and he stared at the innocent gesture.

Gwen's gaze caught his when he hesitated.

The question in her eyes extinguished when she saw the heat in his. Her pupils dilated.

"Aw, hell, Gwen."

He clasped her hand and in one movement had her up and against him. Still holding her hand, he wrapped his arm around her and tugged her hips closer to his. His free hand did what it'd wanted to do since she'd walked back into the house—he grasped the back of her head and pulled her to him.

"Oh…"

Drew pressed his lips to hers. He didn't, couldn't, let her say anything. He didn't want to think.

He slowed down enough to relish the feel of her soft, full lips under his, to savor the pressure she gave back.

She slipped her tongue in his mouth, seeking his, and he was gone.

Lust had never died between them, only the trust to enjoy it without reservations. It'd been so long since she'd allowed him to touch her, since he'd allowed himself to reach for her, to enjoy all that was Gwen.

To make love to her.

She pulled her hand from his and slid both arms around him, holding tight. Giving him permission to feel her, touch her.

Her neck and collarbone were so delicate, so feminine. Her waist, tiny compared to her height, her skin smooth. He thrust his fingers under her T-shirt, pushed it up. He groaned when he finally had a breast in his hand, firm and soft and full… Her hands weren't satisfied to stay at his shoulders and she explored him, as well. Heat rose between them. Drew felt as though he were on a sprint to finish the one-hundred-meter dash. He couldn't stop. His erection, his need to be inside her, was exquisite torture.

Gwen expertly unfastened his pants and only when she held his arousal in her hand did he drag his mouth from hers.

Her flushed cheeks, closed eyes and her hand around his erection sent an unmistakable message.

"Gwen? Open your eyes, baby."

Slowly, as if with reluctance, she did. He'd never forget her eyes as long as he lived. If today was his last day on the planet he'd choose to be with her.

"Is this what you want, Gwen? Are you sure you want this?"

Her eyes, hazy with lust, cleared. He saw the flash of mistrust before her body stiffened, before her fingers withdrew from his pants, before she placed her hands on his chest.

"We're both under a lot of stress, aren't we?"

"This isn't about stress, Gwen."

She shuddered, and he knew she was fortifying herself. "Sure it is, Drew. We're two healthy, fairly young adults. We have a shared history that's powerful. I survived hell for six months, and I miss my baby. You lost a patient, and you're afraid you'll lose your life's dream. It's only natural that we'd reach for each other."

Gwen was making sense. He hated it.

GWEN TURNED AWAY and walked back out to the living room. She had to put some space between them. Not because she didn't wanted to jump Drew's bones and finish what they'd started. But because she did, so badly.

Their relationship wasn't going anywhere; they'd both agreed on it. Sexual compatibility was never enough—not with two driven people like them. Even if they chose to enjoy each other in the moment, it would still end.

The sadness of it all blew her fragile control apart. She couldn't let him see her tears. It wasn't fair to him, not when he was faced with losing the clinic.

And it wasn't fair to her. They weren't going to be together any longer than it took for the case to be resolved, for the adoption to go through and for her to find a place to live while she finished out her squadron tour.

Two months, tops.

She'd already decided she'd take shore orders anywhere but here, to give her a decent amount of time to find a civilian job if she decided to resign her commission. Because if she couldn't get shore orders for the rest of her time until retirement, next tour she was going to resign and give Pax the stability she and Drew had never had in their marriage. She couldn't stay on Whidbey any longer, not after what she and Drew had shared since her return. Her heart couldn't handle it.

No more deployments. No uncertainty.

Pax had had enough moving around and being dislocated in his short life. He deserved stability and security.

He couldn't get to know Drew. Because Drew would become another loss for Pax.

For me, too.

She'd thought she'd finished grieving her marriage, thought she'd moved on, knew what was best for herself.

She'd been mistaken. She needed to move on, yes, but she owed it to herself to mourn her failed marriage and let it go.

And to let Drew go so he could find the love *he* deserved in his life. Being friends hadn't helped either of them in the long run. Until now, when they needed each other.

Their timing had always been crappy.

"Here." He handed her a glass of chilled pinot

grigio, a favorite of hers since they were stationed in Italy for a shore tour all those years ago, when they'd both been active duty. She'd worked at the base outside Naples and he'd been on the NATO staff. On a quick overnight getaway from their responsibilities, they'd gone to Capri's sister island, Ischia. It'd been mid-July and hotter than hell. The pinot grigio had quenched their thirst and cooled their libidos long enough to get them back to their hotel room.

"Thanks."

She sipped the chilled wine and let the taste linger on her tongue. Concentrating on the complexity of the wine was better than thinking about that trip, when she'd lain topless by their hotel pool and then later on the pebble-strewn Mediterranean beach. It was commonplace for Europeans but not for her, not for an Academy grad who wanted to keep her spotless career pristine.

It had been heaven.

"Do you remember Ischia?"

He *had* to bring that up.

"I remember climbing the side of the rock mountain, going from waterfall to waterfall."

"Mmm." He sat on the sofa across from her and sipped his wine.

"You weren't so enamored with all the springs and thermals." She smiled. "Do you remember the looks you got?"

The locals had pointed and laughed at Drew's

Bermuda shorts swim trunks, since he was the most covered-up man on the resort island. The Italian men and international tourists tended to wear G-strings, the women often in topless bikinis.

"Your bikini was memorable."

She dared a glance at him, knowing his eyes smoldered with frustration. He kept his lids downcast.

The drop in her stomach wasn't disappointment. It was certainty—that they shared an unquenchable attraction, no matter what their marital or emotional status.

She wanted to throw her glass of wine against the woodstove and watch it shatter on the cast-iron furnace.

"I'm afraid my bikini days are over. I wouldn't fit into that swimsuit again." Well, she would once she gained her weight back.

"Stop it, Gwen. You're more beautiful than ever."

She caught her breath. After all the horrible fights they'd had in this room… All those nights of giving each other the cold shoulder.

If he hadn't stopped them in the kitchen she'd have allowed him to make love to her.

As if none of the bad memories existed.

She cleared her throat, determined to change the subject. "Any news from the clinic?"

"Nothing. No clients, and I told Serena to stay home until things settle out."

"What about Terri?"

"No need for her to come in with no clients."
He swirled the wine in his glass. "It's for the best.
This will make it easier on both of them when the
clinic closes."

"Now it's your turn to stop it, Drew. You'll have
even more clients once it's proven Dottie died of
natural causes."

"I hope you're right, Gwen. But I can't depend
on that."

"What did your insurance company say?"

"They keep telling me the same thing—that clients and families of clients rarely sue physical therapists."

"That makes sense, since you get to know each
of your clients so well. You improved her quality
of life so much."

"Even so, the client doesn't usually die."

"What family does Dottie have here?"

"I know she has one son who teaches PE and
coaches at the high school. Her daughter is an attorney who lives closer to Seattle. She has grandkids, too, some of whom live here. There's a stepson
in the mix, as well, her husband's son that Dottie
raised." He kicked off his shoes and put his feet on
the coffee table.

"The past month hasn't been easy for either of
us, I'd say. Maybe it's supposed to make us more
grateful or something."

"No God of my understanding would be this
spiteful, Gwen, even to me."

Even to him?

"Don't tell me you're still carrying the weight of the world on your shoulders, Drew. Are you still taking on all the guilt about our divorce?" He'd always accepted the blame for everything that went wrong between them, to the point that she'd accused him of being a martyr.

He shrugged but wouldn't meet her eyes. "Not at all. It was the right decision for us. It doesn't mean we can't be kind to each other, like you said last night. But this situation is going to take a lot more than kindness to fix. It might even be unfixable."

"Wait for the autopsy before you assume anything."

"I'm hanging on by a thread, Gwen." He muttered another earthier phrase under his breath.

She laughed. "I haven't heard such navy raunch in months."

"You used to hate it."

"I would've given anything to hear one of the sailors swear a blue streak while I was out there." Then maybe she would've been rescued a lot earlier. As it was, she'd survived the constant threat of rape while in the camp, saved Pax from that village laid to waste by the insurgents. Somehow she'd kept her sanity in order to save her baby.

It was memories of Drew that saved me.

"There's no way of knowing how fast life can turn sour," Drew said philosophically, apparently still talking about their marriage.

"No, but we didn't appreciate what we had back then, either."

Drew stared at her. "You think you'd appreciate it more now?"

"I'd like to think so. After my jaunt in the jungle, and now your tragedy, some things just aren't as important to me as they once were."

She prayed he didn't ask her for more. Talking about how they'd matured was one thing, but she couldn't handle the what-ifs. Today was all they had.

Today, she and Drew were friends. That was all she could count on.

"Tell me about your time in the PI, Gwen."

She stood up. "Not now. Maybe once the autopsy results are in, and your life's on an even keel again. But not tonight."

She turned back to him on her way to the kitchen. "Oh, I forgot to mention something, but I ran into Opal at the garden center today, and it reminded me that I never told you she came by a couple of days after I got back."

As she related the story, she realized it had been the same day Dottie died, and told him that.

"I'm so sorry I didn't tell you this sooner."

"There was a lot more to worry about that day than Opal making one of her typical drop-ins. She doesn't have a key to the house, Gwen. The back door must've been unlocked. You know how I am."

"I do." She smiled, and it was enough to shatter his determination to keep his distance from her.

They'd had so many fights about his refusal to lock doors. He'd claimed they lived in the "country," so why bother? He should've been more worried about making sure Gwen felt safe.

"I've been gone a long time, Drew. I don't expect you to have been a monk."

He didn't respond to that. "I'll lock up when I leave for work tomorrow."

"I'd appreciate it. I won't be here too much longer. As soon as the adoption—"

He held up a hand. "I know, Gwen. As soon as the adoption clears, you're out of here. I get it."

He looked so defeated she didn't argue with him.

Gwen walked into the kitchen and prepared the dinner she'd planned for them. Drew didn't say much throughout the meal and excused himself to go to bed early.

She knew he wasn't going to be sleeping any more than she was.

THE NEXT MORNING Gwen sipped her tea and wondered why she hadn't corrected Drew. She'd meant to tell him that he didn't need to worry about her request to help out with the adoption. She couldn't possibly burden him now. A counselor could sign off on her health.

"Here." Drew walked into the kitchen and slapped

a shiny key on the counter next to Gwen's mug of tea.

"What's this?"

"A new house key. I changed the locks this morning."

"You must have been up at the crack of dawn!"

"Maybe."

"Any reason?"

"Just a hunch."

"Does the hunch rhyme with 'Opal'?"

"Yes. It doesn't strike me as odd that Opal walked in uninvited that first day. She lets herself in a lot, leaves me leftovers from her coffee shop—pastries, cookies."

"Your relationship with Opal, with anyone else, is just that, Drew. Yours. It's none of my business."

"Fine, but listen. Opal's just a neighbor who once happened to work for me, Gwen. That's it."

"She has major hots for you, Drew."

"She has the hots for *any* man who drives through her coffee shop."

"She's been after you since I can remember." Gwen thought about the way Opal had walked into the house as if she'd owned it. It still didn't sit well with her.

"She's not important to me, Gwen. Your safety and my privacy are." He nodded at the key. "Make sure you lock up, okay?"

CHAPTER ELEVEN

She had to give Drew credit. He waited almost three weeks after she'd returned before he pounced.

"You've got to get back in the saddle, Gwen."

"I'm not ready."

He looked at her over his bowl of rice crisps. Sometime between when she'd left and now, Drew had switched from sugary cereals to rice crisps.

"Gwen, stop avoiding the inevitable. You've been holed up in this house for most of a month."

"The doctors—"

"I don't care what the doctors say. Sure, take six months off, whatever. But you thrive on being a leader, on being in the cockpit. You can't expect to get better without having it in your life."

She swallowed a gulp of coffee and winced when it hit her stomach, its acidity not mixing well with her nerves.

"It's not like anything I've ever gone through before, Drew. I've already missed six months of my command tour. They're doing fine without me. I see no point in going back for the remainder of the squadron's shore time."

"That's the whole point. You *have* to go back. If you don't, you're letting the circumstances that put you in that godforsaken place run the show. You're telling your team you've given up."

"I failed them. I should never have ditched."

"What?"

"I could have made it to Manila, Drew. If I'd listened to the intel reports more closely, if I'd been more conservative in our flight profile, that bird might still be flying."

"You're playing God now, Gwen, and it's not very becoming." Drew stood up and rinsed out his bowl at the sink. "I may just have served out my minimum commitment but I was in the cockpit often enough to know that the P-3 is an old bird that turns into a witch at times. You should've had the P-8, but you were stuck with that old frame."

"Doesn't matter. It was flying fine for the entire workup to deployment."

"Are you kidding? Is it worth the energy you're spending to spit out this BS? Because it's clear to me and any experienced naval aviator that you had no control over when that plane was going to get hit by a missile, much less fall apart. It happened to be on your watch, on your flight, on your mission. That's the way the dice rolled."

She knew Drew wasn't just blowing smoke up her butt, as the junior officers were fond of saying. He was a man of deliberation and didn't shy away from the truth as he saw it.

She also knew he'd always been her strongest supporter; their divorce hadn't changed his professional esteem for her nor hers for him.

"They're champing at the bit to see you, Gwen. Go back where you belong."

The phone calls and meal drop-offs at their front door had started in earnest last week. After the initial few weeks of privacy she'd requested, the squadron didn't hold back their love and support for her. There were no fewer than two dozen casseroles in the freezer and refrigerator, and the kitchen counter was covered with plates of cookies, banana bread, fruit trays and smoked salmon.

"We're never going to eat all the food they've brought."

"It's not about the food, Gwen."

Drew leaned over the breakfast counter toward her.

"Get back out there."

Gwen knew Drew was right; she needed to get back to the squadron, back to work. But she couldn't make herself drive farther than the main shopping area downtown.

Guilt over her reluctance to rejoin her teammates only served to depress her more. She found solace in the backyard while Drew was out at the clinic. He'd returned to his place of work in the face of an apparent unsolved murder. So what was *her* problem?

She fussed with her potted plants while Nappie

dozed in the low-beamed sunlight on the deck. Gwen drew in a deep breath as she transplanted some of her lavender. The scents and sights of the Pacific Northwest were nothing like the Philippines, and for that she was deeply grateful.

She'd appreciated the beauty of the Philippines; in fact, it had kept her going when the days felt as though they stretched to infinity. But her brain, her body, her spirit needed to know without a doubt that she was safe. That she'd healed.

Was she healed?

The gaping hole in her heart left by Pax's absence didn't count. Neither did her deflated ego, flattened by the realization that no matter how significant her epiphanies had been in the jungle, they weren't applicable in her everyday life. More important, they didn't apply to Drew. He made it clear every step of the way that he was here for her as a friend. That was all she'd ever asked of him.

It didn't stop the sting to her pride.

It's not just your pride that hurts.

Maybe not, but her pride could heal, so she had to focus on that.

The sound of raucous voices drifted over to her. She glanced at her watch—four o'clock. The neighborhood kids had all returned home from school an hour ago, so the noise wasn't them getting off the bus.

She stood up and stretched. "Ooh, Nappie, Mommy's getting older." She laughed as she said that to a dog who looked like the poster puppy for geriatric dog food.

As she started to take off her gardening gloves, her sliding glass patio door was thrown open and a stream of loud, young, boisterous people spilled through them.

"Skipper!" "Boss!" "Commander!" She heard so many greetings she couldn't tell who was addressing her as what. It felt as though her heart had swelled and burst. She couldn't keep the huge grin from showing as tears slid down her cheeks. She didn't care. She'd give her life for any one of these fine officers and sailors. Almost had, and with no regrets.

"Green light!" The chorus of navy words heralded the beginning of a surprise party at the CO's house.

"Green light?" Oh, no. That meant the entire squadron wardroom, about one hundred officers, plus spouses, would be piling into her home. Judging by these first visitors, enlisted aircrew had been invited, too.

The house was a mess. It was cluttered. She needed a shower.

"Skipper!" A bear hug crushed her to the massive chest of Rob "Mac" MacAllister. He'd been the engineer on her last flight and while he'd always been a jovial man, he'd never touched her before except when he'd pulled her out of the aircraft as it sank.

"Mac, you look great." She couldn't keep the smile off her face. The hell with her appearance.

"Looking good yourself, Commander." His eyes grew bright as he held on to her. "You saved my life, Skipper. I can't thank you enough."

"You saved the entire crew, Mac, including me. If you hadn't got Lizzie into the life raft..." She shook her head. "You know we wouldn't be here now."

"Hey, let us in, man." The two junior officers who'd piloted the aircraft with her joined the love fest.

"David, Aiden!" Gwen leaned in for a hug from each of her copilots. "How have you been?"

"We're great, Skipper. The real question is how have *you* been?" The deck and backyard were full of her squadron mates. The low murmur of voices quieted and she'd never felt more self-conscious.

"I'm good. It hasn't been easy. I'm still shaky in public and I seem to hear the shots of the insurgents when I'm walking through the grocery store. It's a little awkward when I hit the deck in the pasta aisle." Her attempt to break the tension worked, and the crowd laughed.

"I wouldn't have made it without each and every one of you. And my air crew, you all were so stellar and your exit from the aircraft after we ditched was impeccable. The fact that I was separated from you was no one's fault but the ocean's. There are never any guarantees in a ditch. We all know that."

She took a moment to smile at each and every

person who'd taken the time to come to her home, to wish her well.

"There were many long hours out in that hot jungle. SERE school sure came in handy, but the ability to recall each one of you and what you do day in and day out, with no thanks expected, that's what helped get me through. I'd think of the Frame Shop or the Maintenance Department, keeping those old girls in the air. I'd see the youngest, newest members of our squadron as they rang up my chocolate bar purchase in the Gedunk. All your families were with me, too. I know you all were pulling for me. I felt your prayers, I really did."

Adrenaline pumped through her as if she'd had five coffees. Gwen hadn't felt so good since the day she'd reached the embassy in Manila.

And since the night Drew had made love to her.

"Enough of this serious crap. Thank you all for coming out. Now let's have some fun! You have to help Drew and me eat our way through all the incredible food you've dropped off. Enjoy."

She was immediately surrounded by her subordinates and the new executive officer she'd only met briefly on her return. Bradley Snyder had been flown out to Japan one month into the squadron's deployment for the change of command. He'd filled in for her until now, and from what she'd heard, done a remarkable job of it.

"Bradley, it's great to see you again."

"Call me Brad, and Gwen, it's great to see *you*

again. You made it easy for me. The squadron was totally ready for deployment. We'll talk later, but suffice it to say our success was because the squadron rallied around the hope that you'd be found alive."

"I appreciate that, Brad." The tug at her stomach felt foreign—until she realized it was jealousy. She'd laid all the groundwork, fought like crazy to live and this stranger showed up and gleaned the benefits from it.

It was time to get back to work, just as Drew had said.

Drew.

"Excuse me." She extricated herself from the party and went inside. She looked around the bottom floor and didn't see Drew with any of the clusters of people talking and drinking.

She headed for the stairs. It was hard to be subtle about it, since the open floor plan let everyone see her.

Once in her room she changed into a fresh pair of jeans and a polo shirt with the squadron logo embroidered over the left breast. She found her comfortable sandals in the back of her closet, thankful that she'd painted her toenails the other night. She allowed herself two minutes in the bathroom to brush her teeth and throw on some makeup.

Where was Drew?

A quick check of his room answered her question. "Why aren't you downstairs?"

He was sprawled in their oldest easy chair. Another chair they used to make love in.

"It's for you, Gwen. No one misses me. They don't expect to see me there."

"Is it too much with everything you're going through at the clinic?"

"Not at all."

"Then I think you should come down. You know so many of them, from the other tours, from your work."

"This is your time, Gwen."

"You've helped make it happen, Drew. You got me to this point. Come and share it with me."

"I'll be down in a minute."

"Okay."

DREW WAITED UNTIL Gwen shut the door before he threw the book he hadn't really been reading across the room.

Gwen deserved this time with her squadron. It didn't involve him.

But she'd asked him to come down.

He couldn't refuse her.

He walked downstairs into the din and sought her out.

When Drew saw Gwen laughing while listening to her subordinates tell sea stories, he knew that calling Bradley Snyder on the sly last week had been the right thing to do.

Gwen needed to be around other sailors, other

pilots. It was in her blood, never mind all her talk
about giving it all up so she could be a mom to Pax.
He had no doubt that she was going to be the best
mother, but she deserved to enjoy her career, too.

Of course, providing a baby with a stable environment was a lot easier if the navy wasn't part of
the equation.

Not his problem. He had plenty of his own.

He grabbed a beer out of a cooler and twisted
off the cap.

Tell yourself you don't care.

"Hey, Drew."

Opal stood in front of him, her smile and open
stance welcoming. He saw her every morning at
her coffee shack. The drive-through coffee trailer
was popular with the whole base.

What the hell was she doing here at a squadron
function?

"Opal, how are you doing?"

"Great."

"Who'd you come with?" He had to ask; a green
light was squadron only, spouses optional. Opal
wasn't married to anyone in Gwen's squadron.

"Billy over there." She motioned toward a crowd
of male junior officers. "He invited me. It's okay
that I'm here, right?"

"Sure, but it's supposed to be a squadron-only
function." He wasn't going to be rude to her, but he
was getting tired of Opal showing up everywhere.

"You all make me feel so welcome. And let's face

it, I wouldn't be able to support myself without the business from the squadron."

"You make great coffee." He sipped his beer, trying to get out of the conversation. He looked over her head and his gaze met Gwen's. Gwen was surrounded by squadron mates, yet she'd narrowed in on him and Opal.

If only he didn't care. Then every little incident between him and Gwen wouldn't make his gut tense up. "I buy the best organic beans and I have Pete up at the City Beach coffee shop roast them for me."

"Uh-huh."

"Hey, Opal." A young gun Drew had never met sidled up to them.

Thank God.

As Opal flirted with the newer, younger guy, Drew made his way over to Gwen. She was enjoying herself, unquestionably, but she hadn't done this much since she'd been back. Someone needed to make sure she didn't overdo it.

DREW WALKED TOWARD her with his take-no-prisoners swagger.

"Do you want to call the powers that be and tell them they never should've let us deploy with those old frames?"

Derek's earnestness compelled Gwen to answer positively.

"What I think about more is what a miracle it

is that we've been able to fly these planes for over forty years. Compared to that, the new frame is going to be like flying a kite." The group chuckled.

"We should've been given at least one of the new frames before deployment," Mac chimed in.

"Maybe, but the important thing is that we made the most of what we had."

She felt Drew's presence as he slipped behind her. Quiet, unobtrusive, yet definitely there. *With* her.

"Drew, did you know in your gut the skipper was going to make it?"

"I never doubted it."

Gwen turned sideways and looked back at Drew. His eyes met hers and his complete confidence in her warmed her from the inside out.

"Thanks." She smiled at him and realized with a start that she had the strongest urge to reach up and kiss him.

"It's nice to see you two back together, Skipper. Cheers." Mac raised his bottle of beer and the rest of the crew members gathered around followed. Except for Lizzie.

"I owe you my life, Skipper," she said.

Lizzie's cheeks were red but she gazed steadily at Gwen, pointedly ignoring Drew. "If I were you, I might not have saved me."

"Lizzie, we've put that to rest, haven't we?" Gwen hugged the younger woman. "Life's too short to dwell on our stupid mistakes. I've certainly made my share."

"Thanks, ma'am." Lizzie nodded at Drew, then walked off.

The unexpected desire to kiss Drew was squashed by guilt.

They think we're a real couple again.

God, she hated lying to anyone, but to her crew, the people she was willing to give her life for…

The group started talking, several loud voices at once. Drew grasped her elbow and pulled her over to the side, near the fireplace mantel.

"You doing all right?" His breath caressed her ear, even though he stood several inches away from her. Far enough to keep a safe distance, but too close for her body to ignore its awareness of him.

She nodded. "I'm okay."

The other aviators were spread out across the room, respectful of her privacy with her husband.

"You've got to take it easy," he said.

"I'll have plenty of time to do that after—" Her thoughts caught up with her.

She faced him squarely. "It was you, wasn't it? You called them and told them to show up!"

"I didn't expect the whole damn squadron to pour into my home, but yes, I called Brad and said it might be nice if a few people stopped in. Was I right?"

Anger warred with gratitude. After a full minute, she dropped her shoulders and relaxed.

"Yes. You were right. It *is* time for me to get back to work."

"Hold it. What did you say?"

"I said you were right."

"Did you take some mysterious herbs while you were in the jungle?"

"Hey, I know when I'm wrong."

"You've never admitted it before."

"Maybe I'm changing."

"It's possible." He smiled briefly, then continued to level his stare on her. The look that let her know he missed nothing. "When are you going back in?"

"I can't run in there and immediately start doing full days, but maybe two or three hours to start, then half days as long as I don't have any signs of PTSD."

"It seems to be limited to your nightmares."

"For the most part." She hadn't told him, or anyone except her doctor, about the times the winds blew and the rain fell and she had to remind herself she was on Whidbey and not in the middle of a monsoon. Or about when she felt hot and cold all at once and wanted to drop to the floor, no matter where she was, to hide. She'd actually contemplated crawling into their kitchen cupboards the first few days she'd been back.

"Do you feel stronger?"

She looked into his eyes. "I do. Each day is better. I'm still not one hundred percent. That takes time."

She might never be, but it wasn't something she wanted to talk about. Not now and not with Drew.

Someone hit Gwen lightly on the shoulder.

"Hey, what's going on? I come over to bring you some TLC and you're throwing a bash without me!" Ro, her face flushed with happiness, gave Drew a quick kiss on the cheek before she turned to embrace Gwen.

Gwen accepted her hug and hugged her back. "It's a green light."

"So I see." Ro glanced around the house, the groups of people talking and laughing, the open deck doors that let in the Whidbey breeze. Her gaze landed back on Gwen and Drew.

"This is how your house used to be, how I love it. Filled to the rafters with folks having a great time!"

"I don't know about filled to the rafters, but it's nice to have some energy in here." Despite Drew's smile, Gwen saw the strain underneath his happiness. He was in his own hell with the death at the clinic but still able to muster up a positive response for her.

"I should go say hi to some more folks before they leave." Gwen threw Ro a quick warning look before she walked away. She didn't need her friend playing matchmaker.

DREW TURNED TO RO. "How's Miles?"

Her smile was blinding. Drew hated that he no longer made Gwen smile like this.

"Really well! We're getting the house ready to move into. He's driving me crazy with all his ideas to have the most modern house on Whidbey."

"Working on a house together is a good way for you guys to start things off. We had fun when we built this place."

Neither of them pointed out that this same house was the only thing still keeping him and Gwen legally connected.

"Yes, it's a great project. My house was way too small and he was renting from his friend, who came back from deployment. We both wanted a place in the middle of the woods, one along the lines of your place—modern and spacious." Ro laughed. "You know Miles. He doesn't do things halfway. He wants everything to be perfect before we move in. I just want to get the moving part over with!"

"When's your last day?" He meant her last day on active duty in the navy.

"At the beginning of June. Then I'll go on ninety days terminal leave. It'll be heaven not to *have* to be anywhere for three whole months."

"Didn't you get a new job with that craft store in Coupeville?"

"Gwen told you? I wasn't sure if she realized how serious I am about it. I know it seems weird to her, but I have an artistic side I never got to explore as an intel type."

Ro had decided to go into the fiber-arts business with a retired naval officer's spouse.

"That's great, Ro. Life's too short not to go after your dreams."

"You went after yours." She faltered as they both knew she was referring to his PT practice. A business that was doomed. She placed her hand on his forearm. "How are you *really* doing, Drew? Is the case closed yet?"

He shook his head. "No. Nowhere near it." He wasn't about to delve into the details with Ro, no matter how much he or Gwen trusted her. According to Ramsey, it looked as if someone was either out to kill Dottie or to frame him.

Neither option made for pleasant party conversation.

"I'm sorry. I've known Gwen longer than anyone and…"

"And?"

"She's changed. On a deep level. I'm not pretending I have her all figured out, but she's going to stick by you through this. As are Miles and I."

"I appreciate it, Ro." He didn't doubt that Gwen would continue to be his single best character witness, if not his alibi. He'd been on the phone with her while Dottie was dying.

"It's okay to begin again, Drew." Ro leaned up and gave him a quick kiss on the cheek before she, too, walked away.

Ro didn't get it that he and Gwen had burned their bridges a long time ago.

Before the traumatic events they'd both suffered this year.

His business was destined to fail, and he'd be out of a job. He might even end up in prison. Gwen was fighting her way back to normal and adopting a baby.

A baby who needed a stable environment.

Start over?

Impossible.

GWEN PULLED UP to the drive-through Koffee Hut and peered through the rain at the day's specials. Opal's place was the only one open this early, and the most convenient to the base. Besides, she didn't have anything against Opal—not as far as coffee went.

"How can I help you?" A twentyish male greeted her and she let out a sigh of relief. She wanted a latte to take into the squadron with her, but didn't want to deal with Opal's crush on Drew.

It's none of your business.

"Hi. I'll have a skim, sugar-free almond latte, please. No whip. No, wait—I do want the whip."

"Coming right up."

The barista turned to start her espresso and Gwen looked out the windshield as the wipers moved back and forth. She deserved some whipped cream, darn it. She noted several headlights in her rearview mirror as more cars lined up. Other base workers, no doubt. A familiar figure ran up to the side of the trailer that served as the coffee hut and went inside.

Crap.

Maybe Opal would be too preoccupied with work to notice her.

"Hey, Gwen. Great party!"

Nope, not too busy. And of course Opal knew Gwen's car.

"Thanks, Opal."

"You on your way to go back to work at the base?"

Gwen clenched her teeth at Opal's tone. As if Gwen was some kind of head case.

"Yes, going in to my squadron."

Opal looked at her as if she knew something Gwen didn't.

"Don't they have someone else running it, since you've been, um, gone?"

"Yes, but I'm still the commanding officer. At least the last time I checked." She grudgingly offered Opal a smile.

What a bitch.

"I mean, you weren't here to run it. Someone else had to step in. Didn't they have someone?"

Gwen wanted to scream as her body shook. Not because Opal was so ignorant of the military way of life or because she was being so passive-aggressive. She wanted to tear Opal from limb to limb for her overt flirtation with Drew.

Primal emotions like that had been part of everyday life in the jungle, on the run.

They were pointless, silly, here at home.

"That's three-oh-five." The nice barista held out his hand as he passed Gwen her latte.

"Here you go. Keep the change." Gwen gave him a five. She didn't want to be here for the length of time it would take him to count out the change.

"Thanks!"

"See ya!" She wiggled her fingers at Opal's stunned expression and drove off without answering her question.

Her reaction might be pointless and silly, but her business was none of Opal's.

CHAPTER TWELVE

THE SMELL OF JP-5 hit Gwen the moment she stepped into the hangar, *her* hangar. It was the fuel she'd used to fly her aircraft ever since she'd earned her aviation wings. The hangar doors were wide open but the wind didn't erase all the odor.

She shivered in her green Nomax flight jacket and khaki skirt, the chill of the concrete floor freezing her toes in her brown leather pumps.

"Skipper." A young airman walking to her workstation atop a P-3C that was in for repairs saluted her. Gwen saluted back and aimed her focus on the P-3C that was being towed into the hangar to park alongside the other aircraft. She read the tail number and groaned. It was the airframe she was supposed to have that fateful night nine months ago. But in a split-second decision, she'd taken a different aircraft, an aircraft that lay in pieces at the bottom of the Pacific Ocean.

You could be there with it.

Yes, she could, and so could her entire crew. But they were all safely back and able to continue with their missions. Reminders of what she'd been through were going to be all over the place. She'd better get used to it.

"Skipper! Great to have you back, ma'am." Her XO, Brad, smiled widely and motioned to her office door. They stood in the hallway outside the executive offices, which adjoined an admin space that held four desks.

"It's good to be here, Brad." She followed his gesture and walked into her office. The office she'd never occupied.

Until today.

"It's a nice space. I have to admit that."

"We set it up just like you had it in Japan, Skipper. You'll want to add your own touches, I'm sure."

"No, this is fine for now. After all, it's only for another five months or so." She sank down into the leather office chair positioned behind the wide, glass-topped, maple desk.

"I know you don't drink a lot of coffee but there's an electric kettle and a box of tea bags that the wardroom chipped in on for you."

"That was nice of them!"

"They never gave up believing that you'd be back." Brad spoke quietly, with sincerity.

"We don't know each other, Skipper, but I feel I know you through the squadron. They couldn't wait to have you take over as commanding officer, and were devastated when you were presumed dead."

"I appreciate you telling me that, Brad. They're

a special group of people, and we'd already had a tough deployment up until then."

Up until then they'd flown antiterrorism missions all over the globe, including the Mid-East and Pacific Rim. They'd almost lost a bird in Afghanistan during a night mission when a rogue surface-to-air missile had been launched at them—similar to the missile that took out her engine on that fateful flight.

"I'm here to do whatever you need me to, Skipper. Of course everyone wants a piece of you now, but I can keep them at bay as long as you need."

Gwen studied her executive officer. Young, single, good-looking. And eager to become the CO.

"Thank you for taking on all this while I was gone, Brad. I know it's awkward to have me show up, and now you're back to being the XO again, but like I said, it's only for five months."

"You've read me wrong, Skipper. No one's happier than I am that you're back."

"Thanks, Brad. I'll take my own calls from now on."

"You need to get out of here, Drew."

Startled, Drew looked up from his computer screen at Opal.

"What are you doing here?"

"I've brought you a coffee and your favorite pastry." She shook a paper bag and put down a tall cup with her Koffee Hut logo emblazoned across its circumference.

"Thanks, Opal, but I've got a lot of work to do."

Evidently not deterred, Opal sat on the corner of Drew's desk and leaned over. Just enough so he could see her breasts as they popped out of some bionic push-up bra.

"You need to take a break, Drew. Get out of this office. Doesn't the quiet drive you mad?"

Actually, it made him wonder what Dottie had thought as she died, all alone.

"Come on, Drew, lighten up. I know it's been really hard on you to have Gwen come back out of the blue." She ran her fingers through her hair. "I've wanted to come over more, talk, make you dinner, but I know she's fragile."

"Oh?"

"It's great that the navy's letting her go back to work, don't you think?"

"Yeah. Thanks for the snacks, Opal, but I really do have to work."

"I can take a hint. What I won't take is no for an answer, Drew. You and I have some unfinished business."

"Opal, you were a great worker while you were here, and I'm happy about the success of your business. But as far as you and me…there isn't anything there. You have so many guys from the base asking you out, you sure don't need me."

Her expression went from pouty to pleased in

an instant. But not before he saw the flicker of an emotion he hadn't expected.

Hate? Anger?

"You're not married and Gwen won't be around for much longer, Drew. You can't live like a hermit forever."

She walked out of his office and he held his breath until he heard the front door click shut. He ran out to the reception area and threw the dead bolt on the door.

A cold shiver ran down his neck.

Opal still had her key to the clinic.

"THIS IS LIKE when we were mids at the Academy." Ro plowed her hand into the bucket of artery-clogging movie popcorn she and Gwen were sharing.

"Yeah, but with more money."

They laughed and Gwen licked the extra butter off her fingers, relishing the salt. Popcorn was one of her favorite vices.

"Are you still mad about running into Opal?" Ro never waited for a better moment to talk about private matters; she'd always been ready to dive into any "issues" either of them had. Gwen knew it was one of the main reasons she'd become friends with Ro in the first place, way back at Annapolis. The Naval Academy had been more than a rigorous environment for them, it had been sterile in terms of girl-talk, gossip and heart-to-hearts. Midshipmen, especially female midshipmen, were supposed to live up to a ridiculously high standard of conduct across all facets of their lives.

Gwen and Ro had done what they had to in order to graduate, but still had fun whenever they could.

"I'm not mad about seeing her. It's the other things it brought up."

"Like what?"

"I've never been jealous of Drew, not like this. Before, when I thought he had something going on with someone else, I ignored it. We're divorced, after all. But today, I could've wrestled Opal down and strangled her. It was primal."

"Your brain took over. You view Drew as a father figure for Pax. You're a mother tigress. You'd kill for your cub."

"You're nuts, do you know that? I do not see Drew as a father figure." He'd have to be a husband again first....

She was distracted by an image of Drew throwing Pax in the air, smiling at the beautiful baby.

"If you say so. Look, I'm just telling you what I'm hearing. I'm not here to suck up to you."

They both laughed.

"I'd never expect you to be a suck-up, Ro."

Gwen ate another few kernels of popcorn.

"Maybe it's time to start over with Drew, Gwen. Pretend you just met him, that the past was with someone else."

"Hmph."

"No, really. It's not often that we find someone who understands us, in uniform and out. You have that with Drew."

"Look, you might have a wonderful marriage to the greatest guy on the planet, but that doesn't mean it's for everyone. I'm happy for you, Ro, really, I am. It's great that you and Miles finally got together. You were headed for him all along. You just didn't figure it out right away."

"But?" Ro knew her too well.

No BS.

"But it's not for all of us. At least, it's not for me with Drew. We had our chance and we blew it, or time and maturity ended it. Either way, it is what it is. Can you understand that?"

Ro took a sip of her diet cola. "I can and I do, trust me. But also trust me when I tell you that Drew still can't take his eyes off you. He follows your every move, watches who you talk to, how they talk to you."

"He's always been overprotective. It's his nature."

"Not like this. When you're around, he has a purpose, a drive, that I haven't seen in eons."

"He demonstrated the same kind of purpose when he went after his Ph.D. in physical therapy, after having been a nonmedical undergrad." Gwen had been so proud of Drew. He'd done his undergraduate studies at Embry Riddle in Florida on an NROTC scholarship. But he'd always wanted to work with people on a more personal basis.

Ro shook her head. "It's more than that."

"Shhh!" Several other moviegoers clearly weren't impressed with their chatter.

Ro lowered herself so that her head was even with the edge of the chair.

"Come down here."

"This is ridiculous." Gwen slid down as she whispered, "Can we just watch the movie? We'll talk later."

"We'll be too busy talking about the movie." Ro's face changed color as the coming attractions threw light on the audience.

"I know where you're going with this and it's not happening. A lot of couples don't make it in their first marriage, especially when they got married as young as Drew and I did. It's rarer to stay together in some ways. Enjoy your marital bliss and leave the rest of us out of it."

"You're not just any couple, Gwen. You'll never have the history you have with Drew with someone else. He knew you as a young junior officer, and he grew up right next to you. You helped him leave the navy and get his Ph.D."

"Which he may not be able to use for much longer."

"He'll land on his feet—but he may need you there to spot him."

Gwen's stomach dropped and she looked at Ro but refused to respond. "I'm just sayin', Gwen. He didn't have to be around for you as much as he has since you came back. He could've bolted when you asked him about vouching for your mental health, because of Pax—but he didn't. It seems to me that he's going to need a lot of support to get through whatever comes next. You may have to help him stay out of jail."

"I intend to stay with him through this, Ro. As his friend."

Ro faced front and appeared to be watching the last of the trailers before the movie.

Gwen's interest in the light romantic comedy nosedived into the bottom of the bucket of popcorn when Ro used the words *Drew* and *jail* in the same sentence. It'd be one thing if Drew had to go through an insurance investigation and possible civil suit over Dottie Forsyth's death. But a murder conviction? Drew wasn't a murderer.

He didn't deserve to go to jail.

She'd been on the phone with him. He'd been in his office.

You might be his only hope.

Crap.

GWEN GROANED A week later when the doorbell rang. She'd been home for a few minutes, and had just kicked off her brown pumps. Khakis had been the uniform of the day and she'd worn her skirt. She much preferred her flight suit and boots, but was grateful to be back at work.

Her head itched from the hairpins needed to keep

her hair up in its neat French braid. She planned to let it down as soon as she chucked her uniform and put on some soft, cozy sweats.

She opened the door to a basket of flowering plants at eye level.

"Hello?"

"I thought I owed you these. After barging in and all, I don't want you to think I'm insensitive to what you're dealing with." Opal's face appeared from around the edge of the greenery.

Gwen didn't even try not to smile at the pretty blooms.

"Thank you so much, but really, you didn't have to do this. I get it, Opal. I've been gone a long time, and there's no reason you should've expected me to be in the house when you stopped by."

"You were standoffish at your party, and then I noticed how you clammed up at the Koffee Hut." Opal took a step forward and Gwen was confronted with a decision—either take the basket or let Opal in.

"These are gorgeous." The basket had wooden handles woven into the sides. Opal held it by its bottom, so it was easy for Gwen to lift it from her arms.

"Wait, it's very heavy. I'll put it on the counter."

"Okay." Gwen let go and moved back, allowing Opal access to their house.

Drew's house.

"I made it myself. The flowers are fresh from the nursery, so they should last you awhile."

Opal walked straight to the kitchen counter as if she owned it.

Drew said he and Opal had never been more than work colleagues, that they'd had a boss-employee relationship. He did run a relaxed office, not like the navy had been, and she supposed it might be easy for a certain kind of woman to think it was always open season on Drew, that he was always available.

Of course, he *had* been free for five years.

"Be honest with me, Opal. Were you and Drew dating before I came back?"

Opal grimaced. "He told you?"

"Not in so many words…" God, Opal was a trip and a half. Gwen wished Ro was here to see this. She could hardly believe it herself.

Opal put her hand on Gwen's forearm. "Look, Drew's a catch, I'm not going to lie. But it seems you two have kept a nice friendship, and it's great of him to support you while you get better from your ordeal."

"Yes, it is." She fought to keep her expression neutral while her mind raced. Whether it had been Opal or another woman, the fact was that Drew had every right to initiate another relationship. They both did.

Why was she letting it bother her so much?

Opal fussed with the plants a bit more. "You have to keep them watered or they won't live past July."

"Got it. Thanks again."

Opal looked at her watch. "I've gotta get back to work. It's super busy after three."

Most of the day workers arrived at the base between six and eight in the morning. The long line of exiting vehicles started after three, but Gwen didn't think they'd be buying coffee at that time of day.

"People buy coffee this late in the afternoon?"

"Oh, yeah. More of the dessert drinks, like my frozen coffees."

"I have to hand it to you, Opal. You've been very successful."

Opal shrugged. "I knew what I was doing when I decided to sell an addictive substance."

"Yes, I imagine that's a good business move." It didn't hurt that Opal had positioned her Koffee Hut drive-through on the busiest part of the island, near the base.

"You know, there are four drive-through coffee places outside the base gates. We all do very well. If Drew ever wanted to switch to another business, he could open one."

"It takes a special talent to run a retail business. Sounds like you've got it." Gwen needed to be alone with her thoughts and then call Ro.

"Well, thanks for inviting me in. I'll see you around."

Opal left as quickly as she'd come. But instead of the front door, she went to the kitchen side door and let herself out, unlocking the dead bolt Drew had installed after her last surprise visit.

Gwen stared at the door for a long moment before she walked over and threw the bolt back in place.

She turned and studied the basket. What had looked like a pretty jumble of blooms didn't seem as attractive close-up. The plants had been taken out of their original pots and shoved next to each other with no potting soil to join them. She fingered a spider plant set beside a geranium.

They were only two of at least a half dozen examples of a houseplant being planted with an outdoor garden flower.

Opal might know the coffee business, but she didn't know anything about flowers.

Fine. Lots of people had no interest in gardening. Just as she had no interest in running a business. Opal's choice of plants and the way she'd arranged them seemed so haphazard to Gwen. As though it had been hastily done to please her.

Or fool her.

When Drew didn't come in after she heard the garage door open, she went looking for him.

She found him under the hood of his car.

"I never heard you drive up."

"No reason you should have. Were you getting some rest?" He didn't look up from his task—

checking the oil level in his engine. His T-shirt stretched over his muscles and she remembered why her attraction to him had never truly faded.

"No, I was cleaning out some of the kitchen cupboards."

It wasn't quick enough for her to miss his swift appraisal of her in her workout shirt and exercise tights.

"Were you on the treadmill earlier?"

"Actually, I went for a walk."

He straightened up and closed the hood. His jeans fit snugly in all the right places as he leaned against the car.

"By yourself?"

"Nappie's not up to it. She's getting old, isn't she?"

"That's not the point, Gwen. You shouldn't go out on your own."

"I stayed in the neighborhood, and I'm already driving on my own. I'm going into the squadron every day, for heaven's sake!"

He frowned. "Did you tell anyone else you were going out?"

"No. Look, I appreciate the concern, and I'm not denying that I have PTSD, but I'm fine, Drew. I'm not going to get well doing just half days at work. Besides, a girl can only handle so many episodes on HGTV."

"Text me or Ro next time you decide to take a jaunt. Better yet, why don't you use the base gym?"

Tension shimmered between them and Gwen wished she'd stayed inside instead of seeking him out.

"I'm not your responsibility, Drew."

"Aren't you?" His gaze lowered to her lips. There were at least four feet of space between them, yet that one glance of his made it feel like a mere whisper of air.

She swallowed. "No."

He stared at her lips for a beat too long, and she curled her fingers into her palms. The movement seemed to shake him out of his thoughts.

"Why did you come out here?" he asked. "Did you need to talk to me?"

He moved away from the car; the space between them became even smaller. Gwen reflexively stepped back, only to topple backward over whatever garage junk her feet had hit.

Drew's hands closed over her upper arms the second before she would've landed on the concrete floor. He yanked her up, saving her from a nasty fall.

His body heat, combined with the feel of his hands on her arms, intoxicated her in the time it took her to draw a breath. Attempting a laugh, she raised her eyes to his.

Big. Mistake.

She barely recognized the heat in his eyes before he closed them and lowered his lips to hers.

And dammit, she kissed him back as if *she'd* been the one to start it. As if this was why she'd walked out here.

Isn't it?

He smelled like coffee and gasoline. His scent wasn't the only thing driving her crazy with lust. It was the way his lips were at once gentle yet confident in their touch, the way his hands seemed to revere her while taking very naughty detours in and under her clothes, the way he whirled her around and pressed her against the side of the car.

She tried to lose herself in their kiss, but her mind wouldn't shut up. As much as she tried to compare this to how they'd been before, how they'd kissed and made love during their marriage, nothing came up.

This was different. New.

At that revelation she pulled back, her hands on his chest.

"Drew…"

"If you say 'we can't' I'm going to lose it, Gwen."

"*I* can't."

HER EYES WERE full of his kiss. He'd put that expression on her face, the wondering, the arousal.

"Why are we fighting it, Gwen?"

"I can't do this, Drew. We're having some kind of post-deployment reunion thing here, and it's going to end. I don't want to come close to what either of us went through before. I have a child to consider now."

He dropped his hands to his sides but didn't step back. She was still leaning against the car and he could kiss the common sense out of her.

But he didn't.

CHAPTER THIRTEEN

DREW HEARD THE doorbell through the blare of the football game on television. Nappie snored in her round bed. Poor dog was going deaf. He looked at the digital readout on his laptop, where he was reviewing patient files.

Ten-thirty at night. Not good. He could think of only one person it might be...

"Drew? Did you hear the bell?" Gwen called down from the bedroom where she'd all but hidden from him since he'd rebuffed her attempts to comfort him after Dottie's death.

"I'll get it," he said.

He placed his laptop on the coffee table and got up from the recliner.

A quick look through the peephole confirmed his premonition.

He opened the door. "Cole."

"Drew. Do you have a second?"

"Come on in."

Cole Ramsey stepped across the threshold and wasted no time once Drew shut the door. Cole's face was neutral but his eyes looked as if he'd seen a ghost.

Drew groaned. "Spit it out, Cole."

"We have the autopsy reports."

"And?"

"They're inconclusive, but there are no indications of death by natural causes. No stroke, no cardiac event. The coroner left them at inconclusive only because she didn't have every hallmark of a drowning victim."

"Oh, my God." Drew shook his head. "She wasn't under long enough, Cole. There's no way her lungs could have filled up that quickly. We got her out, got the water out of her in seconds."

They walked into the living area where the television, muted, played the football game. Drew motioned for Cole to sit down.

"What do you think, Cole?"

"I think something is really wrong here. You're positive Serena's happy working for you, that she had no misgivings about Dottie Forsyth?"

"Of course! Serena went through a pretty crazy time last year, but her husband had been killed in the war. That's enough to make anyone crazy."

"Hi, Cole." Gwen had come downstairs.

Shit.

He didn't want her involved in this any more than she already was. And he didn't want to worry about what effect the news would have on her.

But he could tell she'd heard the entire conversation from the landing.

"Gwen." Cole nodded.

"You know Drew and Serena didn't do it, Cole."

"I agree that Drew isn't a murderer, Gwen, but the evidence is damning. With only him and Serena to back themselves up, it's dicey."

"You checked our phone records. You know I was on the phone with Gwen. Everything's matched up with what we told you. Dottie wasn't alone for more than two minutes."

"Actually, it was three minutes. Add another ten or twenty seconds for Serena to write down the notes she did about the call from the orthopedic surgeon who managed one of your clients. I can't prove Serena didn't go to the bathroom, though, or get herself a cup of coffee before she went back to check on the victim. We only have her word and the autopsy evidence, combined with the phone records. The prosecuting attorney won't put personal judgments into the equation."

"Of course Serena didn't get a damned cup of coffee, Cole! I don't run that kind of shop. Serena is top-notch."

"Point taken. But we still have a dead body in your aquatracker while you and Serena were the only two employees present."

"But who would've wanted to kill Dottie? And why?"

"That's what we're trying to figure out."

"What motive could Drew or Serena possibly have to murder a client, much less one they liked?" Gwen asked as Drew sat down.

He might go to prison for something he didn't do. But he sure as hell wasn't going to let Serena hang for this, if it came down to it.

The ultimate accountability was his.

"Are you going to arrest me, Cole?"

"There's no evidence that you had any intent to commit murder, Drew. You're probably going to be charged with negligent homicide by the family, yes. I have no plans to arrest you at the moment."

"*At the moment.* That's encouraging." He'd worked his ass off, hung on for six months thinking he might never see Gwen again, for *this?* To have a tragic accident put his career, his life, on ice?

"Drew, maybe you should call a lawyer *now.*" Gwen's voice broke through his mental screams. He'd never thought she'd stay as long as she had, and he certainly hadn't expected her to stay around and watch his life implode when the Island County Sheriff's Department came knocking.

"I will. Do I need one?" he asked Ramsey. They were pals, had been buds until five minutes ago.

"Not this minute, not tonight, but you'd better get one in the morning." Ramsey put his notepad away. "Drew, the problem is there weren't any prints on the dials. None."

"Which means someone wiped them."

"Yes, or that you normally use a towel when you operate that piece of equipment."

"I told you, we don't. There should've been prints all over that control panel!" His fingers itched to put a fist through the drywall next to him.

This is going to freak Gwen out. She's too fragile right now.

"What do you know about Serena's relationship to Dottie?" Cole asked. The question was unexpected.

"Relationship? Other than that between client and provider?"

"Did Serena or Dottie every mention anything?"

"No. Where is this coming from, Cole?"

Cole tapped his notebook against his thigh. "Turns out Serena was Dottie's biological niece. Dottie's brother fathered her with a housemaid on their family ranch. Her brother never told the family until shortly before his death, and Serena was raised to believe her father was someone else. After Serena's husband was killed, she found out about her biological roots and at Dottie's invitation came out to Whidbey for a fresh start, and to get to know Dottie."

"Serena's related to Dottie?" Drew whistled. "She never mentioned it. Why didn't you tell me this sooner, Cole?"

"I had to make sure you didn't know about it. Part of my job description."

"Damn it, Cole, you know neither Serena nor I did this."

"Needless to say it gives her a motive."

Drew's head snapped up. "Dottie didn't have any money, Cole. Not from what I know."

"But she has a house and left enough to leave someone fairly comfortable."

"Serena has her husband's life insurance from the military. Her son is entitled to benefits for tuition because of his dad's sacrifice. Serena's not your person, Cole."

"I'm only stating the facts, Drew."

Why hadn't Serena said anything to him? Why hadn't Dottie?

Families were complicated.

"What's next?" Drew asked Cole.

Ramsey stared at him. It wasn't the usual friendly expression Ramsey wore when they shared a beer at the Dutch pub in Coupeville.

"Calm down, get a lawyer like I've told you at least twice and go over everyone you come into contact with on a daily basis. Make notes. Someone wants you or Serena pegged for murder."

"Easy for *you* to tell me to calm down. You're not going to jail!"

GWEN TRIED NOT to wince when Drew blew up at Ramsey's comment.

"Drew, I can help you through this. We've been

together almost every minute of the past month, since I've been back." She turned toward Ramsey.

"You verified that we were on the phone at the time of the murder, right? Through the phone-company records? I didn't hear anyone else in the background. The other patients only witnessed him in his office."

"Gwen, stay out of it. Ramsey knows how to do his job."

"I've got the phone records, Gwen, and yes, Drew's alibi is corroborated by witness reports. He didn't go into the aquatracker room until Serena called for help. Look, I believe you," Cole said, raising his hands.

"Drew pulled her body out of the water when it normally takes up to three people. He knows the equipment in his sleep. They had an emergency drill with the aquatracker the week before. Not what someone who was getting ready to kill a patient would do."

"Again, I agree with you. Drew's my friend, too, Gwen. That's why I'm suggesting he get an attorney, and be prepared for the worst. Unless someone comes out of the woodwork with an unexpected explanation, or Serena admits she wanted Dottie dead, Drew is facing full culpability. At least on the insurance front."

Which meant Drew's clinic was done. He might be paying Dottie's family forever.

Gwen looked at Drew. He stood back from her

and Cole, his arms protectively crossed in front of his chest. The misery on his face was heartbreaking.

"We're going to get to the bottom of this," she vowed.

"SMALL SKIM LATTE, and whatever this lady wants." Ro motioned to Gwen.

"I'll have a double whipped almond dream." Gwen smiled at Ro's shock. "Hey, I've earned it. And thank you very much, by the way."

Ro paid for the order and they went to the end of the counter to wait for their drinks. They'd come in Gwen's car to the cute little coffee shop in town, instead of taking a regular lunch break.

"Can we get out of here, maybe go to the beach?" Gwen needed to talk to her best friend.

"Sure, honey. You okay?"

"The noise at the squadron is getting to me. No, make that the people—it's hard to run into so many people and not have anything to say. Everyone looks at me as if I'm a walking head case."

At Ro's concerned glance Gwen rolled her eyes.

"Please, I have to know that you still accept me as the nut I've always been. Otherwise I'm going to take my monster drink and go home."

Ro laughed. "No worries here."

They collected their drinks and walked out to the parking lot together, then piled into Ro's car and took off.

Instead of City Beach, which was two minutes

away, Ro drove them out to West Beach, where the tall cliffs dropped over two hundred feet to the rocky shore.

"Why here, Ro?"

They were parked on the side of the road, facing the ocean.

"It's a great place to watch for whales. Too cloudy today, granted, but still, I love it here." Ro sipped her coffee before she turned to Gwen. "This is where Miles and I started to fall in love."

"Parked in a car on West Beach?"

"Not quite. Over there." Ro pointed toward the beach, a bit south of where they sat. "That's where the body of the sailor killed by the Commodore was found. Do you remember when I had to work that case?"

"Of course I do. I've been through more than I ever thought I could handle, but I still have my memory, thank God."

"I didn't think Miles and I would ever make a go of it. There were times during that investigation that I thought we were done for. But we made it, and now we're married."

"Yes, you are." Gwen envied Ro's bliss but didn't feel like joining in the happy dance.

"Gwen, I'm not telling you this to brag. I'm telling you because no matter how ugly it might look with Drew, I still believe you two have unfinished business. You know I was the first to want to cut off his testicles when you thought he cheated on you."

"Yes. We've already been through this. But he never cheated on me with Lizzie."

"So we both understand that there'll always be Lizzies—and Opals—who go after good-looking, decent men like ours?"

"Sure." Except that Drew was no longer hers. And she and Drew were never going to be back where Ro and Miles were now.

There was no hope for them. *His kisses still burn.* And she still wanted him, painfully so.

"What's eating you, Gwen?"

Gwen waved her hand.

"He's facing murder, or at least negligent homicide, charges. Dottie Forsyth drowned."

Ro frowned at Gwen. "You've never stopped loving him."

"What does that have to do with Drew being charged with murder?"

"You care. You're scared shitless that he's going to take the rap for this. I think you're more scared of that than of not getting Pax."

Gwen shifted in her seat and stared out at the sea. "I had a lot of time to think about things when I wasn't getting bitten by creepy-crawlies. I even thought maybe I'd come back and tell Drew what I'd figured out, that I'd had an epiphany about us. But then I found Pax, and I realized Pax is the child I'm supposed to have. I never agreed to start a family with Drew, and I can't expect him to be Pax's father. Not only that, I don't deserve him, and it'd be best if he met someone else he could begin a new life with."

Before Ro could speak, Gwen went on. "But now he's in trouble. The least I can do is try to help him." Ro put her hand on Gwen's arm.

"Honey, you've got to stop this. First, if you even *think* you might still love Drew, you can't throw that away. You know he's not a murderer. You also have a child you hope to welcome home soon. He's going to need a daddy—one who's not in the brig. And despite what you're assuming, Drew might *want to take on that role*."

Gwen grunted. "It's not that clear-cut, Ro. I do plan to help Drew, but I don't expect it to bring about a miracle."

"I thought you didn't care?"

"I don't." She didn't.

She couldn't.

CHAPTER FOURTEEN

"WE TOLD YOU in no uncertain terms that there weren't any guarantees with your adoption request, Commander Brett." The State Department official's voice over the phone was compassionate, but it didn't lessen the tightness of Gwen's heart. Councillor Darlene Tatem had been so warm and enthusiastic about the adoption when Gwen had briefly met her at the American Embassy in Manila.

It made the woman's message more dire.

"Yes, you did, but you also said it wasn't *impossible* to adopt from the Philippines. Considering that Pax has no relatives—"

"That's the point, ma'am. Several people have approached us, claiming he's related to them."

"Trust me. Anyone related to him perished in the most horrible manner. The village was a five-day hike from the nearest town. We're talking about one of the most remote places on earth. Where are these supposed family members from?"

"Manila."

Rage snarled through Gwen and she fought to maintain control.

"You and I know that this is about money, a chance for a step up out of poverty. I'm the only mother Pax has had since he was six weeks old. Mia," she said, referring to the elderly woman who'd hidden her and Pax for a month, "knew all of his family. She told me there was no one else, that they'd all been killed."

"Yes, but she told you this through her granddaughter, who'd come back from her overseas job, Commander. You admitted that the granddaughter's English was subpar. There's no way of knowing if what Mia said was interpreted correctly."

"What are the odds that Pax would have relatives thousands of miles from where he was born, in a culture where family is so close-knit?"

She heard the councillor's sigh. "Slim, but he's Filipino, as are they. You're the outsider."

"The outsider who saved his life from insurgent monsters!"

The line was silent and Gwen knew she'd hit the wall with Councillor Tatem. The woman wasn't more than five or ten years her senior, yet she sounded like some kind of deity issuing a harsh moral lesson.

"I'm sorry," Gwen muttered. "This is the hardest thing I've ever been through."

Besides the failure of her marriage to Drew, besides watching him face murder charges, but that was none of the councillor's business.

"I understand. I— We're on your side, Gwen.

The Ambassador has weighed in to minimize the perception that you're trying to keep the child as some kind of token of your experience here."

"He's not a souvenir, Councilor Tatem. He's my son."

A vision of Pax's huge brown eyes, his bubbling laughter as she tickled his tummy, enveloped her.

One thing being in the jungle had taught her— nothing happened if she didn't fight for it.

"I'm not saying you won't get Pax, Gwen. It's going to take longer, that's all. Let me see what I can do." Gwen heard the rustle of papers, the click of a keyboard, as though she and the councillor were in the same room and not on phones ten thousand miles apart.

"Thank you. I know this isn't your fault. I'll do whatever it takes to give Pax the home he deserves."

She hung up and faced her biggest fear: never seeing Pax again.

DREW SAT ACROSS from Gwen in the restaurant where he'd agreed to meet her on her lunch break. She'd steadily increased her hours at the squadron and planned to go back to work afterward.

"Thanks for meeting me. I figured you needed to get out of the clinic."

His silence worried her.

"What is it, Drew?"

"I'm going to move out, Gwen."

"Give me a break. If anyone needs to move out, it's me."

Drew's face was lined with stress as he sat across from her in the small retro-style diner. Gwen had to talk to him in a neutral location. After she'd finished her conversation with the State Department official, she'd called and asked him to meet her.

"It's only fair. Living with me is not going to help with your adoption proceedings. If I thought remarrying you for legal purposes would make a difference, I'd do it in a heartbeat. But the game's changed, Gwen. You stand to lose Pax if you stay with me."

She took a gulp of her almond latte to cover her nervous swallow. *Remarry?* Had he just said that?

Had her stomach flipped in hope?

"I know," she murmured. "These are crazy times."

"Crazy, unfair, messed up." His hands gripped the sides of his glass of water; his lunch was hardly touched.

"You've done more than enough for me, Drew. I wouldn't have made it to a command tour without you. I probably wouldn't have survived this last month back on Whidbey with my mind intact." She leaned toward him. "So let *me* be here for *you.* Let me stay until Dottie's case is resolved."

"This isn't your fight, Gwen."

"Helping me reenter and get back on my feet wasn't your fight, either. But you did it."

"And you're doing well. I'm perfectly happy to move out until you find an apartment."

"You're not moving out, and neither am I. How would it look if I moved out now? Or if you did? Like I didn't believe in your innocence. You need someone to back you up. I'm standing by you. It's not going to make a difference as far as the situation with Pax is concerned. At this point it's a question of whether any of his 'relatives' are real." She put her hands on top of his. "Don't you get it? I have complete faith in you."

He stared at her hands for a long moment before he raised his bloodshot, world-weary gaze to hers.

"Why?"

"Because in the time it took me to find my way out of the jungle, I discovered there are more things to life than a career. I don't give a damn if I get another promotion. I'm ready to take an easy shore tour after I finish command, and get out after that."

Drew's eyes widened, but he quickly recovered his noncommittal expression. She had to give him credit; he was in his own hell with the clinic and yet he still seemed to care about what she was telling him. "You're willing to stand by me even after I practically attacked you the first day you were back?"

"It wasn't like that. I wanted it, too."

The memory of her first days back weren't bad ones. She and Drew had needed to reach out to each other, for different reasons that added up to the right thing for both of them. She'd needed to feel human again, like the woman she'd once been.

"Why did *you* do it, Drew? I know I let it happen because I had nothing left. I was afraid I'd turned into some kind of subhuman, existing on so little for so long. I honestly don't know how I survived, much less with Pax in my arms. Being with you so soon—having sex with you—made me feel normal much sooner than I could have any other way. There are songs written about sexual healing, you know."

He nodded once. "I was glad you were alive. I was overwhelmed by it, by you. To have you back in the house, to see that you were still you, still whole, it turned into a need to be with you."

She had called it *sex,* he called it *be with you.* Neither of them said anything about love. But that kiss in the kitchen—she didn't want to bring it up. Nor the one in the garage…

"We don't have to solve it all now, Gwen. I know it's hard for you to understand, but even before Dottie died I'd realized that as much as I love my work, it isn't everything to me. It doesn't define me."

"I understand more than you realize, Drew."

He stretched his arm across the table and held his hand out to her, palm up.

"Give me your hand, Gwen."

After a heartbeat, she placed her hand in his. She was acutely aware of every place their palms connected. Of his pulse, steady under her fingers. Of the firmness of his grip. The warmth generated by their hands moved up her arm and to her throat, breasts, to her insides.

She looked from their intertwined fingers to him.

His gaze had never left her face. His eyes radiated a heat that was at once familiar but also a little frightening. Drew had become the man she'd envisioned when she'd said "I do" as a twenty-something with navy stars in her sights and love for her groom in her heart. Her stupid, foolish, naive heart.

"Drew."

"We'll figure it out, Gwen. We play by our own rules, though, okay? The hell with whatever anyone else is saying or doing. I may end up accused of homicide, you may not end up getting your baby, but we'll work on it together. No more stress over the hows and whys our marriage didn't work. It didn't, and it's over." She tried to pull her hand out of his but he held firm. "The marriage we *had* is over. Our friendship is better, deeper, after only a month of being together. We can work this out so that we give each other what we never could before. Our trust, our promise that we'll work together as friends regardless of the outcome for either of us."

She closed her eyes, fighting tears. Why the hell did she want to cry now? This was good. Really. Friendship was a safe place to be with Drew.

Wasn't it?

Because her stupid, foolish heart was no longer

naive. She couldn't risk even a whisper of hope that she and Drew would ever again be more than friends.

"Gwen?"

She opened her eyes and smiled at him. "We are friends, Drew. The best of friends."

He nodded. "I'm willing to let you be here for me through the inevitable—at the very least a civil trial. If, and only if, it works out, will you consider allowing me to help you with Pax? I'm not asking to be a father figure, but the friend you'll need to establish a life as a single mother."

Now Gwen nodded. "Okay. Deal."

CHAPTER FIFTEEN

A WEEK LATER Gwen pulled into the driveway with the confidence of a woman who'd climbed Mt. Everest.

She'd managed her first month back at the squadron without a hitch. Her exhaustion could still surprise her at the end of a few hours, but her good spirits enabled her to enjoy her shortened workday. Not bad for only two months out of the bush.

Of course she knew the real reason for her sunny mood had nothing to do with surviving her time in the PI or her role as a commanding officer. For the first time in forever, she and Drew had a pact—a real, bona fide commitment to each other. She'd help him get cleared of any wrongdoing in the Forsyth case, and he'd help her with the adoption if necessary.

Rhododendrons were blooming all over the island. Large blossoms of pale yellow, fuchsia, cardinal-red and winter-white covered every neighborhood and portions of the base as the Washington State flower came into season.

When she parked behind Drew's car, she noticed another, smaller car around the curve of their driveway.

Cole Ramsey.

Hadn't his last visit been enough?

"Son of a pile of puppies." She grabbed her tote bag from the passenger seat and opened her door. Drew needed her if Ramsey was here.

"Hey, girlfriend."

She stifled a groan.

"Hi, Opal." Gwen eased out of the car and stood next to Opal. Opal was short and Gwen got a perverse satisfaction out of towering over her too-friendly neighbor.

"Long day after I saw you this morning?" Gwen had stopped at Opal's coffee shack before work. It was important to show that she'd accepted Opal as a woman who'd love to have a relationship with Drew, although Drew wasn't interested. She was no longer a threat, and besides, it was the most convenient place to get a cup of coffee on the way to base.

"No, not at all. Anything I can do for you, Opal? I have to go inside."

"I'll walk in with you. I've brought some extra scones from the shop. They're marionberry, the kind Drew likes. You can freeze them and then heat them up in your toaster oven."

"If you don't mind, I'll take them off your hands now. Drew's in an important meeting."

Opal looked at Ramsey's car and frowned. "Who with?"

None of your business.

"I have to go in," she said again.

Realization dawned on Opal's face. "Fine, don't tell me. I'm sure Drew will fill me in later."

What the hell? "You may be right, Opal."

"Well, don't let me stop you, Gwen. Here, take the scones, and tell Drew I'm sorry I couldn't chat today."

"Sure."

Gwen took the scones and left Opal in the driveway.

ANXIETY GRIPPED HER as soon as she saw Drew.

He sat at the dining-room table with Ramsey, his head in his hands.

Cole looked up at Gwen and motioned for her to sit down, next to Drew.

Gwen dropped her bag and the scones onto the granite kitchen counter and slid into the oak chair. She folded her hands in her lap.

"What's going on?"

"Drew is named in Dottie Forsyth's will. She left him a not insubstantial amount of cash."

"What's *not insubstantial?*"

Cole named the sum and Gwen's shock made her sit up straight.

"Why on earth did she do that?" She turned to Drew, who remained silent.

"Cole's trying to tell you it gives me a motive for killing Dottie."

"Oh, crap."

"Yeah, *oh, crap.*" Drew sighed. "I never treated her any differently from my other patients."

"Which is with respect, kindness and hope. You give all your patients hope that they'll get better, or at least maintain where they are."

"It didn't do Dottie any good."

Gwen shot Cole a look. He wasn't playing the hard-boiled detective; his compassion for Drew's situation was palpable.

"Knock it off, Drew. We have to get to the bottom of this."

She returned her attention to Cole. "Are we absolutely positive it was murder?"

"No, but it's likely, and a jury would probably see it that way."

"So we have to find out who killed her and why. Who are her other relatives?"

Cole managed a smile. "I'm on it, Gwen. It's my job, remember?"

"If it's your job, then why are you in here telling him this instead of out there finding who did it?" Her voice rose on the last few words.

"Drew needed to hear it in private first, before it hits the press. It's going to be all over the internet and local news and you two won't be able to leave the house without a camera flashing in your face."

"Great." Gwen hated how shrewish she sounded.

"I'm sorry for imposing on your exile," Drew said with a cynicism she'd never heard before.

"I'm not worried about me, Drew." Looking at Ramsey again, she said, "This is insane. You know Drew is innocent, and you think someone's trying to frame him. Now he's getting big bucks from Dottie. Does she have her family mentioned in the will?"

Ramsey frowned. "Yes, her kids and stepson are splitting the bulk of her estate. She left her house to her niece Serena."

"That gives *all* of them motive to kill her. Not just Drew."

"Yeah, but even if they all had motive, most of them didn't have means," Drew said. "Besides, she died on my watch, Gwen."

"I'm not buying it." Gwen's mind spun with possibilities.

"Did you get a lawyer yet?" Cole stuck to the practicalities.

"I found one yesterday." Drew wiped his face, shoulders back against the dining-room chair. Gwen longed to smooth his brow.

"He had his choice of several top attorneys. It's obvious that he's innocent." She glanced sharply at Drew. Three lawyers had offered to represent him after she'd contacted them, using the list her mother had given her, and Drew had picked one of them.

"I'd suggest you figure out how or even if you're going to respond to the press. I'd recommend not doing it, but your attorney may have a different strategy."

Cole stood up and Drew followed suit, stretching out his hand.

"Thanks, Cole," he said. "I know this isn't easy for you, either. I don't want to put you in a bad place."

"I am in a bad place, Drew, but it's through no fault of yours—unless I've totally misread you these past years and you're withholding the truth from me."

"I'm not."

"I'll walk you out, Cole," Gwen offered.

She let Cole out the front door and came back inside to find Drew still at the table.

"It'll work out, Drew. I'm sure of that." But Gwen's faith in him obviously wasn't something he wanted to receive at the moment.

She knew him; he believed it couldn't change a damn thing.

DREW ALLOWED GWEN to make dinner and engaged in small talk with her. He refused to talk about the case.

As soon as she went upstairs for her shower, he made a phone call. He left her a note. "Had to go out for a bit. Don't wait up."

"I TAKE IT this isn't a friendly coffee meet-up," Cole said, staring at him across the diner's table.

"At night, when I know you haven't had a moment's rest since Dottie Forsyth died? No, Cole, it's not social."

Drew wrapped his hands around his mug. He needed the warmth. It was a cold, dreary night on Whidbey; Gwen was in his house but still out of reach. "I've been thinking, Cole. I'm not trying to do your job for you, but this is my life, my professional reputation on the line. You can't expect me to sit still while there's a possibility that a murderer's walking around free."

"Go on."

"There are three possible suspects from my clinic—me, Serena and Terri. Terri only works part-time and wasn't in the office when Dottie died, so she's out. I was in my private office, on the phone with Gwen—you have the phone-company records to back that up, I assume."

"You know I can't confirm or deny anything. You have to get the lawyer to do that."

"I know." Drew waved in the air between them. "That's not the issue. Let's assume you have the records and I have an alibi. The security cameras in the front reception area would show me leaving my office but they don't, either."

"Right." Cole didn't try to deny this, to Drew's relief.

"We're leaving out someone I've always thought might be a little off-kilter. Opal Doyle. The gal who runs the coffee stand outside the NAS main gate. She worked for me for a while until she saved up enough capital to start her business, and earned her MBA." Drew shrugged. "I sound desperate—downright insane—don't I?"

"Maybe. But the murder of a PT client while she's using an underwater treadmill is pretty insane, too."

He and Cole Ramsey were poker buddies and they'd had a therapist-client relationship, but more than that they were close friends. As such, they rarely indulged in small talk; they didn't need to.

"You think I might be on to something?" Drew asked.

"What's your relationship with Opal?" Ramsey's gaze was alert, focused.

"I don't have a relationship with her, not in that sense. Never have. She worked for me for about six months. She was a decent employee. I could trust her to multi-task and the patients seemed to love her."

"Seemed?"

"She made them laugh and she was especially

good with the old guys. You know how it is—the male seniors enjoy flirting with a younger gal."

Ramsey nodded. "Where had her last job been?"

"Somewhere in Bellingham, or was it Mount Vernon?" He referred to two small towns on the mainland, both about an hour from Oak Harbor and Whidbey. "Honestly, I don't remember off the top of my head. I have her original application on file. I scan everything and save it."

"I'd like to see that if you don't mind. Do you remember what she did before, in terms of employment?"

"She'd worked in nursing homes as an aide. She doesn't have any formal education that I'm aware of, which I told her was something she might want to consider getting. I trained her on my equipment and had her do some admin work for me. Community college or some other degree program. I thought she'd make a good medical aide. She wasn't drawn to medical services, though. She wanted a business degree."

"What made her interested in the coffee business?"

"Opportunity. She told me and the staff that she'd decided to move to the island to change up her routine. Apparently, she'd lived back East most of her life and wanted a change."

"You never made a pass at her?"

"Are you kidding me? No way! I don't mess with my employees. Besides, she always gave me the feeling that she'd be very needy. I was careful not to encourage her, but that didn't stop her from trying to turn us into a couple."

"Oh?" Cole leaned forward.

"I never talked to you or the poker guys about it because it seemed…silly. When she bought the house next to mine, I thought it was odd but chalked it up to coincidence. But since Gwen's been back, she's unexpectedly shown up at our place more than once. She has a bad habit of letting herself in uninvited."

He filled Cole in on his own bad habit of leaving doors unlocked. He also explained how Opal had recently dropped in at the clinic unannounced.

"I don't want to think of Opal or anyone I know as a murderer—and I don't understand why she'd do something like that, what her motivation might be…but I can't let this go."

"All right. I'd suggest you see that Gwen isn't alone in the house, and that you keep your damn doors locked. If I come up with any hard evidence that could possibly link Opal to the crime, if it was a crime, I *may* be asking for your help in getting Opal to confess. But it's not a sure thing, Drew. And you're not a cop."

"Thanks, Cole. I told you, I'm not trying to do your job. But you're putting the pieces of a puzzle together and I have to make sure you know everything I know."

Cole nodded. "I appreciate it. What can you tell me about Serena?"

"She's the best worker I've ever had. Too smart for her job, actually. She's going back to school for general studies, but we haven't really discussed what she's interested in. Her focus has been on her kid, a boy, since she lost her husband in Afghanistan almost three years ago. I wouldn't normally talk about this, but she was at Beyond the Stars with her son last summer when I went over to San Juan Island for a day."

Cole nodded. Drew had told him about his volunteer time there.

"She's the real deal. Devoted to her son. Still very much the grieving widow. She'll heal, I hope, but it's going to take her longer than a lot of other people."

"Why do you say that?" Cole's interest was piqued.

"She keeps a photo on her desk of her husband holding their son as a newborn. There's no sign that she's dating or even that she has a social life."

"Is she friends with any of the local navy spouses?"

Drew shook his head. "No. Her husband was army. She came out here two years ago, after he died. He was stationed at Fort Hood."

Cole sipped his decaf. "So, what about it, Drew? Are you and Gwen going to patch things up?"

"You don't mess around, do you? And what does

this have to do with Opal or Serena? Are you done asking me questions about them?"

"For now. You say nothing happened between you and either of those ladies. I believe you."

"Nothing happened, on my part. But like I said, Opal's made it clear, still makes it clear, in fact, that her door is open if I'm ever interested."

"Are you?"

"Hell, no! I told you, Opal's not my type. She's a sweet girl, but I always get the feeling she's too needy underneath it all."

"Yeah, you mentioned that. Needy in what way?"

"Nothing I can put my finger on. I see it when she flirts with the other navy guys, though—that air of desperation you sometimes see in old-time barflies."

"You didn't answer my question about Gwen."

Drew shook his head. "Nothing to say there. We've been friends since we divorced, and through some misguided loyalty she's staying with me until we're sure I'm not going to jail. After that, we'll go our separate ways."

He realized he'd be forced off island, probably out of Washington State, to seek employment as a physical therapist. If –when—he was cleared of any wrongdoing in Dottie's death…

"Relationships never come easy." Ramsey's tone grew whimsical and Drew assumed the official questions were over.

"What about you, Cole? Anyone flirting with you lately?"

Ramsey's eyes narrowed but not before Drew saw the glimmer of a smile.

"Hey, you hiding someone from us, Ramsey?"

"I'll let you know when I have something to tell you."

Drew laughed. "That bob and weave might work in the ring but it doesn't fool me, Detective."

"Speaking of which, I haven't had time to go for a run, much less a round." Ramsey stayed in shape by boxing as a hobby.

"It's tough, isn't it? When I was younger I never imagined I wouldn't be exercising each and every day."

"We all had plans like that."

They continued their conversation for another fifteen minutes or so.

"You still need me to stick around the area?" Drew hated to ask, but he hated being a murder suspect even more.

"Just let me know if you're going on a big trip out of state, or up to Vancouver. Are you?"

"No."

All his concerns were local.

DOTTIE FORSYTHE WASN'T supposed to die, damn it. All the controls on the aquatracker, the open door to the room—all of it had been perfectly set up so the old woman only had a bad day.

It was supposed to be a tactic, something to wake Drew up to what mattered. Not a means for his ex-wife to ensnare him in her trap again. Gwen seemed to forget that she was his *ex*-wife. How to get Gwen and that baby from the Philippines out of the way? Out of the picture that was going to have two subjects, neither of which was Gwen or her stupid baby.

Dottie wasn't supposed to die, no, but Gwen—Gwen was different. Gwen needed to be gotten rid of.

Only then could Drew get the love he deserved.

CHAPTER SIXTEEN

DAYLIGHT SLIPPED UNDER the blackout curtains Drew had in his room. The guest room. He'd given her the master suite when she came back and he hadn't returned to it. She saw his shape, still under the covers, only the side of his head showing.

Gwen was careful to open the door slowly so it wouldn't squeak and wake Drew. He needed to rest, and she'd leave him for another twenty minutes. Then he had to get up and get going. She had plans for them today.

She'd only meant to peek in at him. He'd left his door cracked so it wasn't as if she risked barging in on him. The quiet, punctuated by the sound of his breathing, made her stop and take stock of her surroundings.

This wasn't another PTSD precursor. No tremors of fear or anxiety-induced sweats.

The awareness she felt came from something else.

Drew's scent, his breath, his presence.

She missed him.

A movement in the bed caught her attention and

she stood still, expecting him to roll over and catch her spying on him.

But he'd only stretched in his sleep, then turned onto his back. From this angle she could see his profile in the grainy light, and she saw his ear—his ear.

Drew's ears were perfect. Small and flat against his head, unlike her larger, more pronounced ears. They'd joked years ago that they both hoped their kids got his ears. Drew had insisted that he didn't care whose ears they got, as long as he got to be the father of her babies. That was enough for him, he'd said.

She blinked.

And now she'd come back from the dead, blown apart their platonic friendship and announced that she was the mother of a baby she wasn't even sure she'd be able to adopt.

When they were married, their projected time to start a family had always been hazy, but involved both of them achieving major career milestones first. Mostly on the education front. She got her master's degree during a quick ten-month tour in Pennsylvania at the Army War College, on exchange from the navy. He'd earned his Ph.D. in physical therapy.

As a young newlywed she'd believed there'd always be time to have a baby. The truth was that she'd allowed her drive for success and her need for perfection in everything to cloud her common sense.

She was thirty-seven. Even if they were still a

couple, still wanted to have a baby, her ability to get pregnant wasn't guaranteed. After the stress of six months of survival living, she'd bet her chances of conceiving were down to nil. Her cycles had stopped out in the jungle, no doubt due to her weight loss and the shock and fear. The same thing had happened when she was a midshipman at the Academy; her periods had stopped for the better part of her plebe year. Low body fat and a high-stress environment could cause that.

"Gwen?" His gravelly voice interrupted her thoughts.

"I'm sorry, Drew. I was checking to see if you were up yet."

"I am now. Is everything okay?" He leaned toward his nightstand and picked up his cell phone. "Cripes, it's past seven? I slept like the dead."

"You needed it."

She didn't allow herself time to reconsider, just took a breath and plunged right in. "You have twenty minutes to get showered and dressed, and then we're leaving the house for the day. You don't need to bring anything. Oh, and dress casually."

Drew groaned. "I'm not in the mood for this kind of thing, Gwen."

"Relax. It's not like I'm trying to take you on a date or anything. You need a break, Drew. It's in my best interests to keep you healthy if you're going to help me adopt Pax. Staying shut in all weekend like you've been doing isn't good enough."

"I mean what I said. I'm not up to it."

"I wasn't up to going back into the squadron, either. But you gave me a kick in the butt when I needed it and now I'm doing the same thing. Get out of bed, buddy."

She left his room and jogged down the hall to hers. She couldn't risk giving him the opportunity to turn her down.

AN HOUR LATER she'd driven her car onto the ferry's ramp. They got out and stood at the railing watching the island slowly recede.

"I haven't been to Seattle in a long, long time." Drew stood next to her, his elbows on the top rail, hands folded loosely in front of him. The wind blew back his dark hair and she noticed the pronounced streaks of silver glistening.

He'd aged. Between their divorce, her almost-death and return and now Dottie Forsyth's death, he'd become a man with the weight of the world on his shoulders.

"Me, neither. We stopped there when I flew back from Manila, but that was only to use the airport. They took me right to Madigan for the medical routine, and then came back to Oak Harbor." She'd been too afraid to leave her hospital room at that point, even if she'd had the time to travel the forty-five minutes from Tacoma to Seattle.

"Are you sure you'll be okay going so far from

home?" He kept his gaze on the water, obviously taking care to be casual with her.

She hated it but understood.

"I'm fine, Drew. I've been going to work every day. I haven't had a nightmare in ages. I'm doing well." She lied about the nightmares. The one in which she couldn't get to Pax, couldn't save him from an undefined threat, recurred a few times a week.

But today wasn't about her or Pax. It was about Drew and being the friend to him that he'd been to her when she'd first come back.

"Just checking, Gwen."

"I appreciate it. Now tell me, what's your favorite thing to do?"

At his hesitation, she laughed.

"I mean in Seattle, of course."

"I like to have a good meal, preferably off the beaten track."

"What else?"

"Walking through the houseboat neighborhoods?"

"Close, but not quite."

"Let's see—I enjoy the Science Center."

She smiled. "Ding ding ding! Give the man a prize. You're close enough to be right, I suppose. What's near the Science Center that you adore?"

"The IMAX theater?"

"Yes! And today you get to choose whichever movie you want."

"What's showing?"

"A wilderness adventure, a short film about outer space and another one, something about the human body." She waited for comprehension to reflect on his features. It took him a few seconds, but he finally brightened.

"A Body Odyssey?"

"Yes, sir, just for you. A full-length movie that traces a path throughout the entire human body, including its musculoskeletal system!"

"How did you know I wanted to see it?"

"What self-respecting physical therapist wouldn't?" If she could've whipped the words back into her mouth, she would have. As his relaxed expression fell back into the perpetual frown he'd worn since Dottie's death, she groaned.

"Drew, I'm sorry. This is a day to have fun, to try to forget about all the crap that's going on. It's a chance to remember what it's like to live without fear, and with genuine hope that all of this will work out."

"Gwen, I appreciate what you're trying to do here. But I have a murder investigation going on in my workplace—my clinic. The clinic I've built from the ground up."

"And I have to start facing the reality that my odds of adopting Pax are getting lower by the day. Even though I played by all the rules, even though I saved his life I might not get to be the one he calls 'Mommy.' So what's your point?"

She took off her sunglasses so he could see her

eyes, see her stubborn refusal to accept his emotional turmoil as an excuse not to take a break from it all.

He let out a breath that was curiously close to a laugh.

"You've got me there. But no movie about bones or muscles—or anything else that'll remind me of work."

"Fair enough."

THE FERRY DOCKED at Mukilteo on the mainland, and Gwen put the car into drive, prepared to move down the ship's steep ramp and onto the pier.

"I should be driving." He'd always taken the wheel on ferry crossings. Gwen was an experienced pilot but balked at driving in such tight spaces. They'd laughed about it and Drew loved to tease her.

Before. Before it all changed… "I'm fine. Don't be afraid!" She turned from him back to the windshield and slammed on the brakes, catapulting them both to the edge of their seat belts' resistance and stopping the car from crashing into the tiny Fiat in front of them.

"Whoops! Don't worry, I just did that to keep you guessing." She found reverting back to their presplit joking banter came too easily.

"Hell, Gwen, you saved an entire crew from a crash, ditched a plane in rough seas but you still can't drive worth shit."

"Don't get your panties in a wad over it."

Dead silence as she drove down the ramp. As soon as the wheels hit the concrete pier they both laughed.

"I haven't heard that one since we were junior officers."

"It helped to have a sense of humor then, didn't it?" Navy flight school was filled with stress and unrealistic but necessary expectations. Each flight built upon the last completed sortie or mission. Students who failed once risked being out of the entire program within one or two more training flights. There'd been no room for failure.

"Yes, a sense of humor goes a long way in life." He had his hands on his thighs and he stared straight ahead. "I've lost my sense of humor."

"No, you haven't, Drew. It's hard to joke when you think your life is falling apart." She knew; she hadn't laughed a whole lot in the jungle.

They enjoyed the quiet of the car.

"Did you feel like Tom Hanks in *Castaway* over there?"

"Sometimes. When I was hungry and didn't have any food other than what I found growing on the jungle floor. I never had to kill to eat—I'm lucky I met the woman who took us in. She kept Pax and me fed and gave me time to regroup and heal from my crash injuries."

"You never mentioned you'd been hurt in the ditch."

"Nothing life-threatening, obviously. But I had

some scrapes and bruises, that's for sure. The cuts could've gotten infected if I hadn't been able to rest and let them heal properly. I have scars on my legs and the back of my right arm. I remembered feeling some kind of metal brush against my arm when I dragged Lizzie out of the fuselage. It wasn't until I was on the beach that I realized what a gash I had."

"We've never discussed you saving Lizzie."

"What's to discuss? She was one of my crew members. I'd never leave anyone behind."

"Of course not—but there is irony in it."

Gwen drummed her fingers on the steering wheel. "She avoids me at all costs, Drew. We made our peace with each other once we were on deployment—had a girl-to-girl talk about that night, about a lot of things." Lizzie had admitted to being completely mortified by her behavior, and promised she'd never cause Gwen or the squadron any more trouble like that. "She's the best TACCO in the squadron at this point. She'll get command as long as she doesn't have a major screwup between now and the selection board."

"Sounds like you've had a positive influence on her."

"I'm glad she made it back and that she's doing as well as she is." The significance of saving her crews' lives wasn't something she dwelt on. She occasionally thought about it in the quiet, early-morning hours when she couldn't sleep. She'd done what she had to do.

"I'm glad *you* made it, Gwen." What would have been too intimate, too revealing in any other setting, was a sincere and simple statement in the confines of her car.

"I am, too."

Surprisingly, she meant it.

DREW FORCED HIMSELF not to order Gwen to the side of the road so he could escape the car and run for miles until he was too exhausted to think. Being in such close quarters made his focus too narrow, made his awareness of her painful. He wanted to hold her, to kiss the scars she'd talked about, to make up for how rough he'd been with her that first day.

No, he wanted to lose himself in hot sex with Gwen.

Who was he kidding? It wasn't just sex.

He wanted to make love to her.

He was losing it. He hadn't called sex anything but *sex* since their marriage imploded. Since he'd been too tired to fight for it any longer. Since he'd realized Gwen was better off without him, without the encumbrance of a marriage that required so much work.

Guilt niggled at him for not telling her about his insight into Dottie's death but he couldn't, not yet. He'd called Cole to make sure it was okay to go off island, and Cole reminded him to keep it all quiet for now.

"Do you ever wonder why it was so much work to stay together?"

He'd surprised her; she stiffened and her fingers slid to the top of the steering wheel, tightening their grip. He knew her hands like his own. But hers made him hard with a single stroke, a well-placed grasp.

"It wasn't *that* much work, Drew. Not for the first several years. In some respects we were spoiled. We were focused on getting stationed together, and that probably kept us from dealing with the normal stuff that comes up for couples who aren't military and don't have the mobile life we do."

"Civilian couples have to transfer, too."

"Yes, but they don't have to worry about being deployed downrange for a year, not knowing if they'll come back in one piece, with a prosthetic limb or in a body bag."

He winced. Her frankness had always cut through the trivialities, but he didn't want to dwell on the fact that she'd survived more than her share of life-threatening situations.

"I never thought of it that way. If we'd lived together, never moving, for the entire ten years, don't you think we would've gotten to the same point?" She glanced at him and her eyes were assessing. Did she think he couldn't handle her response?

"Hang on." She turned her blinker on and changed lanes, passing a slow-moving, old pickup loaded to the gills with furniture and suitcases, all secured with bungee cords.

"We might not have. But there's no telling. Maybe if we'd been together all the time, never worried about who was going where, never wondering how we were going to get you through PT school, we would've gotten bored with each other."

Bored? Not with Gwen. "Not every marriage ends the way your parents' did."

Her father's death had been one of the roughest spots of her young life.

"What do you want me to say? He committed suicide—the great navy man who'd survived so much, only to be brought to his knees by his alcoholism and his mental illness. It was tough."

"You're not him, Gwen. You have your mother's strength."

"Thank God for that. But I have to admit I don't feel very strong right now."

"You're still processing everything. I'm not convinced you've accepted that you're really back here, safe and sound."

"I'm never going to feel that way until I have Pax in my arms again." She paused. "*Unless* I have him in my arms again."

She spoke quietly, with no accusation. She'd fought so hard when she first got back to get him onboard with supporting her in the adoption. Maybe she'd finally accepted that—as he'd told her himself—he wasn't the best recommendation for her cause.

At his silence she sent him another glance. I-5 wasn't a highway to take one's eyes off, and he shifted, leaning toward her.

"I'm fine. Just getting used to the idea of you being a mother."

"Is it really that difficult to imagine?"

"It's never been difficult to imagine." An image of Gwen, her belly large with their child, threatened to undo his composure. "I'd always hoped we'd have a family."

"I'm sorry it didn't work out for you."

He didn't stop the bark of laughter that shoved its way past the lump in his throat.

"Not for either of us. But if you're sure this is what you want, that it'll make you happy, I hope it all works out."

"That's what I can't explain, Drew. It's beyond 'wanting.' It's…an imperative. Pax needs a mom, and I was there for him at the right time."

"Makes sense." He knew in his bones that otherwise she wouldn't have stopped to consider having kids until it was too late—she was on a fast career track. That, and her need to prove she could do it all on her own.

"I know what you're thinking."

"I doubt it."

"Let me guess. You think that if fate hadn't put this baby in my arms, forced me to live with him in the jungle for months, I wouldn't ever have become a mother."

"You might have." He knew better than to have this conversation on the highway, with her at the wheel.

"No, let's face it. I don't have time to date, much less find someone to spend the rest of my life with. Add the fact that I'd be moving every two years for the next ten, until I retire—"

"You could retire at twenty."

"But not as an O-6."

"There's give and take to everything, Gwen. You could have a life partner who'd help you with the parenting. You don't have to do everything alone."

"Speaking of *give and take,* we have to pick a neighborhood and a place for breakfast. Any preference?" She maneuvered the car into the fast lane, while completely ignoring his salient point.

He didn't argue with her change of subject. It was too hard on both of them to keep bringing up the past choices they'd made, all the might-have-beens.

"As long as there's a place to eat, I'm happy."

"You used to love pancakes."

"Still do." Drew dug into his stack of apple-pecan pancakes while Gwen relished her salted-caramel crepes. They sat in a cozy booth at a favorite Seattle haunt; she'd been delighted to learn via the internet that not only was the place still in business, but it had expanded its menu to include brunch during the week.

"Carb heaven."

"We'll walk it off, I'm sure." She heard the note in his voice. Resignation.

They used to burn off calories in other ways.

Stop.

It had to be the fact that she'd been living under the same roof with him, that she had to see him, hear him, smell him, every day since she'd returned. Not to mention that first day back. It was as though all the sexual urges and needs she'd repressed since they'd gone their separate ways had spilled out.

It was painful enough to face the truth that she wasn't as good at doing things on her own as she used to be. Regardless, she could not allow her sexual needs to get her in too deep with Drew.

"Well, we *do* have all day." She swigged her ice water and studied him. "You're enjoying your pancakes, obviously."

He looked up and gave her a wide grin. "You know it."

Finally. The intensity of the last month retreated into the background, if just for this moment. Drew was eating, talking, smiling.

Relaxing.

"Do you want another order?"

"No, but you could use more."

She glanced down at her plate, almost empty,

and laughed. "I didn't realize how hungry I was. I'll save the rest of my appetite for some madeleines from Nordstrom's."

"No packaged cookies today. Let's go find a bakery."

Gwen laughed again and reached across the table to wipe syrup from Drew's chin. It was pure reflex. Only when he grasped her wrist and held tight, forcing her to meet his eyes, did she recognize that she'd broken her promise to herself.

Her desire for him was getting the better of her.

CHAPTER SEVENTEEN

"CAN YOU CALL Ro and see if she'd mind taking Nappie for the night?" Drew's warm breath tickled her ear as they looked at a particularly evocative display in an art gallery they stumbled upon.

"You're having so much fun that you want to stay?"

His eyes sparkled in response, and Gwen swallowed. Why not? They were two consenting adults. Once they got back on the island Drew might lose his life's work or at least his business, and she'd be gaining a new life or so she hoped—Pax. They'd go their separate ways then.

Just for today I can let it go and enjoy this.

"I'll text her."

Gwen stepped away from his heat, his touch, to pull out her phone. She needed space or she'd jump him right here. Her fingers shook as she punched in the message. Her best friend would stop her if she was being crazy, wouldn't she?

Can you keep Nappie tonight? Also, give Rosie fresh water and a grape.

The phone vibrated with Ro's reply before Gwen could drop it back into her tote.

Should I be popping champagne?—Ro

Get your mind out of the gutter. Thanks for doing this for me—Gwen

My pleasure. Enjoy and forget about the past. Let go of it.—Ro.

Didn't ask for therapy, just take care of the dog and the bird —Gwen

I'm not charging you for my advice, but heed it, anyway. Love you!—Ro

"Can she do it?"

Drew's eyes were intent, his hands in his jeans pockets, which drew her gaze to what lay between those pockets.

Anticipation stroked her insides, pooling heat between her legs.

This was going to be interesting.

"Yes, Ro said it's no problem."

One side of his mouth lifted in a wry grin. "That's not all Ro said, is it?"

"No."

He chuckled and reached for her, sliding his arm

around her waist and urging her to walk with him. "I've always liked Ro."

"You wouldn't talk to her for the longest time."

"What, when we were splitting up? Hell, no, I wouldn't. You two have some kind of blood-sister/ warrior-woman thing going on. I'm not stupid enough to get in the middle of that."

"Even if she never really took sides?"

He grunted. "Ro and Miles are our friends, yes, but she's your friend first. That's just the way it is."

They walked past the contemporary artists' room and wandered into the display of Impressionist paintings, Gwen's favorite.

"I love the colors!" She studied a canvas in the Manet collection on loan from Paris. The blues and greens calmed her nerves, the vibrant yellows made her smile, made her want to heed Ro's suggestion and *let go*.

Just this once.

"I could've done that. A splash here, a splotch there." Drew spoke in a low, serious tone.

She giggled. "Like your work in the master bathroom?"

"Ouch, take the knife out of my back, will you?" He smiled, and she stared at him as the memory of painting the house together came back in a rush of light, laughter and love.

Love.

She'd walked in on him trying out her favorite colors—blue, yellow and green—on the bathroom wall with a scrunched-up plastic grocery bag. They'd watched a home-improvement show a few weeks earlier and she'd commented on how much she'd like that "marbled" effect on a wall in their house.

It'd been two days before their anniversary. She'd been putting in long hours at work, assigned to the patrol wing on shore duty prior to being selected for her department head tour. That was several months before everything had fallen apart between them.

There'd still been a chance to prevent what had happened, or more accurately, what *hadn't* happened.

"Hey, that was one of my best gifts."

"It would've been, if it had looked any good."

"Hey, it wasn't that bad!"

"It was worse than if we'd had the dog paint the wall with her paws."

"Yeah," he said with a shrug, "it was pretty ugly."

Drew had wanted to surprise her but he was in a hurry. He hadn't allowed the paint enough time to dry, so instead of a marbled effect, the wall looked as if he'd applied a glob of gray paint.

She couldn't help laughing. "It was the thought that counted."

"That's not what you said back then."

"No, I was a real bitch about it, wasn't I?"

"It wasn't the paint job that made you angry."

"No."

They'd had so few hours together, and when they

were home, she'd wanted to make the most of it, not do home-improvement projects. She'd walked in on him, back early from a grueling day. All she'd wanted was to get into a steaming-hot bath and then sink into bed and let him spoon her.

Instead, she'd found their bedroom full of everything he'd moved out of the bathroom, the tub full of painting paraphernalia. She'd been furious and taken out her cranky mood on him.

"I was really nasty, Drew. I'm sorry."

"Water under the bridge. That was a hard time for you—make or break as far as getting selected for a command tour. I wasn't around enough to give you the support you deserved."

"What about me not there for you while you studied your butt off? We always thought it would be Easy Street once you had your degrees and I was back on shore duty."

"We were young when we set out those dreams, Gwen. And still pretty young when we achieved them."

"That was only what—six or seven years ago?"

"We've both been through a lot since then."

They had, alone and together.

"Do you think you've changed?" She looked at his profile in the museum light and while she still saw the Drew she'd fallen in love with more than a decade ago, she also saw the lines that had appeared during their breakup. They'd deepened since his clinic's catastrophe.

"Hell, yeah. I'm still me. I've still got a tendency to want things my way, but of course I've changed. It was inevitable—we all have to grow up sometime."

"I didn't change, not really, until after I took my trip to the jungle. Even then, it wasn't until I found Pax that everything started to look different." After she'd discovered that she could put up with any kind of insect crawling over her, that she was willing to kill to save her baby's life.

His gaze at once warmed her and stopped her cold in its seriousness.

"You're still you, Gwen. Under all of what you had to become in order to survive. I see you."

Uninvited tears slipped down her cheeks.

"It wasn't that...that horrible."

"Of course it was."

Mindless of their fellow art patrons, he pulled her into his arms and hugged her tight.

"Of course it was."

"I THOUGHT WE were going to a hotel in the city."

"This will be more fun." Drew had convinced her to let him drive for what she'd figured would be a twenty-minute trip to a convenient overnight hotel.

"Sure, but this was supposed to be my gift to you."

"It is, trust me." He flashed her a smile that made

her stomach flip as though she were sixteen and on a date with her secret crush.

"You weren't expecting to stay overnight, were you? Or was that part of your plan the whole time?"

"You know this wasn't my idea to begin with. I'm going with my gut here, sweetheart, and for once you've given in without too much of a fight." She began to feel apprehensive as they left the outskirts of Seattle; her apprehension grew as he drove them into the deeply forested byways, toward the mountains.

He wouldn't.

He hadn't.

Not *there*.

Yes, he had. He pulled up to the exclusive spa resort where they'd celebrated their anniversary years earlier.

It had been the most romantic night of their marriage.

"Drew, this isn't a good idea."

He shut off the ignition.

"It's a great idea, Gwen. No matter where we each go after this, we have a chance to come full circle. A lot of couples have goodbye sex at the end of their marriage. We never even had a goodbye kiss—we were both so hurt and angry."

"But this, this is—"

"This is our night. One night, Gwen. I hurt you, and it's the least I can do. I can't make up for being an ass and throwing our marriage away, but we can have a great night. I'm not asking you to forgive me—hell, I should be shot for not keeping you first in my life. Keeping us first."

"I'm just as much to blame here, Drew." She gulped. Vulnerability wasn't her strong suit.

HE KNEW THAT if there was anyplace he could make love to her the way she deserved, it was the lodge. They'd had the best sex of their lives here, when they'd celebrated their seventh anniversary.

When they thought they were stronger than life.

She'd probably forgotten, or blocked the happy memories they shared. He understood that. Some things were best left buried. Their split had been necessary for both of them —they'd had to heal from the wounds they'd inflicted on each other.

Gwen was stunning with her hair draped over her shoulders, her top low-cut enough so he could see her cleavage. He still dreamed of losing himself between her breasts.

"I feel a little underdressed." She toyed with her linen napkin as she glanced around the dimly lit dining room. They were seated next to the huge glass wall that offered a magnificent view of Snoqualmie Falls. The other diners were mostly couples who spoke in hushed, reverent tones. The place did have a kind of sacred feel. Of course he could be in a barren desert with her downrange and find it mystical.

"You're beautiful."

Her indrawn breath made her chest rise and the fabric of her shirt tightened over her breasts.

"Drew, no mushy stuff."

He laughed. "Okay, no mush. Do you want to talk gritty?"

"Not exactly my strength, either.

"You, Gwen, are strength personified."

She gulped her ice water.

"Are you blushing?"

"No, it's a hot flash."

"You're a little young for that, sweetheart."

She gave him a halfhearted smile. "You never know. I've been through an awful lot these past few months…"

"Now I know you're feeling better if you're pulling the pity card for your Philippine escapade."

She shrugged. "I get it where I can."

"Have you picked out the massage you want?"

Her eyes filled with tears.

"Gwen, what's wrong?" He reached across the table and grabbed her hand.

"I feel awful having fun when Pax is still so far away."

"And I feel like crap knowing there might be someone out there who killed Dottie and I'm here, doing nothing about it."

"You don't have any control over it, Drew. That's Cole Ramsey's job."

"Just like you have no control over Pax at this point. You've done all the legwork, and the State Department has to finish the job for you."

She sniffed. "I suppose we're in the same boat."

"And your idea to get away was brilliant."

"You didn't want to."

"No, but I'm really glad I'm here. With you. Now." He squeezed her hand.

She nodded. "Me, too."

He picked his menu up.

"Do you want to share an appetizer?"

GWEN WALKED DOWN the hallway from the spa to their room. The massage had been wonderful, but all she'd been able to think about was how it would feel to be with Drew again.

This wasn't like when she'd first come back. That had been an act of need on both their parts. She thrust her hands in the deep pockets of her terry-cloth robe. She and Drew were so good at shoving down their real feelings and needs. Compartmentalizing was a useful skill taught by the navy. It helped pilots, submariners, ship drivers and other operators stay focused on their mission while all hell broke loose around them. It had helped her stay alive in the jungle, and eventually get out.

But when it came to personal relationships, compartmentalization sucked.

The storm wave of emotions she'd had to wade through this past month had proved that to her. Her heart couldn't take another decade of avoiding unwelcome feelings to the point that she could deny their very existence. Whenever she did that, she was cheating herself of whatever lesson she should have been learning in the moment. And more than that, she held back from those she loved.

Love.

Did she still love Drew?

Of course she did; she'd always feel an unconditional love for him. He'd been her first husband, her friend and confidant through the most pivotal times in her life to date.

Liar.

Newfound knowledge fought with her instinct to ignore the voice that said she was still in love with him. That she still wanted him to make love to her as if she were the only woman in the world.

Not as a goodbye.

She slipped her key card into the door slot.

"How was it?"

Drew sat at the window with his iPad. It was criminal, really, that he could look so sexy in his shirt and jeans, his bare feet propped on a generic cocktail table.

"Great. I feel limp as a noodle."

He nodded toward the dresser that ran the length of the room. "I know you're supposed to drink a lot of water after a massage, but I thought you'd enjoy a glass of champagne."

She read the label and groaned. It was her favorite domestic sparkling wine.

"You remembered."

"I like it, too." He was beside her, popping the cork, pouring them each a flute of bubbling rosé.

"You do not. You're a beer guy."

"True, but a glass of nice wine every now and then is okay with me."

"To…" She held out her glass and was horrified when her hand started to tremble. She'd almost said "us."

"New beginnings." He saved her with a clink of his glass against hers before he sipped his drink.

She allowed the effervescence to play with her lips, her tongue.

"Mmm. Even better than I remembered."

"Didn't you have this in the P.I.?" he asked in a tone of mock innocence.

Bubbles went up her nose and she spewed what would have been her second sip. Laughter spurted out of her. Drew maintained his bemused air the entire time, not flinching as she sprayed the sparkling wine all over his face.

"You may claim otherwise," she said, "but you still have your sense of humor."

"You're the only one who laughs at my stupid jokes." He took her glass and placed it with his on the dresser. His hands cupped her face.

Her laughter quieted to an intense awareness.

"I know I've already said this, and I'll keep saying it. You're beautiful, Gwen."

"You're dripping champagne."

He shook his head. "You're more glorious every day. You've always been exceptionally pretty." He stroked her jawline, trailed his fingers along her neck, caressed her collarbone. "But you've become even more gorgeous. The most gorgeous woman I've ever known. The sexiest."

He didn't wait for her to respond, which was just as well. She wanted his lips to stop talking and start kissing.

Gwen raised her head and pressed her lips to his. She licked his top lip and his bottom one with light, soft strokes. Drew's mouth opened, and she fell into the familiar, warm comfort she'd dreamt of even in their darkest moments together. The love had died, or so she thought, but her physical need for him never had. She'd hated herself for it at their lowest points, but now felt grateful it was still there—apparently for both of them.

He moved his hands from her face and grasped her waist as he planted his feet on either side of hers. "My turn."

He thrust his tongue into her mouth. This was still Drew—his scent, his confident sexual appetite, that heavenly way with his fingers. But he introduced an edge to his lovemaking. As though he needed to put his primal stamp on her with each stroke and kiss.

Gwen couldn't get close enough to him, to his hard chest and abdomen. To his erection. She pushed her belly into him and relished his groan when her hand pressed against his jeans, feeling his hard penis under her palm.

In one movement Drew untied her robe and pushed it off her shoulders. He nipped at her neck, her shoulders, until he lowered his head to her breasts.

He paused, his face between her breasts, his hands on either side.

"Don't stop."

"I've missed this so much, Gwen. I've missed you."

"I missed you, too."

He responded by bringing one finger to her lips; she took it in her mouth and sucked hard.

He groaned and put his mouth over her left nipple. The wet heat of his tongue circled and lapped until she had both hands in his hair, drawing him closer, closer.

"My knees are giving out, Drew." She let out a shaky laugh and attempted to back them up toward the bed.

"Not yet." Drew stroked down her belly and slid two fingers into her most private place. She arched her head back. No thought could compete with his magic caresses or with the deep kiss he gave her. Still standing, she looped one leg around his waist to allow him further access. Drew stroked her while moving his fingers in that intoxicating way. *Drew.*

"Oh—" The rest was lost on her scream as his touch sent her into climax. She bit down on his shoulder as her hands gripped his backside. She didn't know if she was falling or flying....

"So sexy, Gwen. Always so sexy." He withdrew his hand and she whimpered.

"Help me, baby." He had his shirt over his head and she pushed him back onto the bed, unbuttoning his jeans as he hit the king-size mattress.

She kissed his abdomen while she got the shirt off. Her tongue had a mind of its own, stroking and licking its way around his navel and down to his erection, which she'd bared when she'd unzipped his jeans. His groan spurred her on, and she tugged off his pants. When he lifted his hips to help her, she took full advantage of having freed his swollen penis from its confines. She lowered her lips to him and didn't stop sucking and licking until he pushed her away with a gasp.

"Gwen!"

"Mmm?"

He sat up and grasped her shoulders, pushing her onto her back.

"I have to have you."

"I'm right here."

He pulled on a condom with shaking hands.

The careful, controlled caresses he'd given earlier were gone as he took her in one strong thrust. He felt larger and hotter than before, and she tightened at the familiar yet long-missed connection.

He stilled, his elbows on either side of her neck.

"Open your eyes, Gwen. Are you okay?"

She opened her eyes and saw the heat, the passion that was distinctly Drew. She also saw his concern—for her. As much as he needed this, he needed her to be okay, not to be uncomfortable.

Drew—the healer.

"I'm beyond okay, Drew."

She grabbed his buttocks and squeezed, urging him to press into her more deeply.

"You're so hot, so tight." He spoke through clenched teeth as he began to move, stroking in and out in an excruciatingly slow rhythm.

"Faster," she gasped.

He let out a quick, sharp laugh. "Patience, sweetheart."

She bit his shoulders and arms with quick, impatient nips.

"Now, Drew!"

He pulled out, slowly, slowly, before plunging back into her again and again until they both yelled out in release.

COLE RAMSEY SAT at his desk and clicked through all his notes on the Forsyth case. He knew Drew as well as he knew any of his friends. But he had to be impartial, unaffected by personal relationships. Because he also knew from the years he'd worked in this field that sociopaths often befriended those around them. They were often charismatic and highly intelligent—and usually impossible to identify.

Dottie's murder had been committed by someone smart enough to leave no trace. Both Drew and Serena fit that bill.

However… He thought Drew might be right about Opal.

Drew was no psychopath and killer; deep down, he knew that.

But if he didn't find a break in this damn case, the DA was going to call for an arraignment, despite the fact that the evidence was entirely circumstantial.

He'd tracked down every relative, every friend of Dottie's. He hadn't met her but she'd been popular in Oak Harbor; he'd been hard-pressed to get anyone to say anything bad about her, except for one neighbor who didn't like how she "grew those wild flowers all over her lawn." Dottie's landscaping, incorporating natural plants into her seasonal blooms, was actually common in Whidbey.

Cole was familiar with plants; he'd been raised by one of the island's best landscapers. His father had been disappointed when Cole chose criminal justice over agriculture, but had held out hope Cole would eventually become interested in at least the business side of the nursery and gift shop.

He fingered the African violets on his desk. He'd inherited his father's green thumb and wished he could be as enthusiastic about plants as he was about fighting for justice. At times, it was a tempting diversion, especially during investigations that went cold and whenever innocents were hurt. That was the worst, the kids he couldn't protect.

Mental images of Anita with her kids brought a smile to his lips. She was the strongest woman he'd ever met.

And the sexiest.

As if summoned by his thoughts, his cell phone buzzed, with her name printed across the display.

"Hey."

"Hi. Is this an okay time to call you?"

"Anytime you call is okay with me, ma'am."

"Cut it out, Detective, or I'll have to call the police."

"At your service, ma'am."

Her laughter would have warmed him to his toes if it hadn't stopped at his groin.

"I want to thank you for the flowers you sent. And for being here for me this past year."

"It was my privilege, sweetheart."

"Seriously, Cole. You've hung in there with me when other men would have fled."

"Their loss."

"The kids and I would like you to come for dinner."

Kids. Anita. Anita and her kids.

"When?"

HE STAYED LATE to finish the other paperwork he'd neglected since taking on the Forsyth case. Working into the evening used to be de rigueur for him, but ever since Anita had welcomed him into her bed he preferred other things to sitting at his desk.

If he got one more file moved into his out box, he was going to call Anita and see if he could stop by and say hi. He never did that when the kids were up; they were both careful to keep their relationship in the background.

Until now... She'd asked him to dinner with the kids. This weekend. His thoughts drifted back to how soft Anita's breast felt in his hand.

"Hey, boss, you have a call on line three." Molly Abernathy, the department's admin assistant, spoke from his doorway. He blinked away the memory of Anita.

"You should've gone home hours ago."

"I like the quiet. It gives me a chance to take care of the mess you guys make all day long." She smiled at him. Petite with shoulder-length black hair, she was the hot single gal on staff everyone wanted to date.

Except Cole. She wasn't his type.

"Something tells me you're just being nice to us."

She laughed. "Actually, I'm using the time to study. I'm back in school."

"Good for you! What're you studying?"

"Paralegal."

"Shoot me now, Molly. The last thing we need around here is another legal anything."

"It'll be a while before you can lump me in with that group. Are you going to take the call?"

He frowned. "Who is it?"

"Some woman, said it was important."

"Then I guess I'd better do my job."

"See you in the morning."

He waved at Molly as he picked up the receiver. "Ramsey."

"Is this Detective Ramsey?" Anxious female, probably somewhere between thirty and forty years old.

"Yes."

"I'm Opal Doyle. I knew Dottie Forsyth and I think I may be able to tell you some things you'd be interested in hearing."

Bingo. The crack they'd hoped for.

"Where do you live?" He checked caller ID. It listed a business on the highway in front of the Air Station.

"I live in Oak Harbor, but I'm calling you from work. I own the coffee shack by the base."

So far, so good. She wasn't lying about where she was.

"I'll need to speak with you in person, Ms. Doyle. Are you available tomorrow?"

"Sure, but I think we should meet sooner."

Cole rubbed his temple and kept his voice level. "Why is that?"

"I believe I know who killed Dottie."

"Stay put in your shop, Ms. Doyle. I'll be there in twenty minutes."

He hung up the phone. His gut told him this gal was nuts, that Drew was smart to figure it out. He looked at his watch.

Shit.

It was later than he thought.

No chance of stopping by Anita's for a good-night kiss.

THE KOFFEE HUT was one of several drive-through coffee shops on the island. Cole knew each and every one and had a special place in his heart for the ones that opened early and closed late.

He saw the light spilling from the business window but the counter was clear of its usual accoutrements—glass canisters stuffed with chocolate-covered espresso beans, madeleine cookies, sugar-free peppermint sticks. The sliding glass window looked as if it was locked tight, and the closed sign indicated that the shop would open with fresh brew at 0500. Just in time for the flight jocks to get a cup on their way to another mission.

He walked up to the service window and peered

in. A blonde woman dressed in a pink hoodie and blue jeans had her back to him, working at a kitchen counter.

Poor judgment on her part to have the place all lit up, showing that she was alone in the trailer. He tapped on the window and she turned around, staring out at him. He waited for her eyes to adjust, to see him clearly as he stood under her motion-detector light.

She unlocked the window and slid it open.

"You're Detective Ramsey?"

"Yes. Ms. Doyle?"

She nodded vigorously. "Yes, it's me. I needed to speak with you immediately."

"So you said. Do you mind coming out of your trailer and talking to me?"

"Oh, no problem. I'd have you come in here but it gets cramped real fast." She shut the window, locked it and disappeared from view. He heard the back door to the trailer slam, followed by her footsteps on the gravel parking lot.

When she turned the corner of the weathered trailer, he was struck by her diminutive stature. She couldn't be much over five feet, but her voice had projected the air of someone bigger, taller. He'd bet money she was the youngest of several siblings.

"Thanks for coming out here on such short notice, Detective."

"It's my job. Can you tell me exactly how you knew Dottie Forsyth?"

"She used to come by my shop, every morning, seven-thirty on the dot." She giggled. "No pun intended."

He refrained from comment.

"She always ordered her latte with a sprinkle of nutmeg."

"Where was she going?"

"Why, to the physical therapist's. Drew's place. At least on Tuesdays and Wednesdays. A lot of seniors come out here in the morning to get themselves going for the day." She shrugged. "I used to work at the PT clinic. When I first moved here, years ago."

"Is that where you met Dottie?"

"Oh, no, I knew her from here, from my coffee stand. I might have met her at the clinic, but I can't say I remember it."

"Why do you think you know who killed her?"

He liked to catch the people he interviewed off guard. Get them comfortable, let them talk then go in for the kill. No pun intended.

"Well, I'm a neighbor of Drew's. I knew him before I worked for him, actually."

"Hmm."

"He's as solid as they come, Detective." She waved her hands. "He's divorced but his ex-wife went missing, and when she came back, she— Never mind that now. Although it is relevant. It does tie together."

"What ties together?"

"The reason she killed her."

"Her? You mean Ms. Forsyth?"

"Yes, of course. It's pretty clear that Gwen killed her. She had a grudge against Drew ever since that squadron party three years ago, when he went home with the wife of one of her colleagues. Why they stayed together for so long afterward is what I didn't understand until I got to know Drew better. He's a healer, which is why he went into physical therapy. He's a caring man and he didn't want to let her down so hard. But their marriage hadn't been good for a long time."

Cole knew people. And he knew as clear as day that Opal Doyle was trying to give Drew a way out, at least in her view. She had the serious hots for the guy. Serious enough to murder Dottie Forsyth?

"That's not a very strong motive for murder." He was used to playing it cool, keeping up a neutral front.

"She's different. You know who I'm talking about, right? She's the one they say survived for six months in the jungle, over in Asia."

He nodded.

"People don't go through that kind of thing and come back normal. Besides, how do we even know she was really lost all that time? Maybe she shacked up with a local."

Cole was surprised his crazy radar hadn't pegged Opal the minute she'd said word one on the phone. Because this woman was definitely off.

Just looking at her didn't reveal anything. She dressed and acted like he'd expect of a woman who ran a drive-through coffee place. Professional, comfortable clothing. It was her words, the wild look in her eyes, that bothered him. Nothing like the serenity he saw when he looked into Anita's eyes.

Anita was different. Self-contained. Unpretentious. Responsible and deeply caring. Whether in gym clothes or her scrubs, she exuded an air of competence and vibrant femininity.

Anita.

Stay on task, Detective.

"Do you have anything else you need to tell me?"

"I saw her, right after Dottie was killed."

"Oh?"

"Yes. She was in her house, in sweats. As if she'd come home and showered after she did it."

"Okay. Anything else?"

Opal looked at a random point to one side. After a long moment, she slowly shook her head.

"No, that's it."

"Thanks very much for your time, Ms. Doyle. It takes a lot of courage to come forward with this kind of information."

"I'm only doing what's right. Drew is innocent. Are you going to arrest his ex now?"

CHAPTER EIGHTEEN

AFTER PERHAPS THE most uninhibited night of their entire relationship, Gwen was quiet on the way home, and she noticed that Drew didn't say much, either. What *was* there to say, when they'd had such a wonderful time but still faced an uncertain future?

She wanted to blame him for the ache in her chest but it was her own doing. She'd allowed Drew back in—she'd let her love for him out of its locked box. Letting him go was going to be infinitely more painful now.

They opted to stay on the highway instead of waiting for a ferry, and were at Ro and Miles's home by early afternoon.

"Your cheeks are awfully rosy, Gwen." Ro poured them each a cup of hot tea while Drew stayed out on the deck with Miles, drinking coffee. They'd stopped by to pick up Nappie on their drive home.

"It's your house—you always keep it so warm. Nappie's never going to want to leave, not after a sleepover with Beau."

"Nice change of subject."

Beau was the Labrador retriever Ro and Miles

had rescued around the same time they'd fallen in love. Beau was such an important part of their family that he'd actually been at their wedding.

"I don't want you to get your hopes up. Drew and I were over ages ago."

"Uh-huh."

"These last months together, even with all the horrible things going on, have given us a chance to get the closure we never had before. Living under the same roof hasn't been as bad as I thought it would be."

"So what happened last night?" Ro looked out at the deck. "Quick. Once they come back in, you won't be able to tell me anything good."

"WE'VE GOTTEN TO know each other well, Drew. You fixed up my aches and pains from that stupid accident." Miles was talking about a motorcycle accident he'd sustained a year ago. It hadn't caused any serious injuries, but since he'd lost his leg in the war, he was prone to more aches and pains in his other leg, the side he'd landed on in the crash.

"You were already in great shape. I didn't do anything but show you the exercises."

"I don't mean the actual PT, Drew. I mean the long talks we had."

"Hmph."

"You've been through too much, man. Too much to give it all up now."

Drew stared at Miles. Miles was the only person on earth to whom he'd confessed his deepest thoughts when Gwen had gone missing—that he'd never stopped loving her, that he'd agreed to the divorce because he believed she was better off without him. Because her career came first.

"I'm not giving anything up, Miles, since I don't *have* anything with Gwen. She doesn't deserve the mess my life is in. Last night, yesterday, was our goodbye."

Bullshit.

"It's not that easy, Drew. Do you still love her?"

"Whether I love her or not isn't the issue. Even if it was a perfect world and we did figure out we still loved each other and wanted to make a go of it—none of that matters. I no longer have anything to offer a woman, much less a mother and child."

"I never took you for the type to throw yourself a pity party."

"It's not self-pity, Miles, it's reality. I could end up in jail before the clinic tragedy shakes out."

"You're not going to jail."

"At the very least I'm losing my business. And if I lose my license to practice, I won't be able to work as a PT. I have no idea what the hell I'd do."

"I'm not trying to push you to make a decision you're not ready to. I know what it's like to feel you don't have a lot to offer someone—trust me." Miles looked up at the sky, as if gathering his thoughts.

It'd taken Miles a long time to feel comfortable asking a woman out on a date after he'd lost his leg, even longer to convince Ro, who, like Gwen, had been hard-core navy.

"The difference is that you had your life together when you realized you loved Ro. Mine's fallen apart."

"Drew, one thing that getting through the war taught me is that nothing will work itself out for me unless I do the footwork." Miles grinned. "Get it, *footwork?* I had to do it with one foot."

"Funny."

"If I'd given up on myself or Ro, you and I wouldn't be having this conversation. She would've taken the next orders out of here and found some other guy."

"Gwen isn't Ro."

"No, but they're cut from the same cloth. Both Academy grads, both women who've made it in a man's world. Ro is tough as nails—I don't have to say that about Gwen. You already know it."

"So your point is?"

"My point is that Gwen doesn't need you to take care of her. She needs you to take care of *yourself,* and if she's the one for you, you need to put yourself first for once and go for it."

"You realize I'm under suspicion for murder, right?"

"I thought my life was over when an IED took my dog and my leg. Someone or something else had a bigger plan for me."

Drew flinched. Miles rarely if ever talked about

the wartime event that had taken his leg. He'd nearly bled out before his Special Forces team was able to reach him. Miles had fought his rescuers because he didn't want to leave his bomb-sniffing dog's corpse behind.

Miles wouldn't be sharing any of this unless he thought it could help Drew.

Maybe it's time to listen to someone else.

"Point taken."

GWEN DIDN'T TELL Ro about the details of her night with Drew. They'd never exchanged such intimacies, even when they were younger and dating midshipmen at the Academy—they used to call it the "ick" factor. Gossiping about men was fine as long as it didn't cross over into "ick," becoming TMI— Too Much Information.

She did, however, admit to Ro that she still had feelings for Drew.

"But it doesn't matter," she went on. "He's made it clear that he's moved on, and expects me to do the same. Not every man and woman who love each other are supposed to make it as a couple. It's not realistic. Besides, I don't see myself married again, Ro. It's not how I want to live my life."

"Love isn't a realistic emotion, Gwen. Marriage is the most unrealistic commitment out there if you take it at face value. Promise yourself to one person only for the rest of your life? Crazy." Ro warmed up their tea with more from her blue ceramic pot.

"I know you need to prove you can make it on your own, no dependency on anyone else. But that isn't how life works, Gwen. Didn't you learn that when you rescued Pax? He wouldn't have made it without you."

Gwen felt as though her heart was jumping in her chest, making it hard to breathe.

"Even if Drew and I had a chance to redo it, or more likely, start over from scratch, this wouldn't be the time."

"There is no perfect time, Gwen! Didn't almost dying teach you anything?" Ro put her arm around Gwen's shoulders and gave her a squeeze. "You need someone to help you when Pax gets here, sis. He *is* going to get here. I feel it in my bones."

Gwen leaned her head against Ro. "Thanks," she mumbled.

Ro patted her back and reached for her tea. "Drew needs someone he can rely on to help him through this ugly mess at the clinic. I can't believe he'll be charged with murder, not without more conclusive evidence from the autopsy report. But he'll probably get sued, maybe even lose his practice. He needs you, Gwen. No one else knows him like you do."

Gwen gripped the dainty teacup to keep her hands from shaking. Anxiety had plagued her since they'd started back home. The closer they got to Whidbey, the more reality cut into the brief reverie she'd shared with Drew.

She shook her head. "It's ironic that I wanted to surprise Drew with an outing to take his mind off the clinic, and it ends up being another major complication for both of us. Neither of us needs a serious relationship right now, even if we've known each other forever."

Even if you admit to yourself that you're in love with him.

"Let go of who you think you're supposed to be, Gwen. Go with it. Just do the next indicated task."

"Like plebe summer?"

Ro laughed. "Hopefully not as difficult." She frowned and bit her lip. "I'm sorry, Gwen. You've been through a thousand plebe summers."

"Worse." It came out as a whisper. She hadn't meant it to.

"How so?" Ro was genuinely curious, yet Gwen knew her friend the intelligence officer wasn't asking about the actual rigors of the jungle, about the insurgents Gwen had run from or about Gwen's specific survival tactics. Ro had been trained for the same rigors, and since she was still on active duty and the wing's intelligence officer, she had full access to the message traffic that had described Gwen's ordeal.

Ro wanted to know about Gwen's heart.

"I had a lot of time to think," she began. "Every night I walked as far as I could. I tried to get to Manila when I wasn't holed up with Pax in that one-room hut. During the day it was too hot to

move, too bright to risk being seen by the enemy."
She looked at Ro. "I know *enemy* might sound a
bit extreme, but when I was out there, those insurgents *were* the enemy." She shuddered as she remembered how frightened she'd been when she'd
arrived at the village with Pax in her arms. The
woman she'd eventually stayed with, who'd saved
her and Pax, had seen her and ran up to her. In that
instant Gwen thought she and the baby were gon-
ers. Even the most innocent-looking person could
be a deadly informant.

Thank God her fears proved false.

"What I thought about the most was my life, of
course, and how much I still wanted to accomplish.
And my blessings. I've served my country, I married the love of my life. We ended up divorced, yes,
but I did have him for a while. That's more than a
lot of people ever get."

"Have you told Drew this?"

"I can't, Ro. That would be like pulling an unfair trump card. If he and I are meant to get back
together—" she shot Ro a warning glance "—it has
to be on fair terms. Saying I thought of him like that
while I was running for my life isn't fair. It wasn't
his fault I was stranded in the jungle."

"It wasn't yours, either. It's not about blame, hon.
Listen to your heart."

CHAPTER NINETEEN

"CONGRATULATIONS, GWEN. PAX'S adoption is official."

Gwen sank into the easy chair, her cell phone at her ear. "That's it?"

Councillor Tatem chuckled.

"Until you get to hold him in your arms, yes. He's going to fly out with one of our FSOs, Foreign Service Officers, tomorrow. Is that soon enough?"

"No, I mean, yes! Oh, this is wonderful news. Thank you!" She'd hoped and prayed, but hadn't expected it to go through so quickly.

"I thought I'd have to fly back to Manila to get him. I still can if you need me to."

"No, no, it's all legal the way it is. Let's get him on U.S. soil with the least amount of fanfare, okay?" Darlene Tatem sounded as relieved as Gwen.

"Of course."

She wrote down the details of the flight with shaky hands.

"Do you need any more signatures from me?"

"No."

"What made it happen so fast?"

"Once we assured the Philippine officials that

Pax is going to the person who rescued him—the person he's already bonded with—they relented. There may have been some other negotiations going on, as well, but I'm not permitted to discuss them. No matter, Pax is your son."

Tears spilled down her cheeks. "I can't thank you enough, Darlene."

"It's me, and the entire State Department, who need to thank *you*, Gwen. Your ability to survive what you did while saving a Filipino baby's life has done more to strengthen U.S.-Philippine relations than anything else in a long while. The fact that you're active-duty military says so much—ever since we pulled our military presence out of here, there's been a PR hole that needed filling."

"I'm only one person, but I appreciate it."

"I'll have my secretary email you the flight details. All you need to do is go directly to customs at SeaTac. Congratulations!"

"Thank you!"

Gwen hung up and started yelling and dancing around the kitchen. Pax was hers! She was going to have her baby back in her arms in fewer than two days.

"Woooooo," Rosie chimed in, her wings outstretched as she strutted about the top of her cage.

Pain shot up Gwen's foot as she stubbed her bare toe on the corner of the kitchen cabinets.

"Oof." She hopped to the center of the room and sank down on the floor.

Nappie came up and licked her face.

As she massaged her toe, her pounding heartbeat slowed to normal, as did her thoughts.

She needed to make a trip to the Base Exchange to pick up baby things, a car seat being the most important.

You need to call Drew.

He'd expect her to move out sooner rather than later.

Tell him you've changed. You know you belong with him.

If only she'd recognized her feelings for Drew earlier, before Dottie's death…

What about their night together? Had it really been goodbye?

"It's never easy, is it?"

Rosie replied with a wolf whistle.

"I'M NOT GOING to SeaTac with you, Gwen."

Her tears of joy threatened to turn bitter at his words.

"I understand."

"No, I don't think you do." He ran his fingers through his hair, his stance wide and defensive. Chirping birds flitted by them as they stood on their deck overlooking the backyard twelve feet below.

"You've known Pax longer than anyone. If I show up at the airport with you, I might scare him. My presence would only add to the chaos of his welcome home."

She gazed out at the grass and the trees several hundred feet beyond. They'd been so lucky to find this piece of land when they'd decided to have a house built. A mountain and water view in front of the house and a forested backyard. It all seemed like a hundred years ago.

"You're okay with this?" He saw her smile.

"Remember when we found this land, Drew? We had no idea what lay ahead of us."

"No one ever does, Gwen. It's called life. You haven't answered me. Do you get what I'm saying?" She got it, all right. He didn't want Pax to have even the slightest chance to think of Drew as a father.

He hadn't changed his mind.

"Sure. You've got enough on your plate, Drew, without adding a baby boy to the mix."

A dandelion puff of seeds floated up and over their heads, caught on the Whidbey breeze.

"He won't get in your way," she promised. "I'll start looking for a new place as soon as I can." She turned to fully face him as she leaned on the redwood deck railing.

"You don't have to do that, Gwen. That's not what I was getting at. Take your time. I'm hardly home as it is." Drew shook his head and looked out at the trees, avoiding her gaze.

"If I could just find out who killed Dottie, I could put it behind me. Have a chance at keeping the clinic. Otherwise…"

"There isn't an *otherwise*. You'll find Dottie's

killer, I *know* it." As she said that, she realized she did believe they'd discover who'd instigated Dottie's death, if not outright murdered her.

"Even if we do, I've probably lost most of my clients, and it'll take a long time to build back up after this. I'd have to attract all new clients, people who don't know about Dottie."

"So what? You might be limited to the newly arriving navy folks, but we're coming up on the big turnover." During the summer months, PCS—Permanent Change of Station—meant that navy families arrived on Whidbey as outgoing sailors left.

"Exactly. Do you really think this will work itself out, Gwen? In any case, I think I'll have to wait until next summer, and a year's too long for any business to be in the red."

"How many times since we've known each other have we thought we were done, whether it was at the Academy when we were trying to pass EE…" She smiled as she referred to the electrical engineering exams. "Or later on, in flight school, when you were sure you failed a sortie? What about when we didn't think we'd get stationed together, but then we did?"

"What about when we decided to live apart—and it all fell apart?"

His sharp retort cut deep. "That's different. We had control over that and we made the wrong decision."

"Was it really the wrong decision? Or did we both know at some level that we weren't going to make it?"

She let out a breath. "I've wondered that, too. What I keep coming up against is that I didn't expect us to ever end. No matter how bad it got—it'd always been Gwen and Drew. But once we were away from the squadron and had time to figure out who we were as a couple, as opposed to what everyone expected, it got…hard. We didn't know how to do things together without the navy telling us our next move."

His eyes were bright as he met hers.

"You have done a lot of thinking about this."

"Of course I have. And it wasn't all in the jungle, either, or because I had nothing else to do. I wanted to figure it out, Drew. I had to know if I could've done anything differently."

"And?"

"Yeah, I could have, we both *could* have. I could've taken orders here instead of downrange between my department head and command tours. That would've kept us together while you finished your Ph.D. Closer, at least."

He shook his head.

"I was living in Seattle. It still would have been a commute on the weekend, for one of us, anyway, if you'd stayed here." After Drew was admitted to the University of Washington's doctorate program in Seattle, they'd promised they'd commute to see each other on weekends whenever possible. It proved impossible most weekends as Gwen had been in Afghanistan, assigned to the command staff.

After that she took ten-month orders to the National Military Defense College in D.C.

"The orders to D.C. were kind of forced on me, you know that." She bit her lip. "But I didn't have to accept them, did I?"

"No more than I had to finish my courses. Look, Gwen, we were hell-bent on our professional goals. And I was putting a lot of pressure on you to have kids, to boot. Especially once you were done with your time in the war."

"You know I couldn't risk having a baby when I was hoping for command?" She refused to be the mom leaving her kid to go to war.

And now she was about to be one—Pax was her son.

"I know. Not everyone gets the chance to command, even fewer women. I never wanted to take that from you. But—"

"You wanted a family and you didn't think I'd ever be ready."

"Yes."

"That's fair, Drew. Not mean or selfish, it's just the way it is."

The breeze waved across the tips of the fir trees and rustled the rhododendrons. They'd lost the last of their blooms since she'd returned. Summer was upon them.

As was her change of command.

"I feel guilty because I'm glad my command tour's almost over. I don't ever want to worry about leaving Pax."

DREW BREATHED IN and relished his surroundings—the redwood deck, the unique Whidbey aroma of pine needles and salt air, the roses that had opened up yesterday in their ceramic pots on the deck. And Gwen.

Gwen's scent was seared in his brain, since the first time he'd kissed her. They'd been so young, so greedy.

He didn't feel any less greedy as he stood next to her now, listening to her plans for her new family that didn't, couldn't, include him. But he felt ancient, wise beyond anything he'd ever imagined.

He'd faced losing her twice already. He had to make this work.

"Why would you feel guilty, Gwen? You've earned every minute of your life—in spades. The navy should be paying you for even staying on active duty. You could opt out, you know."

"I know. It's a definite possibility if I don't get a three-year shore tour, with an option to extend."

"With all the budget cuts, they're more than happy to keep people in one place, don't you think?"

"I'm not sure. I've done well until now, but the truth is, I haven't really commanded my squadron on deployment. I was just two months into it, and now there's only a month and a half left. The majority of my time's been spent saving my own ass from young rebels."

"Young rebels who wouldn't have thought twice about putting a bullet through your head, after they'd raped and tortured you." He walked to the railing and gripped it. He didn't want her to see how badly he was shaking. The sheer force of his rage at the idea of anyone hurting her was bigger than he was.

"They didn't, and I'm here." She put a hand on his forearm.

The warmth of her touch broke through his anger, his deepest fears that she'd been killed.

He let out a harsh laugh. "I'm in the middle of a murder investigation, and it looks like everything I worked for, used up our savings on, is going to go down the drain. And yet I don't give a damn about any of it, as long as you made it out alive." He stopped before he could spit out more. She didn't need to hear how he'd never stopped loving her. Not now, when her dream of getting Pax back was so close.

He heard her take a deep breath. "Drew, how do you think I got through my time in the jungle?"

"Please, Gwen, don't patronize either of us."

"No, listen—it's true. I thought of you each and every moment. I heard your voice in my head, telling me what I needed to do, to remember my SERE school training. I even had dreams of us back at the academy, going through plebe summer. Remember when we had to do the shoring drill? Where we had to stand in that awful tank and stop up the leaks as they poured water into it? You were right behind me, and just when I was going to pack it in, you gave me a shove and told me to keep going. You held my arms on that damned piece of wood so our squad would win."

Her eyes swam with tears that ran down her cheeks, tears he wasn't sure she was even aware of. He wiped her face, then pulled her close.

"Shh. It's okay, you're safe."

She pulled back and pounded a fist on his chest.

"I know I'm safe, Drew, dammit! Will you ever let someone, let *me,* give you a compliment? Let me thank you for getting me through my months in the jungle, the darkest time of my life. It was almost as dark as, as dark as..." She started to hiccup, trademark Gwen when she was overwrought.

"As what?" He braced himself to hear her cry about her fears over losing Pax.

"As when we decided we were done."

He stood still, not wanting to believe she'd said the words.

"I thought you wanted the divorce, Gwen."

"I did—I felt it was best for you at the time, and for me. We'd tortured each other long enough with all the accusations. We both carried too much guilt and self-blame for letting it all go to hell, didn't we?"

"Yes."

He wanted to hug her, to hold her, but it had to be Gwen's move. Just as it'd been her move to get out. He'd made the first move the other night, when he took her to their lodge and made love to her. He'd let her think it was goodbye, and the most fearful part of him had believed it was.

If they reunited now, it had to be with hope.

"I don't want you to think I'm looking for a father for Pax. He'd do fine with me."

"Of course he would."

"But that's not the point, Drew. *I* won't do fine without you. I need you."

It wasn't love, it wasn't a promise. He didn't have hope to give her yet. But this had to be enough for now.

WHEN DREW LEANED IN and kissed her, Gwen closed her eyes and opened her mouth to his without hesitation. It would've been better if they'd had this conversation either before or way after she got the word on Pax, but their timing had never been perfect.

"Gwen, I need you, too, but I don't have anything to give you except this…" He clasped her shoulders and drew her against him. Her breasts were crushed against his chest and she felt her nipples go taut at the friction. She clutched his arms, off balance with the ferocity of his kiss.

"Maybe we should go inside," she whispered as he kissed her neck.

"No one can see us here on the back deck." His voice was low and his naked need for her put Gwen's focus entirely on him.

The deck was covered with a canvas awning and they'd furnished it with rustic wood furniture, except for the long, rattan-framed outdoor sofa they'd purchased when they moved in. They'd bought it with thoughts of future social occasions at their house, but they'd found out the night it was delivered just how comfortable the cushions were.

Gwen shimmied out of her jeans and let them drop to the deck as she lay back on the red cushions. The weather-proof canvas scratched her bare skin but that only served to heighten her awareness of Drew as he, too, removed his pants and joined her. They lay belly to belly, chest to chest on the wide sofa as they kissed.

"Finally." Gwen exhaled a breath of relief as Drew freed her breast from her bra and bent his head toward it. When he sucked on her nipple, she rolled her hips against him and his erection burned into her belly. She squirmed up higher, so that her pelvis was against his, against his hardness.

"Do you like that, sweetheart?" His fingers, his hands, were everywhere as he lovingly attacked her with passion and deliberate strokes of his tongue.

"Kiss me, Drew." She pulled his head up to hers, and looked at him.

His eyes were glazed with desire for her but alert with—

"I love you, Gwen." He didn't allow her to respond as he kissed her deeply.

It wasn't about analyzing words or thoughts or physical attraction. This time between them was about living in the moment, appreciating that they still could do this to each other. For each other.

It was about loving.

CHAPTER TWENTY

GWEN KEPT HER preparations for picking up Pax simple. Drew remained determined to stay behind on Whidbey, and Gwen didn't want her mother coming out, not yet. She was barely a mom herself and wanted time with Pax to reconnect before he was ambushed with overwhelming grandmotherly love.

Which left her best gal pal.

"Thank you for coming with me. And please thank Miles for letting you go."

"Puuuulllleeeeze. He'll live one night without me." Ro drove as they made their way down I-5 to Seattle. Gwen had booked a hotel for the night so they'd be at SeaTac early, at least a few hours before Pax arrived. Otherwise they risked being delayed by traffic, and she wouldn't be able to stand it if she wasn't there to greet Pax when he landed.

"We haven't had a girls' night in a long time."

Ro sent her a smile. "We've both been busy."

"Speak for yourself."

She'd figured out that she loved Drew, more than she ever had. Which was why she had to be willing to let him go, why she couldn't answer him yesterday when he'd told her he loved her. She couldn't ever ask him to do something he didn't want to. His refusal to come with her to get Pax confirmed her deepest fear.

He might love her, but he wouldn't let himself be part of the family she was creating with Pax.

"Hey, don't you have a baby to worry about?"

"I'm not worried about him."

"Liar."

Ro still made her smile.

"He's in the best hands until I get him. I'm really getting him, Ro. I'm a mommy!"

"Yes, you are. But until he shows up tomorrow morning, we are going to have some fun."

"I can't have *too* much fun."

"No. However, we can have a glass or two of the red wine I've brought, and we can do our nails."

"Sounds great." She didn't want to disappoint Ro, but she had no idea how she'd get any sleep tonight, much less calm down enough to paint her nails.

PAX'S ARRIVAL WAS anticlimactic after a long wait in the U.S. Customs office. The State Department Official who'd served as escort was surprisingly young and introduced herself as Stefanie Quinn.

"Thank you so much." Gwen spoke to Stefanie but her gaze was on Pax. Her stomach flip-flopped as she looked at her son. Her son!

"Come here, sweetie pie. It's Mommy." She held out her arms and after a brief, heart-stopping pause accompanied by a stare, Pax giggled and reached for Gwen.

"My baby boy." She hugged him to her, burying her face in his warm, dark hair.

"Mamamamamama…!" Pax screeched before he giggled again and kicked his legs against her.

"Yes, I'm your mama."

She was dimly aware of flashes as Ro took the first photos of Gwen and Pax on American soil.

Gwen would never forget the softness of Pax's skin as she pressed her cheek to his, the way his fingers grabbed at her hair, the solid feel of his little body in her embrace. She had him back.

Yet through all the joy and the tears of reunion, a somber thought raced through her mind and closed tight around her heart. There was one person on earth she wished she could share this with, and he wasn't here.

Drew.

DREW GOT INTO the shower after he'd mowed the lawn and cleaned out the refrigerator. He couldn't pinpoint when, but sometime between his chat with Ramsey this morning and the text from Gwen saying they were on their way home, he knew this was it.

His chance to maybe, just maybe, make things right with her. To show her that he could be a father for Pax, but more important, a husband for her.

He soaped up and tried to relax under the hot

water. He'd planned to be the best father for their child one day, and he'd thought he had it all figured out. Gwen would get pregnant on or about their thirtieth birthdays, they'd have three kids, she'd get out of the navy as he had. He'd be able to support her with his job, with the clinic.

Hell's bells. The clinic. He'd suddenly remembered, and like a wall of ice, the reality of his predicament slammed into him. He couldn't offer Gwen or Pax anything. Not yet. Not while the case was still open. His clinic was going to close. Even if Dottie's death was found to be accidental, or if his hunches about Opal proved true, who would ever trust him or his staff again? Gwen believed in his innocence. But it wasn't enough.

Stay focused. You've got to finish it out.

A movement outside the glass shower walls caught his eye and he stilled.

"Gwen?"

They weren't due back for over an hour, longer with traffic or ferry delays.

"No, Drew, it's me, Opal. Open up, sweetie."

DREW REALIZED THAT Opal had taken the bait. He'd texted her and let her know Gwen was going to pick up the baby this morning, and thanked Opal for supporting them.

Opal had shown up a little early, since he was supposed to be dressed and wired with the equipment Ramsey had given him *before* she got into the house.

He peered through the steamed window.

She was naked.

Holy freaking crap.

He'd served in the navy. He could do this.

"Get the hell out of here!" He played it the way he and Ramsey had planned. No way on God's green earth was he going to have her ruin whatever chance he had left in life.

Gwen.

Thank God Opal had shown up while Gwen and Pax were still far away. Far from danger.

"I mean it, Opal, you have to leave."

He shut the shower off and reached outside the stall for his towel.

"Looking for this?"

Opal stood just out of reach, the towel dangling from her fingers.

He gritted his teeth and kept his eyes on her face. He hadn't been wrong to think she'd killed Dottie. She was insane.

"Get. Out." He stalked over to the linen closet and grabbed a towel off the shelf, nearly shoving her aside as he wrapped it around his waist.

"Drew, that's not very nice." He heard the excitement in her voice. Just like Ramsey had predicted. Sociopaths thrived on the distress of others. Perceived or real.

"You know I can't be with you, Opal."

He held open the bathroom door and waited for her to walk into the bedroom where, he noted, her clothes lay in a pile in front of the bed.

His and Gwen's bed.

Get her to talk.

"Can I please have some privacy to get dressed? And would you do the same?"

"You don't have to be such a jerk, Drew."

She took her time putting her clothes back on. He stood, covered by the towel and waited. When she wasn't looking at him, he dared a glance at his clothes. The wires were concealed; she hadn't seen them unless she'd messed with his clothes on her way into the bathroom.

"Do you like watching me get dressed, Drew?"

He didn't answer but instead walked to the bedroom door and opened it, motioning for her to leave.

"Go."

As soon as she was in the hallway, he threw his clothes on, taking care with the tiny recording device. He couldn't risk texting Ramsey. It would take too much time. He'd have to trust that Cole's equipment was catching everything.

APPREHENSION TRILLED INSIDE Gwen as she carried Pax the brief distance from the car to the house. She'd dropped Ro off at home; Ro had insisted that the first time Drew met Pax, it should be as quiet as possible, with little fanfare.

For all concerned.

Gwen knew Ro was praying this would be a true family event, one that included Drew.

She was afraid to hope....

Still, her hands shook as she unlocked the door and called out. "Drew?"

Pax squealed in her arms, trying to get down.

"Just a few more minutes, sweetie." She walked over to the sofa and dumped everything but Pax onto it—the oversize diaper bag, a toy, her purse, a water bottle.

"I'm going to have to get a little more organized for you, aren't I?"

Pax strained against her arms and she laughed.

"Okay, big boy, here you go. Nappie, good girl, stay there." She set Pax down on the living-room rug and sank down next to him. He immediately started to crawl, checking out every nook and cranny around him.

"You've learned to do a lot while we've been apart."

She angled her face toward the upstairs loft. "Drew?"

Still no answer. His car was in the driveway, so he was here somewhere. Maybe in the shower, or in the basement on the treadmill.

She'd texted him to let him know when she'd be back.

He hasn't guaranteed you anything.

In fact, he'd seemed relieved when she'd mentioned finding a place for her and Pax. He clearly hadn't wanted to engage in any conversation about Pax or her future plans.

Neither of them owed each other anything.

It's not about that. It's about love.

"It's always about love, Pax." No man made love to a woman the way Drew had to her unless his feelings were real. Unless the possibility of a future existed.

She leaned over to grab the elastic waist on Pax's baby jeans and stop him from investigating the electrical cord under one of the end tables.

"No, you don't, buddy."

He cried out in distress and she laughed.

"I know this won't be funny in a few days when we're both tired, but right now you are the most adorable kid ever." She lifted his little T-shirt and planted a kiss on his belly, which made him giggle.

Nappie trotted up to them and Gwen realized the old dog was jealous.

"I'll get your belly next, Nappie."

The sound of voices upstairs made her pause in midtickle.

Voices.

Male and female.

Oh. God.

Not again.

Before she could react, the upstairs master bedroom door burst open and Opal came out, face red, hair in disarray.

The bedroom door slammed shut behind her.

Please tell me Drew threw her out.

Opal saw them and headed down the stairs.

Nappie leaned her warm body against Gwen's calf. She held Pax in her arms, the overwhelming urge to run out of the house making her legs shake.

"Gwen, what the hell are you doing here? Don't you know Drew needs his own life?"

"It's okay, Pax," she whispered in his ear, her gaze never leaving Opal. It wouldn't surprise her if Opal pulled a weapon. The crazed, haunted shadows in her eyes weren't unfamiliar to Gwen; she'd seen them in her captors' eyes. "Opal, leave Gwen alone and go."

Opal paused halfway down the stairs and turned to face Drew, who'd emerged from the bedroom in a polo shirt and jeans. Gwen noticed that his hair was dripping wet.

What the hell? Had he been in the shower with Opal?

"It's always been about her, hasn't it, Drew? You led me on."

Drew held up his hands as if in surrender as he walked to the landing and started down the stairs.

"No, I didn't lead you on, Opal. You've made up your entire version of my life, haven't you? You've invented your own life *and* mine."

Opal backed down the stairs as Drew closed the gap.

"Maaaaama!" Pax squirmed in her arms.

Opal reached the bottom step and turned toward Gwen.

"Aren't you the perfect little mother?" Her lip lifted in a snarl and Gwen tightened her hold on Pax, taking a step backward.

Nappie growled in warning, the vibration reassuring against Gwen's leg.

"Oh, what a cute baby," Opal cooed and she smiled at Pax.

More like leered, Gwen thought.

"We're just on our way out." She couldn't think of anything else to say.

"Wait, Gwen." Drew was beside her, anger rolling off him. And something else. Was he guilty?

No. He'd never do this to you.

"What do you see in her, anyway?" Opal stared at Gwen with her crazy eyes, speaking as if Gwen and Pax were inanimate.

"Okay, Opal, you win. Let's tell Gwen everything."

Opal's head snapped toward Drew.

"What do you mean, *everything?*"

"Why don't you start with Dottie Forsyth, Opal? The truth or I'll never be able to trust you."

"The truth?" Opal laughed. "The truth is you and I had a smooth road ahead of us, Drew. But then you—" she poked Gwen with her finger, hard "—had to come back from the dead, didn't you?"

Drew frowned but didn't make a move.

Gwen angled Pax away from Opal. Her gaze fell on a window, where a familiar shape surprised her.

Uniformed agents.

This was some kind of setup.

Trust Drew.

"Don't touch me, Opal," she said.

"Don't touch you? I wish I didn't have to."

"Opal! You haven't finished your story." Drew was closer, close enough to grab Opal if need be. But he didn't.

What was Drew up to? Gwen had seen him in plenty of high-stress situations. He had that edge of adrenaline; she saw the vein at his temple jumping. But his demeanor remained calm, in control.

Like he's holding back his anger.

"What story?" Opal crossed her arms over her chest. "Do you want me to spell it out for you?"

"Just tell me the truth, Opal."

"I only did it so you'd see that we belong together, Drew. We got along so well before *she* came back."

"What did you do, Opal?"

"I only meant for Dottie to have a little accident. I never meant for the old bat to die. She was in good shape for her age!"

"What did you do? I have to know."

Opal frowned. "If I tell you in front of her, we're going to have to take care of her."

"Don't worry, we'll sort it out. Tell me, Opal."

Great. She had to stand here and trust that Drew

knew what the hell he was doing, that he'd get her and Pax safely through this, SWAT team or no.

"It's your fault, really. You never asked for the clinic keys back. It was easy to go in through the back door of the aquatracker room. All I did was turn up the motor a bit. Dottie wasn't supposed to be under that long, Drew."

"How did you keep your fingerprints off the equipment?"

"Oh, I didn't. I wiped the knobs down after I turned them back to normal, after she passed out."

"But she hadn't passed out, had she? You killed her!" Gwen couldn't keep it in any longer. Opal threatened her whole future.

"Gwen, stay out of it!" Drew yelled.

Before Gwen could respond, the back door burst open and Cole Ramsey walked in with two deputies. There was a commotion in the foyer as the front door opened, as well, and more uniformed officers poured into the house.

"You lied to me!" Opal screamed at Drew, who wasn't even looking at her.

He was staring at Gwen.

"Opal Doyle, you're under arrest." Cole read her Miranda rights and one of his deputies had Opal in cuffs as she ranted and raved at all of them.

"Take her out of here." The deputies followed Cole's orders and in a matter of minutes the house was empty again except for Cole, Drew, Gwen and Pax.

Gwen wasn't sure what she wanted to do more—run upstairs and cuddle Pax all night, punch Drew or hand Pax to Cole so she could kiss Drew.

"Let me guess—you're wired."

"Cole and I will explain. But first…" Drew's hair was still wet, dripping water onto his shirt, but his gaze was steady on the newcomer. He leaned over and grasped Pax's hand.

"Hello, Pax."

PAX SLEPT QUIETLY in the portable playpen Gwen had purchased on her way up to SeaTac. She needed to go furniture shopping for the little guy—her son! Maybe tomorrow, after she'd managed a good night's sleep.

Judging from the anguished expression on Drew's face, that might be impossible.

"I wish you'd told me you were planning to catch her at her own game, Drew. She's crazy. She could have killed you!"

"I couldn't tell you. I didn't know for sure she killed Dottie, not until after you and I came back from our overnight. I went by the Koffee Hut this morning, and she was downright mean about you. I called Cole, and we came up with this plan."

She looked at him and was unable to look away. His gaze was inscrutable.

"I never meant for you and Pax to be involved. It was all supposed to be over by the time you got back home."

"She could have taken us all out if she'd been armed." Gwen spoke the words he wouldn't.

"Opal is crazy, and a murderer, but to the best of our knowledge, she hadn't progressed to buying a weapon. Cole's team checked it out. If we thought she had a gun of any kind I wouldn't have lured her into our home."

"*Our* home?"

"We had a great night—nights—since we went to Seattle. I believe it could be a new beginning, and I think you do, too."

He hadn't said anything about love.

Or about Pax.

He stood up, pacing the room before he came back and sat next to her on the couch. She saw him steal a glance at Pax, to make sure he was still sleeping. Hope sparked deep in her heart.

"I've been like an expectant father, Gwen. I couldn't wait to meet Pax, and it was all I could do not to text you each and every minute. I wanted you home. But I had to be absolutely certain you were coming home to a safe place, to a man who could offer you more than broken dreams."

"I'd take you no matter what, Drew. I don't care if you're a physical therapist, a janitor, a bricklayer."

"How about a stay-at-home dad?"

She laughed. "Now I know you're joking."

"Actually, I'm not. There won't be any criminal charges against me, and with luck Dottie's family won't press civil charges, not with Opal's confession. But for the time being my practice is done. It's difficult to lose the taint something like this leaves behind. I'll be lucky to find a contract job as a therapist at the base hospital or down in Coupeville."

"I don't care, Drew. Tell me more about the family part."

He inched closer and pulled on a lock of her hair. "I want to be with you for the rest of our lives, Gwen. It won't be like before—"

"Shhh." She put her fingers to his lips. "No, it won't. I'm going to get out of the navy."

"That's my point. I don't want you to get out—you love the navy. There's no reason you can't continue. If you get reassigned, I can follow you."

"But what about me, Drew? I'm through with the moving, chasing the next rung in the career ladder." She glanced at Pax's sleeping form.

"I want to be here for Pax."

"You can, honey. You have shore duty from now on if there's no further war. We can go overseas, and you can take whatever assignment you want. I'll be the steady one who's here for Pax. Let me be here for *you,* too, Gwen."

They met each other halfway and kissed. Deep, long kisses and reverent caresses of the other's face expressed the need they'd never lost.

"I love you, Drew."

"I love you, too, sweetheart. But you already know that."

After several more soul-rending kisses, Drew lifted his head. "Gwen?"

"Mmm?"

"Is Pax too young to be a ring bearer?"

CHAPTER TWENTY-ONE

Six Months Later

GWEN HAD NEVER been happier. The baby on her hip as she stood at the podium in front of her squadron was a huge part of that, as was the handsome husband who stood beside her. They smiled for the cameras as her Change of Command ceremony ended; all that would remain of the day were the official photos and the memories. She started her shore job as the Naval Airstation's Executive Officer in two weeks. No moving for at least three years.

"How much longer do we have to pose?" She complained halfheartedly as she hoisted Pax higher in her arms.

"Want to give them a shot they'll remember?" Drew's whispered response made her laugh.

The huge American flag hung behind them as a backdrop to the ceremony. As a reminder of all she'd sacrificed to get to this moment. Gwen smiled. She knew she'd do it all again if the ending was the same—she, Drew and Pax together as a family.

They had a vacation to Disneyland in California planned for part of her leave, after which they were leaving Pax with Brenda and George for a few nights. Drew wanted to take her to Napa Valley for a belated second honeymoon.

It wasn't just love that buoyed Gwen's spirits. It was hope.

Hope that she and Drew had a future.

They'd been remarried by the base chaplain within a week of Pax's homecoming, just two days after Drew and his clinic were cleared of any culpability in Dottie's death.

Opal had been deemed criminally insane and was far from Whidbey Island, serving time at Western State Hospital. If Drew had gone to prison, Gwen would have convinced him to remarry her, anyway. It'd taken her too long, but she finally understood that although she was fine on her own, capable of taking care of herself, life was infinitely better with the man she loved at her side.

"Let's go see Auntie Ro!" She eased Pax down to the stage and held his hand as he practiced walking with her support.

Pax screamed and insisted on running toward the edge of the platform.

"Oh, no, you don't, pal." Drew scooped him up and placed him on his shoulders.

"Thanks. You always know how to handle him." She kissed Drew full on the lips, public display of affection regulations be damned. Her dress whites had cake stains on the sleeves from where Pax's hands had held on to her, and she prized those marks more than any of the ribbons or medals she wore on her chest.

"It's a guy thing, Mom. Right, bud?" Drew wiggled Pax's feet.

Pax laughed delightedly.

Before they reached Ro, Cole Ramsey approached them, a statuesque blonde on his arm.

"Congrats, Gwen. I'd like you and Drew to meet my fiancée, Anita."

"Hey, congrats right back at you, Cole! A fiancée? Hi, Anita, nice to meet you." Gwen gave Cole a quick hug and smiled at Anita, who beamed with a smile so white Gwen thought she could be a toothpaste model.

"Cole." Drew gave his buddy a bear hug and offered his hand to Anita. "You've got a good man here, Anita."

"I know."

Pax ran up to Ro, who'd closed the distance between them. "How does it feel to be done with flying, Gwen?" she asked.

"Strangely calm. Maybe it hasn't hit me yet."

"Or something else is distracting her," Drew said with a wink.

"Stop it." Gwen punched him playfully in the shoulder.

"What am I missing?" Ro's glance bounced like a video cursor between them.

Drew gave Gwen a questioning look.

She nodded.

"Fine with me."

Drew grinned. "Ro, have you noticed that Gwen's uniform is a little, um, tight?"

Ro cocked her head and studied Gwen. "You're finally back to your normal weight—oh. My. Gosh. Tell me it ain't so."

Gwen grinned.

"Yeah, it's so. Pax is going to be a big brother."

Ro squealed and threw her arms around Gwen. Gwen returned the hug as best she could in full dress whites.

"What's the big celebration?"

"Serena! Thank you for coming. Hi, Pepe." Drew answered for both of them. "We're excited because Gwen is going to have a baby."

Pepe didn't seem very impressed.

"I'm so happy for you both, Drew." Serena smiled and hugged each of them. "I wish you'd reconsider the clinic, Drew. You could start again. Your clients love you."

Gwen watched Drew as he slowly shook his head. "No, not yet. I've found a great position over at Beyond the Stars, on San Juan. I'll be offering my services to the Gold Star families."

"That's wonderful! You know how much Pepe and I got out of our time there."

"What will you do for work, Serena?" Gwen felt

awful that Serena was without a job when she had a young child to take care of.

"I'm not sure. We have some time. As you know by now, Dottie was my biological aunt and she left me her house and property. Pepe and I can hang out for a bit before I figure out my next move."

"There's a huge backyard for me to play in!" Pepe said excitedly.

"How long is your shore duty here, Gwen?"

"Only a few years. After that—who knows? Maybe we'll move to San Juan Island. After I hit my twenty I'm looking into flying for the local commuter airline another vet started up a few years ago."

She smiled up at Drew. "The 'where' isn't the issue for me anymore." She kissed him. "Right?"

"Mmm." Drew kissed her back. Ro, Serena and the squadron personnel who'd gathered around to offer their farewells started to clap. Pax, still on his father's shoulders, pulled on Drew's hair and knocked Gwen's cover off her head.

His parents didn't notice.

* * * * *

Navy Rescue/Whidbey Island Series Acronyms

AAA – anti-aircraft artillery

Aquatracker – based on actual underwater treadmills, this is my fictional name for the equipment in Drew's physical therapy clinic

BTS – Beyond the Stars. Fictional therapeutic resort for Gold Star families of service members

CO – commanding officer

Cover – name for a uniform hat, whether it is a squadron's ball cap, a khaki uniform hat or the traditional navy uniform hat

FE – flight engineer. On a P-3 this is often the senior enlisted person of the aircrew. Sits behind the pilot and copilot in the cockpit

Gedunk – a place in a squadron where snacks, sodas and other food is sold

Gold Star Family – a family who has lost a loved one, usually to war, while on active duty

ICS – internal communications system

KIA – killed in action

LPA – life preserver assembly

MIA – missing in action

NAS – naval air station. Land-based, comparable to an army post or air force base

NCIS – Naval Criminal Investigative Service

P-3C Orion – The U.S. Navy's long-range aircraft (4-engine turboprop) used for reconnaissance (traditionally antisubmarine warfare, especially during the Cold War). Is being replaced by the P-8

PT – physical therapy, but in the navy it means physical training

PTSD – post-traumatic stress disorder

SERE – Survival Evasion Resistance Escape school, training required of all aircrew

SGLI – Servicemember's group life insurance. Provided for all active duty in the event of their death. Beneficiary is assigned by the servicemember

Skipper – nickname for the commanding officer of a squadron

TACCO – tactical coordinator. A naval flight officer (not a pilot) who is in charge of prosecuting the tactical mission

XO – executive officer (#2 to the CO)